SCM 4.95

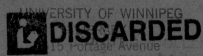

BY JAMES BALDWIN

Going to Meet the Man

by James Baldwin

THE DIAL PRESS NEW YORK 1965

Acknowledgement is made to the following magazines in whose
pages the following stories were originally published:
Commentary, October, 1948, for "Previous Condition"; *New Story*,
1951, for "The Outing"; *Partisan Review*, Summer, 1957, for
"Sonny's Blues"; *Mademoiselle*, March, 1958, for "Come Out
the Wilderness"; *Atlantic Monthly*, September, 1960, for "This
Morning, This Evening, So Soon."

Library of Congress Catalog Card number: 65-15331
Designed by Klaus Gemming
Manufactured in the United States of America

for Beauford Delaney

CONTENTS

Going to Meet the Man

The Rockpile

ACROSS THE STREET from their house, in an empty lot between two houses, stood the rockpile. It was a strange place to find a mass of natural rock jutting out of the ground; and someone, probably Aunt Florence, had once told them that the rock was there and could not be taken away because without it the subway cars underground would fly apart, killing all the people. This, touching on some natural mystery concerning the surface and the center of the earth, was far too intriguing an explanation to be challenged, and it invested the rockpile, moreover, with such mysterious importance that Roy felt it to be his right, not to say his duty, to play there.

Other boys were to be seen there each afternoon after school and all day Saturday and Sunday. They fought on the rockpile. Sure footed, dangerous, and reckless, they rushed each other and grappled on the heights, sometimes disappearing down the other side in a confusion of dust and screams and upended, flying feet. "It's a wonder they don't kill themselves," their mother said, watching sometimes from the fire escape. "You children stay away from there, you hear me?" Though she said "children," she was looking at Roy, where he sat beside John on the fire escape. "The good Lord knows," she continued, "I don't want you to come home bleeding like a hog every day the Lord sends." Roy shifted impatiently, and continued to stare at the street, as though in this gazing he might somehow acquire wings. John said nothing. He had not really been spoken to: he was afraid of the rockpile and of the boys who played there.

Each Saturday morning John and Roy sat on the fire escape and watched the forbidden street below. Sometimes their mother sat in the room behind them, sewing, or dressing their younger sister, or nursing the baby, Paul. The sun fell across them and across the fire escape with a high, benevolent indifference; below them, men and women, and boys and girls, sinners all, loitered; sometimes one of the church-members passed and saw them and waved. Then, for the moment that they waved decorously back, they were intimidated. They watched the saint, man or woman, until he or she had disappeared from sight. The passage of one of the redeemed made them consider, however vacantly, the wickedness of the street, their own latent wickedness in sitting where they sat; and made them think of their father, who came home early on Saturdays and who would soon be turning this corner and entering the dark hall below them.

But until he came to end their freedom, they sat, watching and longing above the street. At the end of the street nearest their house was the bridge which spanned the Harlem River and led to a city called the Bronx; which was where Aunt Florence lived. Nevertheless, when they saw her coming, she did not come from the bridge, but from the opposite end of the street. This, weakly, to their minds, she explained by saying that she had taken the subway, not wishing to walk, and that, besides, she did not live in *that* section of the Bronx. Knowing that the Bronx was across the river, they did not believe this story ever, but, adopting toward her their father's attitude, assumed that she had just left some sinful place which she dared not name, as, for example, a movie palace.

In the summertime boys swam in the river, diving off the wooden dock, or wading in from the garbage-heavy bank. Once a boy, whose name was Richard, drowned in the river. His mother had not known where he was; she had even come to their house, to ask if he was there. Then, in the evening, at six o'clock, they had heard from the street a woman screaming and wailing; and they ran to the windows and looked out. Down the street came the woman, Richard's mother, screaming, her face raised to the sky and tears running down her face. A woman walked beside her, trying to make her quiet and trying to hold her up. Behind them walked a man, Richard's father, with Richard's body in his arms. There were two white policemen walking in the gutter, who did not seem to know what should be done. Richard's father and Richard were wet, and Richard's body lay across his father's arms like a cotton baby. The woman's screaming filled all the street; cars slowed down and the people in the cars stared; people opened their windows and looked out and came rushing out of doors to stand in the gutter, watching. Then the small procession disappeared within the house which stood beside the rockpile. Then, *"Lord, Lord, Lord!"* cried Elizabeth, their mother, and slammed the window down.

One Saturday, an hour before his father would be coming home, Roy was wounded on the rockpile and brought screaming upstairs. He and John had been sitting on the fire escape and their mother had gone into the kitchen to sip tea with Sister McCandless. By and by Roy became bored and sat beside John in restless silence; and John began drawing into his schoolbook a newspaper advertisement which featured a new electric locomotive. Some friends of Roy passed beneath the fire escape and called him. Roy began to fidget, yelling down to them through the bars. Then a silence fell. John looked up. Roy stood looking at him.

"I'm going downstairs," he said.

"You better stay where you is, boy. You know Mama don't want you going downstairs."

"I be right *back*. She won't even know I'm gone, less you run and tell her."

"I ain't *got* to tell her. What's going to stop her from coming in here and looking out the window?"

"She's talking," Roy said. He started into the house.

"But Daddy's going to be home soon!"

"I be back before *that*. What you all the time got to be so *scared* for?" He was already in the house and he now turned, leaning on the windowsill, to swear impatiently, "I be back in *five* minutes."

John watched him sourly as he carefully unlocked the door and disappeared. In a moment he saw him on the sidewalk with his friends. He did not dare to go and tell his mother that Roy had left the fire escape because he had practically promised not to. He started to shout, *Remember, you said five minutes!* but one of Roy's friends was looking up at the fire escape. John looked down at his schoolbook: he became engrossed again in the problem of the locomotive.

When he looked up again he did not know how much time had passed, but now there was a gang fight on the rockpile. Dozens of boys fought each other in the harsh sun: clambering up the rocks and battling hand to hand, scuffed shoes sliding on the slippery rock; filling the bright air with curses and jubilant cries. They filled the air, too, with flying weapons: stones, sticks, tin cans, garbage, whatever could be picked up and thrown. John watched in a kind of absent amazement—until he remembered that Roy was still downstairs, and that he was one of the boys on the rockpile. Then he was afraid; he could not see his brother among the figures in the sun; and he stood up, leaning over the fire-escape railing. Then Roy appeared from the other side of the rocks; John saw that his shirt was torn; he was laughing. He moved until he stood at the very top of the rockpile. Then, something, an empty tin can, flew out of the air and hit him on the forehead, just above the eye. Immediately, one side of Roy's face ran with blood, he fell and rolled on his face down the rocks. Then for a moment there was no movement at all, no sound, the sun, arrested, lay on the street and the sidewalk and the arrested boys. Then someone screamed or shouted; boys began to run away, down the street, toward the bridge. The figure on the ground, having caught its breath and felt its own blood, began to shout. John cried, "Mama! Mama!" and ran inside.

"Don't fret, don't fret," panted Sister McCandless as they rushed down the dark, narrow, swaying stairs, "don't fret. Ain't a boy been born don't get his knocks every now and again. *Lord!*" they hurried into the sun. A man had picked Roy up and now walked slowly toward them. One or two boys sat silent on their stoops; at either end of the street there was a group of boys watching. "He ain't hurt bad," the man said, "Wouldn't be making this kind of noise if he was hurt real bad."

Elizabeth, trembling, reached out to take Roy, but Sister McCandless, bigger, calmer, took him from the man and threw him over her shoulder as she once might have handled a sack of cotton. "God bless you," she said to the man, "God bless you, son." Roy was still screaming. Elizabeth stood behind Sister McCandless to stare at his bloody face.

"It's just a flesh wound," the man kept saying, "just broke the skin, that's all." They were moving across the sidewalk, toward the house. John, not now afraid of the staring boys, looked toward the corner to see if his father was yet in sight.

Upstairs, they hushed Roy's crying. They bathed the blood away, to find, just above the left eyebrow, the jagged, superficial scar. "Lord, have mercy," murmured Elizabeth, "another inch and it would've been his eye." And she looked with apprehension toward the clock. "Ain't it the truth," said Sister McCandless, busy with bandages and iodine.

"When did he go downstairs?" his mother asked at last.

Sister McCandless now sat fanning herself in the easy chair, at the head of the sofa where Roy lay, bound and silent. She paused for a moment to look sharply at John. John stood near the window, holding the newspaper advertisement and the drawing he had done.

"We was sitting on the fire escape," he said. "Some boys he knew called him."

"When?"

"He said he'd be back in five minutes."

"Why didn't you tell me he was downstairs?"

He looked at his hands, clasping his notebook, and did not answer.

"Boy," said Sister McCandless, "you hear your mother a-talking to you?"

He looked at his mother. He repeated:

"He said he'd be back in five minutes."

"He said he'd be back in five minutes," said Sister McCandless with scorn, "don't look to me like that's no right answer. You's the man of the house, you supposed to look after your baby brothers and sisters—you ain't supposed to let them run off and get half-killed. But I expect," she added, rising from the chair, dropping the cardboard fan, "your Daddy'll make you tell the truth. Your Ma's way too soft with you."

He did not look at her, but at the fan where it lay in the dark red, depressed seat where she had been. The fan advertised a pomade for the hair and showed a brown woman and her baby, both with glistening hair, smiling happily at each other.

"Honey," said Sister McCandless, "I got to be moving along. Maybe I drop in later tonight. I don't reckon you going to be at Tarry Service tonight?"

Tarry Service was the prayer meeting held every Saturday night at church to strengthen believers and prepare the church for the coming of the Holy Ghost on Sunday.

"I don't reckon," said Elizabeth. She stood up; she and Sister McCandless kissed each other on the cheek. "But you be sure to remember me in your prayers."

"I surely will do that." She paused, with her hand on the door knob, and looked down at Roy and laughed. "Poor little man," she said, "reckon he'll be content to sit on the fire escape *now*."

Elizabeth laughed with her. "It sure ought to be a lesson to him. You don't reckon," she asked nervously, still smiling, "he going to keep that scar, do you?"

"Lord, no," said Sister McCandless, "ain't nothing but a scratch. I declare, Sister Grimes, you worse than a child. Another couple of weeks and you won't be able to *see* no scar. No, you go on about your housework, honey, and thank the Lord it weren't no worse." She opened the door; they heard the sound of feet on the stairs. "I expect that's the Reverend," said Sister McCandless, placidly, "I *bet* he going to raise cain."

"Maybe it's Florence," Elizabeth said. "Sometimes she get here about this time." They stood in the doorway, staring, while the steps reached the landing below and began again climbing to their floor. "No," said Elizabeth then, "that ain't her walk. That's Gabriel."

"Well, I'll just go on," said Sister McCandless, "and kind of prepare his mind." She pressed Elizabeth's hand as she spoke and started into the hall, leaving the door behind her slightly ajar. Elizabeth turned slowly back into the room. Roy did not open his eyes, or move; but she knew that he was not sleeping; he wished to delay until the last possible moment any contact with his father. John put his newspaper and his notebook on the table and stood, leaning on the table, staring at her.

"It wasn't my fault," he said. "I couldn't stop him from going downstairs."

"No," she said, "you ain't got nothing to worry about. You just tell your Daddy the truth."

He looked directly at her, and she turned to the window, staring into the street. What was Sister McCandless saying? Then from her bedroom she heard Delilah's thin wail and she turned, frowning, looking toward the bedroom and toward the still open door. She knew that John was watching her. Delilah continued to wail, she thought, angrily, *Now that girl's getting too big for that,* but she feared that Delilah would awaken Paul and she hurried into the bedroom. She tried to soothe

Delilah back to sleep. Then she heard the front door open and close—too loud, Delilah raised her voice, with an exasperated sigh Elizabeth picked the child up. Her child and Gabriel's, her children and Gabriel's: Roy, Delilah, Paul. Only John was nameless and a stranger, living, unalterable testimony to his mother's days in sin.

"What happened?" Gabriel demanded. He stood, enormous, in the center of the room, his black lunchbox dangling from his hand, staring at the sofa where Roy lay. John stood just before him, it seemed to her astonished vision just below him, beneath his fist, his heavy shoe. The child stared at the man in fascination and terror—when a girl down home she had seen rabbits stand so paralyzed before the barking dog. She hurried past Gabriel to the sofa, feeling the weight of Delilah in her arms like the weight of a shield, and stood over Roy, saying:

"Now, ain't a thing to get upset about, Gabriel. This boy sneaked downstairs while I had my back turned and got hisself hurt a little. He's alright now."

Roy, as though in confirmation, now opened his eyes and looked gravely at his father. Gabriel dropped his lunchbox with a clatter and knelt by the sofa.

"How you feel, son? Tell your Daddy what happened?"

Roy opened his mouth to speak and then, relapsing into panic, began to cry. His father held him by the shoulder.

"You don't want to cry. You's Daddy's little man. Tell your Daddy what happened."

"He went downstairs," said Elizabeth, "where he didn't have no business to be, and got to fighting with them bad boys playing on that rockpile. That's what happened and it's a mercy it weren't nothing worse."

He looked up at her. "Can't you let this boy answer me for hisself?"

Ignoring this, she went on, more gently: "He got cut on the forehead, but it ain't nothing to worry about."

"You call a doctor? How you know it ain't nothing to worry about?"

"Is you got money to be throwing away on doctors? No, I ain't called no doctor. Ain't nothing wrong with my eyes that I can't tell whether he's hurt bad or not. He got a fright more'n anything else, and you ought to pray God it teaches him a lesson."

"You got a lot to say *now*," he said, "but I'll have *me* something to say in a minute. I'll be wanting to know when all this happened, what you was doing with your eyes *then*." He turned back to Roy, who had lain quietly sobbing eyes wide open and body held rigid: and who now, at his father's touch, remembered the height, the sharp, sliding rock beneath his feet, the sun, the explosion of the sun, his plunge into darkness and his salty blood; and recoiled, beginning to scream, as his father touched his forehead. "Hold still, hold still," crooned his father, shaking, "hold still. Don't cry. Daddy ain't going to hurt you, he just wants to see this bandage, see what they've done to his little man." But Roy continued to scream and would not be still and Gabriel dared not lift the bandage for fear of hurting him more. And he looked at Elizabeth in fury: "Can't you put that child down and help me with this boy? John, take your baby sister from your mother—don't look like neither of you got good sense."

John took Delilah and sat down with her in the easy chair. His mother bent over Roy, and held him still, while his father, carefully—but still Roy screamed—lifted the bandage and stared at the wound. Roy's sobs began to lessen. Gabriel readjusted the bandage. "You see," said Elizabeth, finally, "he ain't nowhere near dead."

"It sure ain't your fault that he ain't dead." He and Elizabeth considered each other for a moment in silence. "He came mightly close to losing an eye. Course, his eyes ain't as big as your'n, so I reckon you don't think it matters so much." At this her face hardened; he smiled. "Lord, have mercy," he said, "you think you ever going to learn to do right? Where was you when all this happened? Who let him go downstairs?"

"Ain't nobody let him go downstairs, he just went. He got a head just like his father, it got to be broken before it'll bow. I was in the kitchen."

"Where was Johnnie?"

"He was in here?"

"Where?"

"He was on the fire escape."

"Didn't he know Roy was downstairs?"

"I reckon."

"What you mean, you reckon? He ain't got your big eyes for nothing, does he?" He looked over at John. "Boy, you see your brother go downstairs?"

"Gabriel, ain't no sense in trying to blame Johnnie. You know right well if you have trouble making Roy behave, he ain't going to listen to his brother. He don't hardly listen to me."

"How come you didn't tell your mother Roy was downstairs?"

John said nothing, staring at the blanket which covered Delilah.

"Boy, you hear me? You want me to take a strap to you?"

"No, you ain't," she said. "You ain't going to take no strap to this boy, not today you ain't. Ain't a soul to blame for Roy's lying up there now but you—you because you done spoiled him so that he thinks he can do just anthing and get away with it. I'm here to tell you that ain't no way to raise no child. You don't pray to the Lord to help you do better than you been doing, you going to live to shed bitter tears that the Lord didn't take his soul today." And she was trembling. She moved, unseeing, toward John and took Delilah from his arms. She looked back at Gabriel, who had risen, who stood near the sofa, staring at her. And she found in his face not fury alone, which would not have surprised her; but hatred so deep as to become insupportable in its lack of personality. His eyes were struck alive, unmoving, blind with malevolence—she felt, like the pull of the earth at her feet, his longing to witness her perdition. Again, as though it might be propitiation, she moved the child in her arms. And at this his eyes changed, he looked at Elizabeth, the mother of his children, the helpmeet given by the Lord. Then her eyes clouded; she moved to leave the room; her foot struck the lunchbox lying on the floor.

"John," she said, "pick up your father's lunchbox like a good boy."

She heard, behind her, his scrambling movement as he left the easy chair, the scrape and jangle of the lunchbox as he picked it up, bending his dark head near the toe of his father's heavy shoe.

The Outing

Each summer the church gave an outing. It usually took place on the Fourth of July, that being the day when most of the church-members were free from work; it began quite early in the morning and lasted all day. The saints referred to it as the 'whosoever will' outing, by which they meant that, though it was given by the Mount of Olives Pentecostal Assembly for the benefit of its members, all men were free to join them, Gentile, Jew or Greek or sinner. The Jews and the Greeks, to say nothing of the Gentiles—on whom, for their livelihood, most of the saints depended—showed themselves, year after year, indifferent to the invitation; but sinners of the more expected hue were seldom lacking. This year they were to take a boat trip up the Hudson as far as Bear Mountain where they would spend the day and return as the moon rose over the wide river. Since on other outings they had merely taken a subway ride as far as Pelham Bay or Van Cortlandt Park, this year's outing was more than ever a special occasion and even the deacon's two oldest boys, Johnnie and Roy, and their friend, David Jackson, were reluctantly thrilled. These three tended to consider themselves sophisticates, no longer, like the old folks, at the mercy of the love or the wrath of God.

The entire church was going and for weeks in advance talked of nothing else. And for weeks in the future the outing would provide interesting conversation. They did not consider this frivolous. The outing, Father James declared from his pulpit a week before the event, was for the purpose of giving the children of God a day of relaxation; to breathe a purer air and to worship God joyfully beneath the roof of heaven; and there was nothing frivolous about *that*. And, rather to the alarm of the captain, they planned to hold church services aboard the ship. Last year Sister McCandless had held an impromptu service in the unbelieving subway car she played the tambourine and sang and exhorted sinners and passed through the train distributing tracts. Not everyone had found this admirable, to some it seemed that Sister McCandless was being a little ostentatious. "I praise my Redeemer wherever I go," she retorted defiantly. "Holy Ghost don't leave *me* when I leave the church. I got a every day religion."

Sylvia's birthday was on the third, and David and Johnnie and Roy had been saving money for her birthday present. Between them they had five dollars but they could not decide what to give her. Roy's suggestion that they give her underthings was rudely shouted down: did he want Sylvia's mother to kill the girl? They were all frightened of the great, rawboned, outspoken Sister Daniels and for Sylvia's sake went to great pains to preserve what remained of her good humor. Finally, and at the suggestion of David's older sister, Lorraine, they bought a small, gold-plated pin cut in the shape of a butterfly. Roy thought that it was cheap and grumbled angrily at their combined bad taste ("Wait till it starts turning her clothes green!" he cried) but David did not think it was so bad; Johnnie thought it pretty enough and he was sure that Sylvia would like it anyway; ("When's *your* birthday?" he asked David). It was agreed that David should present it to her on the day of the outing in the presence of them all. ("Man, I'm the oldest cat here," David said, "you know that girl's crazy about me"). This was the summer in which they all abruptly began to grow older, their bodies becoming troublesome and awkward and even dangerous and their voices not to be trusted. David perpetually boasted of the increase of down on his chin and professed to have hair on his chest—"and somewhere else, too," he added slyly, whereat they all laughed. "You ain't the only one," Roy said. "No," Johnnie said, "I'm almost as old as you are." "Almost ain't got it," David said. "Now ain't this a hell of a conversation for church boys?" Roy wanted to know.

The morning of the outing they were all up early; their

father sang in the kitchen and their mother, herself betraying an excitement nearly youthful, scrubbed and dressed the younger children and laid the plates for breakfast. In the bedroom which they shared Roy looked wistfully out of the window and turned to Johnnie.

"Got a good mind to stay home," he said. "Probably have more fun." He made a furious gesture toward the kitchen. "Why doesn't *he* stay home?"

Johnnie, who was looking forward to the day with David and who had not the remotest desire to stay home for any reason and who knew, moreover, that Gabriel was not going to leave Roy alone in the city, not even if the heavens fell, said lightly, squirming into clean underwear: "Oh, he'll probably be busy with the old folks. We can stay out of his way."

Roy sighed and began to dress. "Be glad when I'm a man," he said.

Lorraine and David and Mrs. Jackson were already on the boat when they arrived. They were among the last; most of the church, Father James, Brother Elisha, Sister McCandless, Sister Daniels and Sylvia were seated near the rail of the boat in a little semi-circle, conversing in strident tones. Father James and Sister McCandless were remarking the increase of laxity among God's people and debating whether or not the church should run a series of revival meetings. Sylvia sat there, saying nothing, smiling painfully now and then at young Brother Elisha, who spoke loudly of the need for a revival and who continually attempted to include Sylvia in the conversation. Elsewhere on the boat similar conversations were going on. The saints of God were together and very conscious this morning of their being together and of their sainthood; and were determined that the less enlightened world should know who they were and remark upon it. To this end there were a great many cries of "Praise the Lord!" in greeting and the formal holy kiss. The children, bored with the familiar spectacle, had already drawn apart and amused themselves by loud cries and games that were no less exhibitionistic than that being played by their parents. Johnnie's nine year old sister, Lois, since she professed salvation, could not very well behave as the other children did; yet no degree of salvation could have equipped her to enter into the conversation of the grown-ups; and she was very violently disliked among the adolescents and could not join them either. She wandered about, therefore, unwillingly forlorn, contenting herself to some extent by a great display of virtue in her encounters with the unsaved children and smiling brightly at the grown-ups. She came to Brother Elisha's side. "Praise the Lord," he cried, stroking her head and continuing his conversation.

Lorraine and Mrs. Jackson met Johnnie's mother for the first time as she breathlessly came on board, dressed in the airy and unreal blue which Johnnie would forever associate with his furthest memories of her. Johnnie's baby brother, her youngest, happiest child, clung round her neck; she made him stand, staring in wonder at the strange, endless deck, while she was introduced. His mother, on all social occasions, seemed fearfully distracted, as though she awaited, at any moment, some crushing and irrevocable disaster. This disaster might be the sudden awareness of a run in her stocking or private knowledge that the trump of judgment was due, within five minutes, to sound: but, whatever it was, it lent her a certain agitated charm and people, struggling to guess what it might be that so claimed her inward attention, never failed, in the process, to be won over. She talked with Lorraine and Mrs. Jackson for a few moments, the child tugging at her skirts, Johnnie watching her with a smile; and at last, the child becoming always more restive, said that she must go—into what merciless arena one dared not imagine—but hoped, with a despairing smile which clearly indicated the improbability of such happiness, that she would be able to see them later. They watched her as she walked slowly to the other end of the boat, sometimes pausing in conversation, always (as though it were a duty) smiling a little and now and then considering Lois where she stood at Brother Elishas' knee.

"She's very friendly," Mrs. Jackson said. "She looks like you, Johnnie."

David laughed. "Now why you want to say a thing like that, Ma? That woman ain't never done nothing to you."

Johnnie grinned, embarrassed, and pretended to menace David with his fists.

"Don't you listen to that old, ugly boy," Lorraine said. "He just trying to make you feel bad. Your mother's real good-looking. Tell her I said so."

This embarrassed him even more, but he made a mock bow and said, "Thank you, Sister." And to David: "Maybe now you'll learn to keep your mouth shut."

"Who'll learn to keep whose mouth shut? What kind of talk is that?"

He turned and faced his father, who stood smiling on them as from a height.

"Mrs. Jackson, this is my father," said Roy quickly. "And this is Miss Jackson. You know David."

Lorraine and Mrs. Jackson looked up at the deacon with polite and identical smiles.

"How do you do?" Lorraine said. And from Mrs. Jackson: "I'm very pleased to meet you."

"Praise the Lord," their father said. He smiled. "Don't you let Johnnie talk fresh to you."

"Oh, no, we were just kidding around," David said. There was a short, ugly silence. The deacon said: "It looks like a good day for the outing, praise the Lord. You kids have a good time. Is this your first time with us, Mrs. Jackson?"

"Yes," said Mrs. Jackson. "David came home and told me about it and it's been so long since I've been in the country I just decided I'd take me a day off. And Lorraine's not been feeling too strong, I thought the fresh air would do her some good." She smiled a little painfully as she spoke. Lorraine looked amused.

"Yes, it will, nothing like God's fresh air to help the feeble." At this description of herself as feeble Lorraine looked ready to fall into the Hudson and coughed nastily into her handkerchief. David, impelled by his own perverse demon, looked at Johnnie quickly and murmured, "That's the truth, deacon." The deacon looked at him and smiled and turned to Mrs. Jackson. "We been hoping that your son might join our church someday. Roy brings him out to service every Sunday. Do you like the services, son?" This last was addressed in a hearty voice to David; who, recovering from his amazement at hearing Roy mentioned as his especial pal (for he was Johnnie's friend, it was to be with Johnnie that he came to church!) smiled and said, "Yes sir, I like them alright," and looked at Roy, who considered his father with an expression at once contemptuous, ironic and resigned and at Johnnie, whose face was a mask of rage. He looked sharply at the deacon again; but he, with his arm around Roy, was still talking.

"This boy came to the Lord just about a month ago," he said proudly. "The Lord saved him just like that. Believe me, Sister Jackson, ain't no better fortress for nobody, young or old, than the arms of Jesus. My son'll tell you so, ain't it, Roy?"

They considered Roy with a stiff, cordial curiosity. He muttered murderously, "Yes sir."

"Johnnie tells me you're a preacher," Mrs. Jackson said at last. "I'll come out and hear you sometime with David."

"Don't come out to hear me," he said. "You come out and listen to the Word of God. We're all just vessels in His hand. Do you know the Lord, sister?"

"I try to do His will," Mrs. Jackson said.

He smiled kindly. "We must all grow in grace." He looked at Lorraine. "I'll be expecting to see you too, young lady."

"Yes, we'll be out," Lorraine said. They shook hands. "It's very nice to have met you," she said.

"Goodbye." He looked at David. "Now you be good. I want to see you saved soon." He released Roy and started to walk away. "You kids enjoy yourselves. Johnnie, don't you get into no mischief, you hear me?"

He affected not to have heard; he put his hands in his pants' pockets and pulled out some change and pretended to count it. His hand was clammy and it shook. When his father repeated his admonition, part of the change spilled to the deck and he bent to pick it up. He wanted at once to shout to his father the most dreadful curses that he knew and he wanted to weep. He was aware that they were all intrigued by the tableau presented by his father and himself, that they were all vaguely cognizant of an unnamed and deadly tension. From his knees on the deck he called back (putting into his voice as much asperity, as much fury and hatred as he dared):

"Don't worry about me, Daddy. Roy'll see to it that I behave."

There was a silence after he said this; and he rose to his feet and saw that they were all watching him. David looked pitying and shocked, Roy's head was bowed and he looked apologetic. His father called:

"Excuse yourself, Johnnie, and come here."

"Excuse me," he said, and walked over to his father. He looked up into his father's face with an anger which surprised and even frightened him. But he did not drop his eyes, knowing that his father saw there (and he wanted him to see it) how much he hated him.

"What did you say?" his father asked.

"I said you don't have to worry about me. I don't think I'll get into any mischief." And his voice surprised him, it was more deliberately cold and angry than he had intended and there was a sardonic stress on the word 'mischief.' He knew that his father would then and there have knocked him down if they had not been in the presence of saints and strangers.

"You be careful how you speak to me. Don't you get grown too fast. We get home, I'll pull down those long pants and we'll see who's the man, you hear me?"

Yes we will, he thought and said nothing. He looked with a deliberate casualness about the deck. Then they felt the lurch of the boat as it began to move from the pier. There was an excited raising of voices and "I'll see you later," his father said and turned away.

He stood still, trying to compose himself to return to Mrs. Jackson and Lorraine. But as he turned with his hands in his pants' pockets he saw that David and Roy were coming toward him and he stopped and waited for them.

"It's a bitch." Roy said.

David looked at him, shocked. "That's no language for a saved boy." He put his arm around Johnnie's shoulder. "We're off to Bear Mountain," he cried, "*up* the glorious Hudson"— and he made a brutal gesture with his thumb.

"Now suppose Sylvia saw you do that," said Roy, "what would you say, huh?"

"We needn't worry about her," Johnnie said. "She'll be sitting with the old folks all day long."

"Oh, we'll figure out a way to take care of *them*," said David. He turned to Roy. "Now you the saved one, why don't you talk to Sister Daniels and distract her attention while we talk to the girl? You the baby, anyhow, girl don't want to talk to you."

"I ain't got enough salvation to talk to that hag," Roy said. "I got a Daddy-made salvation. I'm saved when I'm with Daddy." They laughed and Roy added, "And I ain't no baby, either, I got everything my Daddy got."

"And a lot your Daddy don't dream of," David said.

Oh, thought Johnnie, with a sudden, vicious, chilling anger, *he doesn't have to dream about it!*

"Now let's act like we Christians," David said. "If we was real smart now, we'd go over to where she's sitting with all those people and act like we wanted to hear about God. Get on the good side of her mother."

"And suppose *he* comes back?" asked Johnnie.

Gabriel was sitting at the other end of the boat, talking with his wife. "Maybe he'll stay there," David said; there was a note of apology in his voice.

They approached the saints.

"Praise the Lord," they said sedately.

"Well, praise Him," Father James said. "How are you young men today?" He grabbed Roy by the shoulder. "Are you coming along in the Lord?"

"Yes, sir," Roy muttered, "I'm trying." He smiled into Father James's face.

"It's a wonderful thing," Brother Elisha said, "to give up to the Lord in your youth." He looked up at Johnnie and David. "Why don't you boys surrender? Ain't nothing in the world for you, I'll tell you that. He says, 'Remember thy Creator in the days of thy youth when the evil days come not.' "

"Amen," said Sister Daniels. "We're living in the last days, children. Don't think because you're young you got plenty of time. God takes the young as well as the old. You got to hold yourself in readiness all the time lest when He comes He catch you unprepared. Yes sir. Now's the time."

"You boys going to come to service today, ain't you?" asked Sister McCandless. "We're going to have service on the ship, you know." She looked at Father James. "Reckon we'll start as soon as we get a little further up the river, won't we, Father?"

"Yes," Father James said, "we're going to praise God right in the middle of the majestic Hudson." He leaned back and released Roy as he spoke. "Want to see you children there. I want to hear you make a *noise* for the Lord."

"I ain't never seen none of these young men Shout," said

Sister Daniels, regarding them with distrust. She looked at David and Johnnie. "Don't believe I've ever even heard you testify."

"We're not saved yet, sister," David told her gently.

"That's alright," Sister Daniels said. "You *could* get up and praise the Lord for your life, health and strength. Praise Him for what you got, He'll give you something more."

"That's the truth," said Brother Elisha. He smiled at Sylvia. "I'm a witness, bless the Lord."

"They going to make a noise yet," said Sister McCandless. "Lord's going to touch everyone of these young men one day and bring them on their knees to the altar. You mark my words, you'll see." And she smiled at them.

"You just stay around the house of God long enough," Father James said. "One of these days the Spirit'll jump on you. I won't never forget the day It jumped on me."

"That *is* the truth," Sister McCandless cried, "so glad It jumped on me one day, hallelujah!"

"Amen," Sister Daniels cried, "amen."

"Looks like we're having a little service right now," Brother Elisha said smiling. Father James laughed heartily and cried, "Well, praise Him anyhow."

"I believe next week the church is going to start a series of revival meetings," Brother Elisha said. "I want to see you boys at every one of them, you hear?" He laughed as he spoke and added as David seemed about to protest, "No, no, brother, don't want no excuses. You *be* there. Get you boys to the altar, then maybe you'll pay more attention in Sunday School."

At this they all laughed and Sylvia said in her mild voice, looking mockingly at Roy, "Maybe we'll even see Brother Roy Shout." Roy grinned.

"Like to see you do some Shouting too," her mother grumbled. "You got to get closer to the Lord." Sylvia smiled and bit her lip; she cast a glance at David.

"Now everybody ain't got the same kind of spirit," Brother
Elisha said, coming to Sylvia's aid. "Can't *all* make as much
noise as you make," he said, laughing gently, "we all ain't got
your energy."

Sister Daniels smiled and frowned at this reference to her
size and passion and said, "Don't care, brother, when the Lord
moves inside you, you bound to do something. I've seen that
girl Shout all night and come back the next night and Shout
some more. I don't believe in no dead religion, no sir. The
saints of God need a revival."

"Well, we'll work on Sister Sylvia," said Brother Elisha.

Directly before and behind them stretched nothing but the
river, they had long ago lost sight of the point of their departure. They steamed beside the Palisades, which rose rough and
gigantic from the dirty, broad and blue-green Hudson. Johnnie
and David and Roy wandered downstairs to the bottom deck,
standing by the rail and leaning over to watch the white,
writhing spray which followed the boat. From the river there
floated up to their faces a soft, cool breeze. They were quiet
for a long time, standing together, watching the river and the
mountains and hearing vaguely the hum of activity behind
them on the boat. The sky was high and blue, with here and
there a spittle-like, changing cloud; the sun was orange and
beat with anger on their uncovered heads.

And David muttered finally, "Be funny if they were right."

"If who was right?" asked Roy.

"Elisha and them—"

"There's only one way to find out," said Johnnie.

"Yes," said Roy, "and I ain't homesick for heaven yet."

"You always got to be so smart," David said.

"Oh," said Roy, "you just sore because Sylvia's still up there
with Brother Elisha."

"You think they going to be married?" Johnnie asked.

"Don't talk like a fool," David said.

"Well it's a cinch you ain't never going to get to talk to her till you get saved," Johnnie said. He had meant to say 'we.' He looked at David and smiled.

"Might be worth it," David said.

"*What* might be worth it?" Roy asked, grinning.

"Now be nice," David said. He flushed, the dark blood rising beneath the dark skin. "How you expect me to get saved if you going to talk that way? You supposed to be an example."

"Don't look at me, boy," Roy said.

"I want you to talk to Johnnie," Gabriel said to his wife.

"What about?"

"That boy's pride is running away with him. Ask him to tell you what he said to me this morning soon as he got in front of his friends. He's your son, alright."

"What did he say?"

He looked darkly across the river. "You ask him to tell you about it tonight. I wanted to knock him down."

She had watched the scene and knew this. She looked at her husband briefly, feeling a sudden, outraged anger, barely conscious; sighed and turned to look at her youngest child where he sat involved in a complicated and strenuous and apparently joyless game which utilized a red ball, jacks, blocks and a broken shovel.

"I'll talk to him," she said at last. "He'll be alright." She wondered what on earth she would say to him; and what he would say to her. She looked covertly about the boat, but he was nowhere to be seen.

"That proud demon's just eating him up," he said bitterly. He watched the river hurtle past. "Be the best thing in the world if the Lord would take his soul." He had meant to say 'save' his soul.

Now it was noon and all over the boat there was the activity of lunch. Paper bags and huge baskets were opened. There was then revealed splendor: cold pork chops, cold chicken, bananas, apples, oranges, pears, and soda-pop, candy and cold lemonade. All over the boat the chosen of God relaxed; they sat in groups and talked and laughed; some of the more worldly gossiped and some of the more courageous young people dared to walk off together. Beneath them the strong, indifferent river raged within the channel and the screaming spray pursued them. In the engine room children watched the motion of the ship's gears as they rose and fell and chanted. The tremendous bolts of steel seemed almost human, imbued with a relentless force that was not human. There was something monstrous about this machine which bore such enormous weight and cargo.

Sister Daniels threw a paper bag over the side and wiped her mouth with her large handkerchief. "Sylvia, you be careful how you speak to these unsaved boys," she said.

"Yes, I am, Mama."

"Don't like the way that little Jackson boy looks at you. That child's got a demon. You be careful."

"Yes, Mama."

"You got plenty of time to be thinking about boys. Now's the time for you to be thinking about the Lord."

"Yes'm."

"You *mind* now," her mother said.

"Mama, I want to go home!" Lois cried. She crawled into her mother's arms, weeping.

"Why, what's the matter, honey?" She rocked her daughter gently. "Tell Mama what's the matter? Have you got a pain?"

"I want to go home, I want to go home." Lois sobbed.

"A very fine preacher, a man of God and a friend of mine will run the service for us," said Father James.

"Maybe you've heard about him—a Reverend Peters? A real man of God, amen."

"I thought," Gabriel said, smiling, "that perhaps I could bring the message some Sunday night. The Lord called me a long time ago. I used to have my own church down home."

"You don't want to run too fast, Deacon Grimes," Father James said. "You just take your time. You been coming along right well on Young Ministers' Nights." He paused and looked at Gabriel. "Yes, indeed."

"I just thought," Gabriel said humbly, "that I could be used to more advantage in the house of God."

Father James quoted the text which tells us how preferable it is to be a gate-keeper in the house of God than to dwell in the tent of the wicked; and started to add the dictum from Saint Paul about obedience to those above one in the Lord but decided (watching Gabriel's face) that it was not necessary yet.

"You just keep praying," he said kindly. "You get a little closer to God. He'll work wonders. You'll see." He bent closer to his deacon. "And try to get just a little closer to the *people*."

Roy wandered off with a gawky and dazzled girl named Elizabeth. Johnnie and David wandered restlessly up and down the boat alone. They mounted to the topmost deck and leaned over the railing in the deserted stern. Up here the air was sharp and clean. They faced the water, their arms around each other.

"Your old man was kind of rough this morning," David said carefully, watching the mountains pass.

"Yes," Johnnie said. He looked at David's face against the sky. He shivered suddenly in the sharp, cold air and buried his

face in David's shoulder. David looked down at him and tightened his hold.

"Who do you love?" he whispered. "Who's your boy?"

"You," he muttered fiercely, "I love you."

"Roy!" Elizabeth giggled, "*Roy Grimes*. If you *ever* say a
thing like that *again*."

Now the service was beginning. From all corners of the boat
there was the movement of the saints of God. They gathered
together their various possessions and moved their chairs from
top and bottom decks to the large main hall. It was early
afternoon, not quite two o'clock. The sun was high and fell
everywhere with a copper light. In the city the heat would
have been insupportable; and here, as the saints filed into the
huge, high room, once used as a ballroom, to judge from the
faded and antique appointments, the air slowly began to be
oppressive. The room was the color of black mahogany and
coming in from the bright deck, one groped suddenly in darkness; and took one's sense of direction from the elegant grand
piano which stood in the front of the room on a little plat-
form.

They sat in small rows with one wide aisle between them,
forming, almost unconsciously, a hierarchy. Father James sat
in the front next to Sister McCandless. Opposite them sat Gabriel and Deacon Jones and, immediately behind them, Sister
Daniels and her daughter. Brother Elisha walked in swiftly,
just as they were beginning to be settled. He strode to the
piano and knelt down for a second before rising to take his
place. There was a quiet stir, the saints adjusted themselves,
waiting while Brother Elisha tentatively ran his fingers over
the keys. Gabriel looked about impatiently for Roy and Johnnie, who, engaged no doubt in sinful conversation with David,
were not yet in service. He looked back to where Mrs. Jackson

sat with Lorraine, uncomfortable smiles on their faces, and glanced at his wife, who met his questioning regard quietly, the expression on her face not changing.

Brother Elisha struck the keys and the congregation joined in the song, *Nothing Shall Move Me from the Love of God,* with tambourine and heavy hands and stomping feet. The walls and the floor of the ancient hall trembled and the candelabra wavered in the high ceiling. Outside the river rushed past under the heavy shadow of the Palisades and the copper sun beat down. A few of the strangers who had come along on the outing appeared at the doors and stood watching with an uneasy amusement. The saints sang on, raising their strong voices in praises to Jehovah and seemed unaware of those unsaved who watched and who, some day, the power of the Lord might cause to tremble.

The song ended as Father James rose and faced the congregation, a broad smile on his face. They watched him expectantly, with love. He stood silent for a moment, smiling down upon them. Then he said, and his voice was loud and filled with triumph:

"Well, let us all say, Amen!"

And they cried out obediently, "Well, Amen!"

"Let us all say, praise Him!"

"Praise Him!"

"Let us all say, hallelujah!"

"Hallelujah!"

"Well, glory!" cried Father James. The Holy Ghost touched him and he cried again, "Well, bless Him! Bless His holy name!"

They laughed and shouted after him, their joy so great that they laughed as children and some of them cried as children do; in the fullness and assurance of salvation, in the knowledge that the Lord was in their midst and that each heart, swollen to anguish, yearned only to be filled with His glory. Then, in that moment, each of them might have mounted with wings like eagles far past the sordid persistence of the flesh, the depthless iniquity of the heart, the doom of hours and days and weeks; to be received by the Bridegroom where He waited on high in glory; where all tears were wiped away and death had no power; where the wicked ceased from troubling and the weary soul found rest.

"Saints, let's praise Him," Father James said. "Today, right in the middle of God's great river, under God's great roof, beloved, let us raise our voices in thanksgiving that God has seen fit to save us, amen!"

"Amen! Hallelujah!"

"—and to keep us saved, amen, to keep us, oh glory to God, from the snares of Satan, from the temptation and the lust and the evil of this world!"

"Talk about it!"

"Preach!"

"Ain't nothing strange, amen, about worshiping God *wherever* you might be, ain't that right? Church, when you get this mighty salvation you just can't keep it in, hallelujah! you got to talk about it—"

"Amen!"

"You got to live it, amen. When the Holy Ghost touches you, you *move*, bless God!"

"Well, it's so!"

"Want to hear some testimonies today, amen! I want to hear some *singing* today, bless God! Want to see some *Shouting*, bless God, hallelujah!"

"Talk about it!"

"And I don't want to see none of the saints hold back. If the Lord saved you, amen, He give you a witness *every*where you go. Yes! My soul is a witness, bless our God!"

"Glory!"

"If you ain't saved, amen, get up and praise Him anyhow.

Give God the glory for sparing your sinful life, *praise* Him for the sunshine and the rain, praise Him for all the works of His hands. Saints, I want to hear some praises today, you hear me? I want you to make this old boat *rock*, hallelujah! I want to *feel* your salvation. Are you saved?"

"Amen!"

"Are you sanctified?"

"Glory?"

"Baptized in fire?"

"Yes! So glad!"

"Testify!"

Now the hall was filled with a rushing wind on which forever rides the Lord, death or healing indifferently in His hands. Under this fury the saints bowed low, crying out "holy!" and tears fell. On the open deck sinners stood and watched, beyond them the fiery sun and the deep river, the black-brown-green, unchanging cliffs. That sun, which covered earth and water now, would one day refuse to shine, the river would cease its rushing and its numberless dead would rise; the cliffs would shiver, crack, fall and where they had been would then be nothing but the unleashed wrath of God.

"Who'll be the first to tell it?" Father James cried. "Stand up and talk about it!"

Brother Elisha screamed, "Have mercy, Jesus!" and rose from the piano stool, his powerful frame possessed. And the Holy Ghost touched him and he cried again, bending nearly double, while his feet beat ageless, dreadful signals on the floor, while his arms moved in the air like wings and his face, distorted, no longer his own face not the face of a young man, but timeless, anguished, grim with ecstasy, turned blindly toward heaven. *Yes, Lord,* they cried, *yes!*

"Dearly beloved . . ."

"Talk about it!"

"Tell it!"

"I want to thank and praise the Lord, amen . . ."

"Amen!"

". . . for being here, I want to thank Him for my life, health, and strength. . . ."

"Amen!"

"Well, glory!"

". . . I want to thank Him, hallelujah, for saving my soul one day. . . ."

"*Oh!*"

"Glory!"

". . . for causing the light, bless God, to shine in *my* heart one day when I was still a child, amen, I want to thank Him for bringing me to salvation in the days of my *youth*, hallelujah, when I have all my faculties, amen, before Satan had a chance to destroy my body in the world!"

"Talk about it!"

"He saved me, dear ones, from the world and the things of the world. Saved me, amen, from cardplaying . . ."

"Glory!"

". . . saved me from drinking, bless God, saved me from the streets, from the movies and all the filth that is in the world!"

"I *know* it's so!"

"He saved me, beloved, and sanctified me and filled me with the blessed Holy Ghost, *hallelujah!* Give me a new song, amen which I didn't know before and set my feet on the King's highway. Pray for me beloved, that I will stand in these last and evil days."

"Bless your name, Jesus!"

During his testimony Johnnie and Roy and David had stood quietly beside the door, not daring to enter while he spoke. The moment he sat down they moved quickly, together, to the front of the high hall and knelt down beside their seats to pray. The aspect of each of them underwent always, in this company a striking, even an exciting change; as though their youth, barely begun, were already put away; and the animal, so vividly restless and undiscovered, so tense with power, ready to spring had been already stalked and trapped and offered, a perpetual blood-sacrifice, on the altar of the Lord. Yet their bodies continued to change and grow, preparing them, mysteriously and with ferocious speed, for manhood. No matter how careful their movements, these movements suggested, with a distinctness dreadful for the redeemed to see, the pagan lusting beneath the blood-washed robes. In them was perpetually and perfectly poised the power of revelation against the power of nature; and the saints, considering them with a baleful kind of love, struggled to bring their souls to safety in order, as it were, to steal a march on the flesh while the flesh still slept. A kind of storm, infernal, blew over the congregation as they passed; someone cried, "Bless them, Lord!" and immediately, honey-colored Sister Russell, while they knelt in prayer, rose to her feet to testify.

From the moment that they closed their eyes and covered their faces they were isolated from the joy that moved everything beside them. Yet this same isolation served only to make the glory of the saints more real, the pulse of conviction, however faint, beat in and the glory of God then held an undertone of abject terror. Roy was the first to rise, sitting very straight in his seat and allowing his face to reveal nothing; just as Sister Russell ended her testimony and sat down, sobbing, her head thrown back and both hands raised to heaven. Immediately Sister Daniels raised her strong, harsh voice and hit her tambourine, singing. Brother Elisha turned on the piano stool and hit the keys. Johnnie and David rose from their knees and as they rose the congregation rose, clapping their hands singing. The three boys did not sing; they stood together, carefully ignoring one another, their feet steady on the slightly tilting floor but their bodies moving back and forth as the music grew more savage. And someone cried aloud, a timeless

sound of wailing; fire splashed the open deck and filled the
doors and bathed the sinners standing there; fire filled the
great hall and splashed the faces of the saints and a wind,
unearthly, moved above their heads. Their hands were arched
before them, moving, and their eyes were raised to heaven.
Sweat stained the deacon's collar and soaked the tight head-
bands of the women. Was it true then? and had there indeed
been born one day in Bethlehem a Saviour who was Christ the
Lord? who had died for them—for *them!*—the spat-upon and
beaten with rods, who had worn a crown of thorns and seen
His blood run down like rain; and who had lain in the grave
three days and vanquished death and hell and risen again in
glory—*was it for them?*

Lord, I want to go, show me the way!

For unto us a child is born, unto us a son is given—and
His name shall be called Wonderful, the mighty God, the everlasting Father, the Prince of Peace. Yes, and He was coming
back one day, the King of glory; He would crack the face of
heaven and descend to judge the nations and gather up His
people and take them to their rest.

Take me by my hand and lead me on!

Somewhere in the back a woman cried out and began the
Shout. They looked carefully about, still not looking at one
another, and saw, as from a great distance and through intoler-
able heat, such heat as might have been faced by the Hebrew
children when cast bound into the fiery furnace, that one of
the saints was dancing under the arm of the Lord. She danced
out into the aisle, beautiful with a beauty unbearable, graceful
with grace that poured from heaven. Her face was lifted up,
her eyes were closed and the feet which moved so surely now
were not her own. One by one the power of God moved others
and—as it had been written—the Holy Ghost descended from
heaven with a Shout. Sylvia raised her hands, the tears poured
down her face, and in a moment, she too moved out into the

aisle, Shouting. Is it true then? the saints rejoiced, Roy beat the tambourine. David, grave and shaken, clapped his hands and his body moved insistently in the rhythm of the dancers. Johnnie stood beside him, hot and faint and repeating yet again his struggle, summoning in panic all his forces, to save him from this frenzy. And yet daily he recognized that he was black with sin, that the secrets of his heart were a stench in God's nostrils. *Though your sins be as scarlet they shall be white as snow. Come, let us reason together, saith the Lord.*

Now there was a violent discord on the piano and Brother Elisha leapt to his feet, dancing. Johnnie watched the spinning body and listened, in terror and anguish, to the bestial sobs. Of the men it was only Elisha who danced and the women moved toward him and he moved toward the women. Johnnie felt blow over him an icy wind, all his muscles tightened, as though they furiously resisted some imminent bloody act, as the body of Isaac must have revolted when he saw his father's knife, and, sick and nearly sobbing, he closed his eyes. It was Satan, surely, who stood so foully at his shoulder; and what, but the blood of Jesus, should ever set him free? He thought of the many times he had stood in the congregation of the righteous—and yet he was not saved. He remained among the vast army of the doomed, whose lives—as he had been told, as he now, with such heart-sickness, began to discover for himself—were swamped with wretchedness and whose end was wrath and weeping. Then, for he felt himself falling, he opened his eyes and watched the rejoicing of the saints. His eyes found his father where he stood clapping his hands, glittering with sweat and overwhelming. Then Lois began to shout. For the first time he looked at Roy; their eyes met in brief, wry wonder and Roy imperceptibly shrugged. He watched his mother standing over Lois, her own face obscurely troubled. The light from the door was on her face, the entire room was filled with this strange light. There was no sound now except the sound of

Roy's tambourine and the heavy rhythm of the saints; the
sound of heavy feet and hands and the sound of weeping.
Perhaps centuries past the children of Israel led by Miriam had
made just such a noise as they came out of the wilderness. *For
unto us is born this day a Saviour who is Christ the Lord.*

Yet, in the copper sunlight Johnnie felt suddenly, not the
presence of the Lord, but the presence of David; which
seemed to reach out to him, hand reaching out to hand in the
fury of flood-time, to drag him to the bottom of the water or to
carry him safe to shore. From the corner of his eye he watched
his friend, who held him with such power; and felt, for that
moment, such a depth of love, such nameless and terrible joy
and pain, that he might have fallen, in the face of that company, weeping at David's feet.

Once at Bear Mountain they faced the very great problem of
carrying Sylvia sufficiently far from her mother's sight to
present her with her birthday present. This problem, difficult
enough, was made even more difficult by the continual presence of Brother Elisha; who, inspired by the afternoon's service and by Sylvia's renewal of her faith, remained by her side
to bear witness to the goodness and power of the Lord. Sylvia
listened with her habitual rapt and painful smile. Her mother,
on the one side and Brother Elisha on the other, seemed almost to be taking turns in advising her on her conduct as a
saint of God. They began to despair, as the sun moved visibly
westward, of ever giving her the gold-plated butterfly which
rested uncomfortably in David's waistcoat pocket.

Of course, as Johnnie once suggested, there was really no
reason they could not go up to her, surrounded as she was, and
give her the jewel and get it over with—the more particularly
as David evinced a desire to explore the wonders of Bear
Mountain until this mission should have been fulfilled. Sister
Daniels could scarcely object to an innocuous memento from

three young men, all of whom attended church devoutly and one of whom professed salvation. But this was far from satisfactory for David, who did not wish to hear Sylvia's "thank-you's" in the constricting presence of the saints. Therefore they waited, wandering about the sloping park, lingering near the lake and the skating rink and watching Sylvia.

"God, why don't they go off somewhere and sleep? or pray?" cried David finally. He glared at the nearby rise where Sylvia and her mother sat talking with Brother Elisha. The sun was in their faces and struck from Sylvia's hair as she restlessly moved her head, small blue-black sparks.

Johnnie swallowed his jealousy at seeing how Sylvia filled his comrade's mind; he said, half-angrily, "I still don't see why we don't just go over and give it to her."

Roy looked at him. "Boy, you sound like you ain't got good sense," he said.

Johnnie, frowning, fell into silence. He glanced sidewise at David's puckered face (his eyes were still on Sylvia) and abruptly turned and started walking off.

"Where you going, boy?" David called.

"I'll be back" he said. And he prayed that David would follow him.

But David was determined to catch Sylvia alone and remained where he was with Roy. "Well, make it snappy," he said; and sprawled, full length, on the grass.

As soon as he was alone his pace slackened; he leaned his forehead against the bark of a tree, shaking and burning as in the teeth of a fever. The bark of the tree was rough and cold and though it offered no other comfort he stood there quietly for a long time, seeing beyond him—but it brought no peace— the high clear sky where the sun in fading glory traveled; and the deep earth covered with vivid banners, grass, flower, thorn and vine, thrusting upward forever the brutal trees. At his back he heard the voices of the children and the saints. He knew that he must return, that he must be on hand should David at last outwit Sister Daniels and present her daughter with the golden butterfly. But he did not want to go back, now he realized that he had no interest in the birthday present, no interest whatever in Sylvia—that he had had no interest all along. He shifted his stance, he turned from the tree as he turned his mind from the abyss which suddenly yawned, that abyss, depthless and terrifying, which he had encountered already in dreams. And he slowly began to walk, away from the saints and the voices of the children, his hands in his pockets, struggling to ignore the question which now screamed and screamed in his mind's bright haunted house.

It happened quite simply. Eventually Sister Daniels felt the need to visit the ladies' room, which was a long ways off. Brother Elisha remained where he was while Roy and David, like two beasts crouching in the underbrush, watched him and waited their opportunity. Then he also rose and wandered off to get cold lemonade for Sylvia. She sat quietly alone on the green rise, her hands clasped around her knees, dreaming.

They walked over to her, in terror that Sister Daniels would suddenly reappear. Sylvia smiled as she saw them coming and waved to them merrily. Roy grinned and threw himself on his belly on the ground beside her. David remained standing, fumbling in his waistcoat pocket.

"We got something for you," Roy said.

David produced the butterfly. "Happy birthday, Sylvia," he said. He stretched out his hand, the butterfly glinted oddly in the sun, and he realized with surprise that his hand was shaking. She grinned widely, in amazement and delight, and took the pin from him.

"It's from Johnnie too," he said. "I—we—hope you like it—"

She held the small gold pin in her palm and stared down at it; her face was hidden. After a moment she murmured, "I'm so surprised." She looked up, her eyes shining, almost wet. "Oh, it's wonderful," she said. "I never expected anything. I don't know what to say. It's marvelous, it's wonderful." She pinned the butterfly carefully to her light blue dress. She coughed slightly. "Thank you," she said.

"Your mother won't mind, will she?" Roy asked. "I mean—" he stammered awkwardly under Sylvia's sudden gaze—"we didn't know, we didn't want to get you in any trouble—"

"No," David said. He had not moved; he stood watching Sylvia. Sylvia looked away from Roy and up at David, his eyes met hers and she smiled. He smiled back, suddenly robbed of speech. She looked away again over the path her mother had taken and frowned slightly. "No," she said, "no, she won't mind."

Then there was silence. David shifted uncomfortably from one foot to the other. Roy lay contentedly face down on the grass. The breeze from the river, which lay below them and out of sight, grew subtly more insistent for they had passed the heat of the day; and the sun, moving always westward, fired and polished the tips of trees. Sylvia sighed and shifted on the ground.

"Why isn't Johnnie here?" she suddenly asked.

"He went off somewhere," Roy said. "He said he'd be right back." He looked at Sylvia and smiled. She was looking at David.

"You must want to grow real tall," she said mockingly. "Why don't you sit down?"

David grinned and sat down cross-legged next to Sylvia. "Well, the ladies like 'em tall." He lay on his back and stared up at the sky. "It's a fine day," he said.

She said, "Yes," and looked down at him; he had closed his eyes and was bathing his face in the slowly waning sun. Abruptly, she asked him:

"Why don't you get saved? You around the church all the time and you not saved yet? Why don't you?"

He opened his eyes in amazement. Never before had Sylvia mentioned salvation to him, except as a kind of joke. One of the things he most liked about her was the fact that she never preached to him. Now he smiled. uncertainly and stared at her.

"I'm not joking," she said sharply. "I'm perfectly serious. Roy's saved—at least he *says* so—" and she smiled darkly, in the fashion of the old folks, at Roy—"and anyway, you ought to be thinking about your soul."

"Well, I don't know," David said. "I *think* about it. It's—well, I don't know if I can—well, live it—"

"All you got to do is make up your mind. If you really want to be saved, He'll save you. Yes, and He'll keep you too." She did not sound at all hysterical or transfigured. She spoke very quietly and with great earnestness and frowned as she spoke. David, taken off guard, said nothing. He looked embarrassed and pained and surprised. "Well, I don't know," he finally repeated.

"Do you ever pray?" she asked. "I mean, *really* pray?"

David laughed, beginning to recover himself. "It's not fair,' he said, "you oughtn't to catch me all unprepared like that. Now I don't know what to say." But as he looked at her earnest face he sobered. "Well, I try to be decent. I don't bother nobody." He picked up a grass blade and stared at it. "I don't know," he said at last. "I do my best."

"*Do* you?" she asked.

He laughed again, defeated. "Girl," he said, "you *are* a killer."

She laughed too. "You black-eyed demon," she said, "if I don't see you at revival services I'll never speak to you again." He looked up quickly, in some surprise, and she said, still smiling, "Don't look at me like that. I mean it."

"All right, sister," he said. Then: "If I come out can I walk you home?"

"I got my mother to walk me home—"

"Well, let your mother walk home with Brother Elisha," he said, grinning, "Let the old folks stay together."

"Loose him, Satan!" she cried, laughing, "loose the boy!"

"The brother needs prayer," Roy said.

"Amen," said Sylvia. She looked down again at David. "I want to see you at church. Don't you forget it."

"All right," he said. "I'll be there."

The boat whistles blew at six o'clock, punctuating their holiday; blew, fretful and insistent, through the abruptly dispirited park and skaters left the skating rink; boats were rowed in furiously from the lake. Children were called from the swings and the seesaw and the merry-go-round and forced to leave behind the ball which had been lost in the forest and the torn kite which dangled from the top of a tree. ("Hush now," said their parents, "we'll get you another one—come along." *"Tomorrow?"*—"Come along, honey, it's time to go!") The old folks rose from the benches, from the grass, gathered together the empty lunch-basket, the half-read newspaper, the Bible which was carried everywhere; and they started down the hillside, an army in disorder. David walked with Sylvia and Sister Daniels and Brother Elisha, listening to their conversation (good Lord, thought Johnnie, don't they ever mention anything but sin?) and carrying Sylvia's lunch-basket. He seemed interested in what they were saying; every now and then he looked at Sylvia and grinned and she grinned back. Once, as Sylvia stumbled, he put his hand on her elbow to steady her and held her arm perhaps a moment too long. Brother Elisha, on the far side of Sister Daniels, noticed this and a frown passed over his face. He kept talking, staring now and then hard at Sylvia and trying, with a certain almost humorous helplessness, to discover what was in her mind. Sister Daniels talked of nothing but the service on the boat and of the forthcoming revival. She scarcely seemed to notice David's presence, though once she spoke to him, making some remark about the need, on his part, of much prayer. Gabriel carried the sleeping baby in his arms, striding beside his wife and Lois—who stumbled perpetually and held tightly to her mother's hand. Roy was somewhere in the back, joking with Elizabeth. At a turn in the road the boat and the dock appeared below them, a dead gray-white in the sun.

Johnnie walked down the slope alone, watching David and Sylvia ahead of him. When he had come back, both Roy and David had disappeared and Sylvia sat again in the company of her mother and Brother Elisha; and if he had not seen the gold butterfly on her dress he would have been aware of no change. She thanked him for his share in it and told him that Roy and David were at the skating rink.

But when at last he found them they were far in the middle of the lake in a rowboat. He was afraid of water, he could not row. He stood on the bank and watched them. After a long while they saw him and waved and started to bring the boat in so that he could join them. But the day was ruined for him; by the time they brought the boat in, the hour, for which they had hired it, was over; David went in search of his mother for more money but when he came back it was time to leave. Then he walked with Sylvia.

All during the trip home David seemed preoccupied. When he finally sought out Johnnie he found him sitting by himself on the top deck, shivering a little in the night air. He sat down beside him. After a moment Johnnie moved and put his head on David's shoulder. David put his arms around him. But now where there had been peace there was only panic and where there had been safety, danger, like a flower, opened.

The Man Child

As the sun began preparing for her exit, and he sensed the waiting night, Eric, blond and eight years old and dirty and tired, started homeward across the fields. Eric lived with his father, who was a farmer and the son of a farmer, and his mother, who had been captured by his father on some far-off, unblessed, unbelievable night, who had never since burst her chains. She did not know that she was chained anymore than she knew that she lived in terror of the night. One child was in the churchyard, it would have been Eric's little sister and her name would have been Sophie: for a long time, then, his mother had been very sick and pale. It was said that she would never, really, be better, that she would never again be as she had been. Then, not long ago, there had begun to be a pounding in his mother's belly, Eric had sometimes been able to hear it when he lay against her breast. His father had been pleased. *I did that,* said his father, big, laughing, dreadful, and red, and Eric knew how it was done, he had seen the horses and the blind and dreadful bulls. But then, again, his mother had been sick, she had had to be sent away, and when she came back the pounding was not there anymore, nothing was there anymore. His father laughed less, something in his mother's face seemed to have gone to sleep forever.

Eric hurried, for the sun was almost gone and he was afraid the night would catch him in the fields. And his mother would be angry. She did not really like him to go wandering off by himself. She would have forbidden it completely and kept Eric under her eye all day but in this she was overruled: Eric's father liked to think of Eric as being curious about the world and as being daring enough to explore it, with his own eyes, by himself.

His father would not be at home. He would be gone with his friend, Jamie, who was also a farmer and the son of a farmer, down to the tavern. This tavern was called the Rafters. They went each night, as his father said, imitating an Englishman he had known during a war, *to destruct the Rafters, sir.* They had been destructing The Rafters long before Eric had kicked in his mother's belly, for Eric's father and Jamie had grown up together, gone to war together, and survived together—never, apparently, while life ran, were they to be divided. They worked in the fields all day together, the fields which belonged to Eric's father. Jamie had been forced to sell his farm and it was Eric's father who had bought it.

Jamie had a brown and yellow dog. This dog was almost always with him; whenever Eric thought of Jamie he thought also of the dog. They had always been there, they had always been together: in exactly the same way, for Eric, that his mother and father had always been together, in exactly the same way that the earth and the trees and the sky were together. Jamie and his dog walked the country roads together, Jamie walking slowly in the way of country people, seeming to see nothing, heads lightly bent, feet striking surely and heavily on the earth, never stumbling. He walked as though he were going to walk to the other end of the world and knew it was a long way but knew that he would be there by the morning. Sometimes he talked to his dog, head bent a little more than usual an turned to one side, a slight smile playing about the edges of his granite lips; and the dog's head snapped up, perhaps he leapt upon his master, who cuffed him down lightly, with one hand. More often he was silent. His head was carried in a cloud of blue smoke from his pipe. Through this cloud, like a ship on a foggy day, loomed his dry and steady face. Set far back, at an unapproachable angle, were those eyes of his, smoky and thoughtful, eyes which seemed always to be considering the horizon. He had the kind of eyes which no one had ever looked into—except Eric, only once. Jamie had been walking these roads and across these fields, whistling for his dog in the evenings as he turned away from Eric's house, for years, in silence. He had been married once, but his wife had run away. Now he lived alone in a wooden house and Eric's mother kept his clothes clean and Jamie always ate at Eric's house.

Eric had looked into Jamie's eyes on Jamie's birthday. They had had a party for him. Eric's mother had baked a cake and filled the house with flowers. The doors and windows of the great kitchen all stood open on the yard and the kitchen table was placed outside. The ground was not muddy as it was in winter, but hard, dry, and light brown. The flowers his mother so loved and so labored for flamed in their narrow borders against the stone wall of the farmhouse; and green vines covered the grey stone wall at the far end of the yard. Beyond this wall were the fields and barns, and Eric could see, quite far away, the cows nearly motionless in the bright green pasture. It was a bright, hot, silent day, the sun did not seem to be moving at all.

This was before his mother had had to be sent away. Her belly had been beginning to grow big, she had been dressed in blue, and had seemed—that day, to Eric—younger than she was ever to seem again.

Though it was still early when they were called to table, Eric's father and Jamie were already tipsy and came across the fields, shoulders touching, laughing, and telling each other stories. To express disapproval and also, perhaps, because she had heard their stories before and was bored, Eric's mother was quite abrupt with them, barely saying, "Happy Birthday, Jamie" before she made them sit down. In the nearby village church bells rang as they began to eat.

It was perhaps because it was Jamie's birthday that Eric was held by something in Jamie's face. Jamie, of course, was very old. He was thirty-four today, even older than Eric's father, who was only thirty-two. Eric wondered how it felt to have so many years and was suddenly, secretly glad that he was only eight. For today, Jamie *looked* old. It was perhaps the one additional year which had done it, this day, before their very eyes—a metamorphosis which made Eric rather shrink at the prospect of becoming nine. The skin of Jamie's face, which had never before seemed so, seemed wet today, and that rocky mouth of his was loose; loose was the word for everything about him, the way his arms and shoulders hung, the way he sprawled at the table, rocking slightly back and forth. It was not that he was drunk. Eric had seen him much drunker. Drunk, he became rigid, as though he imagined himself in the army again. No. He was old. It had come upon him all at once, today, on his birthday. He sat there, his hair in his eyes, eating, drinking, laughing now and again, and in a very strange way, and teasing the dog at his feet so that it sleepily growled and snapped all through the birthday dinner.

"Stop that," said Eric's father.

"Stop what?" asked Jamie.

"Let that stinking useless dog alone. Let him be quiet."

"Leave the beast alone," said Eric's mother—very wearily, sounding as she often sounded when talking to Eric.

"Well, now," said Jamie, grinning, and looking first at Eric's father and then at Eric's mother, "it *is* my beast. And a man's got a right to do as he likes with whatever's his."

"That dog's got a right to bite you, too," said Eric's mother, shortly.

"This dog's not going to bite me," said Jamie, "he knows I'll shoot him if he does."

"That dog knows you're not going to shoot him," said Eric's father. "Then you *would* be all alone."

"All alone," said Jamie, and looked around the table. "All alone." He lowered his eyes to his plate. Eric's father watched him. He said, "It's pretty serious to be all alone at *your* age." He smiled. "If I was you, I'd start thinking about it."

"I'm thinking about it," said Jamie. He began to grow red.

"No, you're not," said Eric's father, "you're dreaming about it."

"Well, goddammit," said Jamie, even redder now, "it isn't as though I haven't tried!"

"Ah," said Eric's father, "that was a *real* dream, that was. I used to pick *that* up on the streets of town every Saturday night."

"Yes," said Jamie, "I bet you did."

"I didn't think she was as bad as all that," said Eric's mother, quietly. "*I* liked her. I was surprised when she ran away."

"Jamie didn't know how to keep her," said Eric's father. He looked at Eric and chanted: *"Jamie, Jamie, pumkin-eater, had a wife and couldn't keep her!"* At this, Jamie at last looked up, into the eyes of Eric's father. Eric laughed again, more shrilly, out of fear. Jamie said:

"Ah, yes, you can talk, you can."

"It's not my fault," said Eric's father, "if you're getting old— and haven't got anybody to bring you your slippers when night comes—and no pitter-patter of little feet—"

"Oh, leave Jamie alone," said Eric's mother, "he's *not* old, leave him alone."

Jamie laughed a peculiar, high, clicking laugh which Eric had never heard before, which he did not like, which made him want to look away and, at the same time, want to stare. "Hell, no," said Jamie, "I'm not old. I can still do all the things we used to do." He put his elbows on the table, grinning. "I haven't ever told you, have I, about the things we used to do?"

"No, you haven't," said Eric's mother, "and I certainly don't want to hear about them now."

"He wouldn't tell you anyway," said Eric's father, "he knows what I'd do to him if he did."

"Oh, sure, sure," said Jamie, and laughed again. He picked

up a bone from his plate. "Here," he said to Eric, "why don't you feed my poor mistreated dog?"

Eric took the bone and stood up, whistling for the dog; who moved away from his master and took the bone between his teeth. Jamie watched with a smile and opened the bottle of whiskey and poured himself a drink. Eric sat on the ground beside the dog, beginning to be sleepy in the bright, bright sun.

"Little Eric's getting big," he heard his father say.

"Yes," said Jamie, "they grow fast. It won't be long now."

"Won't be long *what?*" he heard his father ask.

"Why, before he starts skirt-chasing like his Daddy used to do," said Jamie. There was mild laughter at the table in which his mother did not join; he heard instead, or thought he heard, the familiar, slight, exasperated intake of her breath. No one seemed to care whether he came back to the table or not. He lay on his back, staring up at the sky, wondering—wondering what he would feel like when he was old—and fell asleep.

When he awoke his head was in his mother's lap, for she was sitting on the ground. Jamie and his father were still sitting at the table; he knew this from their voices, for he did not open his eyes. He did not want to move or speak. He wanted to remain where he was, protected by his mother, while the bright day rolled on. Then he wondered about the uncut birthday cake. But he was sure, from the sound of Jamie's voice, which was thicker now, that they had not cut it yet; or if they had, they had certainly saved a piece for him.

"—ate himself just as full as he could and then fell asleep in the sun like a little animal," Jamie was saying, and the two men laughed. His father—though he scarcely ever got as drunk as Jamie did, and had often carried Jamie home from The Rafters—was a little drunk, too.

Eric felt his mother's hand on his hair. By opening his eyes very slightly he would see, over the curve of his mother's thigh, as through a veil, a green slope far away and beyond it the everlasting, motionless sky.

"—she was a no-good *bitch*," said Jamie.

"She was beautiful," said his mother, just above him.

Again, they were talking about Jamie's wife.

"Beauty!" said Jamie, furious. "Beauty doesn't keep a house clean. Beauty doesn't keep a bed warm, neither."

Eric's father laughed. "You were so—poetical—in those days, Jamie," he said. "Nobody thought you cared much about things like that. I guess she thought you didn't care, neither."

"I cared," said Jamie, briefly.

"In fact," Eric's father continued, "I *know* she thought you didn't care."

"*How* do you know?" asked Jamie.

"She told me," Eric's father said.

"What do you mean," asked Jamie, "what do you mean, she told you?"

"I mean just that. She told me."

Jamie was silent.

"In those days" Eric's father continued after a moment, "all you did was walk around the woods by yourself in the daytime and sit around The Rafters in the evenings with me."

"You two were always together then," said Eric's mother.

"Well," said Jamie, harshly, "at least that hasn't changed."

"Now, you know," said Eric's father, gently, "it's not the same. Now I got a wife and kid—and another one coming—"

Eric's mother stroked his hair more gently, yet with something in her touch more urgent, too, and he knew that she was thinking of the child who lay in the churchyard, who would have been his sister.

"Yes," said Jamie, "you really got it all fixed up, you did. You got it all—the wife, the kid, the house, and all the land."

"I didn't steal your farm from you. It wasn't my fault you

lost it. I gave you a better price for it than anybody else would have done."

"I'm not blaming you. I know all the things I have to thank you for."

There was a short pause, broken, hesitantly, by Eric's mother. "What I don't understand," she said, "is why, when you went away to the city, you didn't *stay* away. You didn't really have anything to keep you here."

There was the sound of a drink being poured. Then, "No. I didn't have nothing—*really*—to keep me here. Just all the things I ever knew—all the things—*all* the things—I ever cared about."

"A man's not supposed to sit around and mope," said Eric's father, wrathfully, "for things that are over and dead and finished, things that can't *ever* begin again, that can't ever be the same again. That's what I mean when I say you're a dreamer—and if you hadn't kept on dreaming so long, you might not be alone now."

"Ah, well," said Jamie, mildly, and with a curious rush of affection in his voice, 'I know you're the giant-killer, the hunter, the lover—the real old Adam, that's you. I know you're going to cover the earth. I know the world depends on men like you."

"And you're damn right," said Eric's father, after an uneasy moment.

Around Eric's head there was a buzzing, a bee, perhaps, a blue-fly, or a wasp. He hoped that his mother would see it and brush it away, but she did not move her hand. And he looked out again, through the veil of his eyelashes, at the slope and the sky, and then saw that the sun had moved and that it would not be long now before she would be going.

"—just like you already," Jamie said.

"You think my little one's like me?" Eric knew that his father was smiling—he could almost feel his father's hands.

"Looks like you, walks like you, talks like you," said Jamie.

"*And* stubborn like you," said Eric's mother.

"Ah, yes," said Jamie, and sighed. "You married the stubbornest, most determined—most selfish—man I know."

"I didn't know you felt that way," said Eric's father. He was still smiling.

"I'd have warned you about him," Jamie added, laughing, "if there'd been time."

"Everyone who knows you feels that way," said Eric's mother, and Eric felt a sudden brief tightening of the muscle in her thigh.

"Oh, *you*," said Eric's father, "I know *you* feel that way, women like to feel that way, it makes them feel important. But," and he changed to the teasing tone he took so persistently with Jamie today, "I didn't know my fine friend, Jamie, here—"

It was odd how unwilling he was to open his eyes. Yet, he felt the sun on him and knew that he wanted to rise from where he was before the sun went down. He did not understand what they were talking about this afternoon, these grown-ups he had known all his life; by keeping his eyes closed he kept their conversation far from him. And his mother's hand lay on his head like a blessing, like protection. And the buzzing had ceased, the bee, the blue-fly, or the wasp seemed to have flown away.

"—if it's a boy this time," his father said, "we'll name it after you."

"That's touching," said Jamie, "but that really won't do me— or the kid—a hell of a lot of good."

"Jamie can get married and have kids of his own any time he decides to," said Eric's mother.

"No," said his father, after a long pause, "Jamie's thought about it too long."

And, suddenly, he laughed and Eric sat up as his father slapped Jamie on the knee. At the touch, Jamie leaped up, shouting, spilling his drink and overturning his chair, and the dog beside Eric awoke and began to bark. For a moment, before Eric's unbelieving eyes, there was nothing in the yard but noise and flame.

His father rose slowly and stared at Jamie. "What's the matter with you?"

"What's the matter with me!" mimicked Jamie, "what's the matter with me? what the hell do you care what's the matter with me! What the hell have you been riding me for all day like this? What do you want? what do you *want?*"

"I want you to learn to hold your liquor for one thing," said his father, coldly. The two men stared at each other. Jamie's face was red and ugly and tears stood in his eyes. The dog, at his legs, kept up a furious prancing and barking. Jamie bent down and, with one hand, with all his might, slapped his dog, which rolled over, howling, and ran away to hide itself under the shadows of the far grey wall.

Then Jamie stared again at Eric's father, trembling, and pushed his hair back from his eyes.

"You better pull yourself together," Eric's father said. And, to Eric's mother. "Get him some coffee. He'll be all right."

Jamie set his glass on the table and picked up the overturned chair. Eric's mother rose and went into the kitchen. Eric remained sitting on the ground, staring at the two men, his father and his father's best friend, who had become so unfamiliar. His father, with something in his face which Eric had never before seen there, a tenderness, a sorrow—or perhaps it was, after all, the look he sometimes wore when approaching a calf he was about to slaughter—looked down at Jamie where he sat, head bent, at the table. "You take things too hard," he said. "You always have. I was only teasing you for your own good."

Jamie did not answer. His father looked over to Eric, and smiled.

"Come on," he said. "You and me are going for a walk."

Eric, passing on the side of the table farthest from Jamie, went to his father and took his hand.

"Pull yourself together," his father said to Jamie. "We're going to cut your birthday cake as soon as me and the little one come back."

Eric and his father passed beyond the grey wall where the dog still whimpered, out into the fields. Eric's father was walking too fast and Eric stumbled on the uneven ground. When they had gone a little distance his father abruptly checked his pace and looked down at Eric, grinning.

"I'm sorry," he said. "I guess I said we were going for a walk, not running to put out a fire."

"What's the matter with Jamie?" Eric asked.

"Oh," said his father, looking westward where the sun was moving, pale orange now, making the sky ring with brass and copper and gold—which, like a magician, she was presenting only to demonstrate how variously they could be transformed —"Oh," he repeated, "there's nothing wrong with Jamie. He's been drinking a lot," and he grinned down at Eric, "and he's been sitting in the sun—you know, his hair's not as thick as yours," and he ruffled Eric's hair, "and I guess birthdays make him nervous. Hell," he said, "they make me nervous, too."

"Jamie's *very* old," said Eric, "isn't he?"

His father laughed. "Well, butch, he's not exactly ready to fall into the grave yet—he's going to be around awhile, is Jamie. Hey," he said, and looked down at Eric again, "you must think I'm an old man, too."

"Oh," said Eric, quickly, "I know you're not as old as Jamie."

His father laughed again. "Well, thank you, son. That shows real confidence. I'll try to live up to it."

They walked in silence for awhile and then his father said, not looking at Eric, speaking to himself, it seemed, or to the air: "No, Jamie's not so old. He's not as old as he should be."

"How old *should* he be?" asked Eric.

"Why," said his father, "he ought to be his age," and, looking down at Eric's face, he burst into laughter again.

"Ah," he said, finally, and put his hand on Eric's head again, very gently, very sadly, "don't you worry now about what you don't understand. The time is coming when you'll have to worry—but that time hasn't come yet."

Then they walked till they came to the steep slope which led to the railroad tracks, down, down, far below them, where a small train seemed to be passing forever through the countryside, smoke, like the very definition of idleness, blowing out of the chimney stack of the toy locomotive. Eric thought, resentfully, that he scarcely ever saw a train pass when he came here alone. Beyond the railroad tracks was the river where they sometimes went swimming in the summer. The river was hidden from them now by the high bank where there were houses and where tall trees grew.

"And this," said his father, "is where your land ends."

"What?" said Eric.

His father squatted on the ground and put one hand on Eric's shoulder. "You know all the way we walked, from the house?" Eric nodded. "Well," said his father, "that's your land."

Eric looked back at the long way they had come, feeling his father watching him.

His father, with a pressure on his shoulder made him turn; he pointed: "And over there. It belongs to you." He turned him again. "And that," he said, "that's yours, too."

Eric stared at his father. "Where does it end?" he asked.

His father rose. "I'll show you that another day," he said. "But it's further than you can walk."

They started walking slowly, in the direction of the sun.

"When did it get to be mine?" asked Eric.

"The day you were born," his father said, and looked down at him and smiled.

"My father," he said, after a moment, "had some of this land
—and when he died, it was mine. He held on to it for me. And
I did my best with the land I had, and I got some more. I'm
holding on to it for you."

He looked down to see if Eric was listening. Eric was listening, staring at his father and looking around him at the great
countryside.

"When I get to be a real old man," said his father, "even
older than old Jamie there—you're going to have to take care
of all this. When I die it's going to be yours." He paused and
stopped; Eric looked up at him. "When you get to be a big
man, like your Papa, you're going to get married and have
children. And all this is going to be theirs."

"And when *they* get married?" Eric prompted.

"All this will belong to *their* children," his father said.

"Forever?" cried Eric.

"Forever," said his father.

They turned and started walking toward the house.

"Jamie," Eric asked at last, "how much land has *he* got?"

"Jamie doesn't have any land," his father said.

"Why not?" asked Eric.

"He didn't take care of it," his father said, "and he lost it."

"Jamie doesn't have a wife anymore, either, does he?" Eric
asked.

"No," said his father. "He didn't take care of her, either."

"And he doesn't have any little boy," said Eric—very sadly.

"No," said his father. Then he grinned. "But *I* have."

"*Why* doesn't Jamie have a little boy?" asked Eric.

His father shrugged. "Some people do, Eric, some people
don't."

"Will I?" asked Eric.

"Will you what?" asked his father.

"Will I get married and have a little boy?"

His father seemed for a moment both amused and checked.
He looked down at Eric with a strange, slow smile. "Of course

you, will," he said at last. "Of course you will." And he held out
his arms. "Come," he said, "climb up. I'll ride you on my shoulders home."

So Eric rode on his father's shoulders through the wide
green fields which belonged to him, into the yard which held
the house which would hear the first cries of his children. His
mother and Jamie sat at the table talking quietly in the silver
sun. Jamie had washed his face and combed his hair, he
seemed calmer, he was smiling.

"Ah," cried Jamie, "the lord, the master of this house arrives!
And bears on his shoulders the prince, the son, and heir!" He
described a flourish, bowing low in the yard. "My lords! Be-
hold your humble, most properly chastised servant, desirous of
your—compassion, your love, and your forgiveness!"

"Frankly," said Eric's father, putting Eric on the ground,
"I'm not sure that this is an improvement." He looked at Jamie
and frowned and grinned. "Let's cut that cake."

Eric stood with his mother in the kitchen while she lit the
candles—thirty-five, one, as they said, to grow on, though
Jamie, surely, was far past the growing age—and followed
her as she took the cake outside. Jamie took the great, gleaming knife and held it with a smile.

"Happy Birthday!" they cried—only Eric said nothing—and
then Eric's mother said, "You have to blow out the candles,
Jamie, before you cut the cake."

"It looks so pretty the way it is," Jamie said.

"Go ahead," said Eric's father, and clapped him on the back,
"be a man."

Then the dog, once more beside his master, awoke, growl-
ing, and this made everybody laugh. Jamie laughed loudest.
Then he blew out the candles, all of them at once, and Eric
watched him as he cut the cake. Jamie raised his eyes and
looked at Eric and it was at this moment, as the suddenly
blood-red sun was striking the topmost tips of trees, that Eric

had looked into Jamie's eyes. Jamie smiled that strange smile of an old man and Eric moved closer to his mother.

"The first piece for Eric", said Jamie, then, and extended it to him on the silver blade.

That had been near the end of summer, nearly two months ago. Very shortly after the birthday party, his mother had fallen ill and had had to be taken away. Then his father spent more time than ever at The Rafters; he and Jamie came home in the evenings, stumbling drunk. Sometimes, during the time that his mother was away, Jamie did not go home at all, but spent the night at the farm house; and once or twice Eric had awakened in the middle of the night, or near dawn, and heard Jamie's footsteps walking up and down, walking up and down, in the big room downstairs. It has been a strange and dreadful time, a time of waiting, stillness, and silence. His father rarely went into the fields, scarcely raised himself to give orders to his farm hands—it was unnatural, it was frightening, to find him around the house all day, and Jamie was there always, Jamie and his dog. Then one day Eric's father told him that his mother was coming home but that she would not be bringing him a baby brother or sister, not this time, nor in any time to come. He started to say something more, then looked at Jamie who was standing by, and walked out of the house. Jamie followed him slowly, his hands in his pockets and his head bent. From the time of the birthday party, as though he were repenting of that outburst, or as though it had frightened him, Jamie had become more silent than ever.

When his mother came back she seemed to have grown older—old; she seemed to have shrunk within herself, away from them all, even, in a kind of storm of love and helplessness, away from Eric; but, oddly, and most particularly, away from Jamie. It was in nothing she said, nothing she did—or perhaps it was in everything she said and did. She washed and cooked for Jamie as before, took him into account as much as before as a part of the family, made him take second helpings at the table, smiled good night to him as he left the house—it was only that something had gone out of her familiarity. She seemed to do all that she did out of memory and from a great distance. And if something had gone out of her ease, something had come into it, too, a curiously still attention, as though she had been startled by some new aspect of something she had always known. Once or twice at the supper table, Eric caught her regard bent on Jamie, who, obliviously, ate. He could not read her look, but it reminded him of that moment at the birthday party when he had looked into Jamie's eyes. She seemed to be looking at Jamie as though she were wondering why she had not looked at him before; or as though she were discovering, with some surprise, that she had never really liked him but also felt, in her weariness and weakness, that it did not really matter now.

Now, as he entered the yard, he saw her standing in the kitchen doorway, looking out, shielding her eyes against the brilliant setting sun.

"Eric!" she cried, wrathfully, as soon as she saw him, "I've been looking high and low for you for the last hour. You're getting old enough to have some sense of responsibility and I wish you wouldn't worry me so when you know I've not been well."

She made him feel guilty at the same time that he dimly and resentfully felt that justice was not all on her side. She pulled him to her, turning his face up toward hers, roughly, with one hand.

"You're filthy," she said, then. "Go around to the pump and wash your face. And hurry, so I can give you your supper and put you to bed."

And she turned and went into the kitchen, closing the door

lightly behind her. He walked around to the other side of the
house, to the pump.

On a wooden box next to the pump was a piece of soap and
a damp rag. Eric picked up the soap, not thinking of his
mother, but thinking of the day gone by, already half asleep:
and thought of where he would go tomorrow. He moved the
pump handle up and down and the water rushed out and wet
his socks and shoes—this would make his mother angry, but he
was too tired to care. Nevertheless, automatically, he moved
back a little. He held the soap between his hands, his hands
beneath the water.

He had been many places, he had walked a long way and
seen many things that day. He had gone down to the railroad
tracks and walked beside the tracks for awhile, hoping that a
train would pass. He kept telling himself that he would give
the train one more last chance to pass; and when he had given
it a considerable number of last chances, he left the railroad bed and climbed a little and walked through the high,
sweet meadows. He walked through a meadow where there
were cows and they looked at him dully with their great dull
eyes and moo'd among each other about him. A man from the
far end of the field saw him and shouted, but Eric could not
tell whether it was someone who worked for his father or not
and so he turned and ran away, ducking through the wire
fence. He passed an apple tree, with apples lying all over the
ground—he wondered if the apples belonged to him, if he
were still walking on his own land or had gone past it—but he
ate an apple anyway and put some in his pockets, watching a
lone brown horse in a meadow far below him nibbling at the
grass and flicking his tail. Eric pretended that he was his father
and was walking through the fields as he had seen his father
walk, looking it all over calmly, pleased, knowing that everything he saw belonged to him. And he stopped and pee'd as he
had seen his father do, standing wide-legged and heavy in the

middle of the fields; he pretended at the same time to be smoking and talking, as he had seen his father do. Then, having watered the ground, he walked on, and all the earth, for that moment, in Eric's eyes, seemed to be celebrating Eric.

Tomorrow he would go away again, somewhere. For soon it would be winter, snow would cover the ground, he would not be able to wander off alone.

He held the soap between his hands, his hands beneath the water; then he heard a low whistle behind him and a rough hand on his head and the soap fell from his hands and slithered between his legs onto the ground.

He turned and faced Jamie, Jamie without his dog.

"Come on, little fellow," Jamie whispered. "We got something in the barn to show you."

"Oh, did the calf come yet?" asked Eric—and was too pleased to wonder why Jamie whispered.

"Your Papa's there," said Jamie. And then: "Yes. Yes, the calf is coming now."

And he took Eric's hand and they crossed the yard, past the closed kitchen door, past the stone wall and across the field, into the barn.

"But *this* isn't where the cows are!" Eric cried. He suddenly looked up at Jamie, who closed the barn door behind them and looked down at Eric with a smile.

"No," said Jamie, "that's right. No cows here." And he leaned against the door as though his strength had left him. Eric saw that his face was wet, he breathed as though he had been running.

"Let's go see the cows," Eric whispered. Then he wondered why he was whispering and was terribly afraid. He stared at Jamie, who stared at him.

"In a minute," Jamie said, and stood up. He had put his hands in his pockets and now he brought them out and Eric stared at his hands and began to move away. He asked, "Where's my Papa?"

"Why," said Jamie, "he's down at The Rafters, I guess. I have to meet him there soon."

"I have to go," said Eric. "I have to eat my supper." He tried to move to the door, but Jamie did not move. "I have to go," he repeated, and, as Jamie moved toward him the tight ball of terror in his bowels, in his throat, swelled and rose, exploded, he opened his mouth to scream but Jamie's fingers closed around his throat. He stared, stared into Jamie's eyes.

"That won't do you any good," said Jamie. And he smiled. Eric struggled for breath, struggled with pain and fright. Jamie relaxed his grip a little and moved one hand and stroked Eric's tangled hair. Slowly, wondrously, his face changed, tears came into his eyes and rolled down his face.

Eric groaned—perhaps because he saw Jamie's tears or because his throat was so swollen and burning, because he could not catch his breath, because he was so frightened—he began to sob in great, unchildish gasps. 'Why do you hate my father?'

"I love your father," Jamie said. But he was not listening to Eric. He was far away—as though he were struggling, toiling inwardly up a tall, tall mountain. And Eric struggled blindly, with all the force of his desire to live, to reach him, to stop him before he reached the summit.

"Jamie," Eric whispered, "you can have the land. You can have all the land."

Jamie spoke, but not to Eric: "I don't want the land."

"I'll be your little boy," said Eric. "I'll be your little boy forever and forever and forever—and you can have the land and you can live forever! Jamie!"

Jamie had stopped weeping. He was watching Eric.

"We'll go for a walk tomorrow," Eric said, "and I'll show it to you, all of it—really and truly—if you kill my father I can be your little boy and we can have it all!"

"This land," said Jamie, "will belong to no one."

"Please!" cried Eric, "oh, please! Please!"

He heard his mother singing in the kitchen. Soon she would

come out to look for him. The hands left him for a moment. Eric opened his mouth to scream, but the hands then closed around his throat.

Mama. Mama.

The singing was further and further away. The eyes looked into his, there was a question in the eyes, the hands tightened. Then the mouth began to smile. He had never seen such a smile before. He kicked and kicked.

Mama. Mama. Mama. Mama. Mama.

Far away, he heard his mother call him.

Mama.

He saw nothing, he knew that he was in the barn, he heard a terrible breathing near him, he thought he heard the sniffling of beasts, he remembered the sun, the railroad tracks, the cows, the apples, and the ground. He thought of tomorrow— he wanted to go away again somewhere tomorrow. *I'll take you with me,'* he wanted to say. He wanted to argue the question, the question he remembered in the eyes—wanted to say, *I'll tell my Papa you're hurting me.* Then terror and agony and darkness overtook him, and his breath went violently out of him. He dropped on his face in the straw in the barn, his yellow head useless on his broken neck.

Night covered the countryside and here and there, like emblems, the lights of houses glowed. A woman's voice called, "Eric! Eric!"

Jamie reached his wooden house and opened his door; whistled, and his dog came bounding out of darkness, leaping up on him; and he cuffed it down lightly, with one hand. Then he closed his door and started down the road, his dog beside him, his hands in his pockets. He stopped to light his pipe. He heard singing from The Rafters, then he saw the lights; soon, the lights and the sound of singing diminished behind him. When Jamie no longer heard the singing, he began to whistle the song that he had heard.

Previous Condition

I woke up shaking, alone in my room. I was clammy cold with sweat; under me the sheet and the mattress were soaked. The sheet was gray and twisted like a rope. I breathed like I had been running.

I couldn't move for the longest while. I just lay on my back, spread-eagled, looking up at the ceiling, listening to the sounds of people getting up in other parts of the house, alarm clocks ringing and water splashing and doors opening and shutting and feet on the stairs. I could tell when people left for work: the hall doorway downstairs whined and shuffled as it opened and gave a funny kind of double slam as it closed. One thud and then a louder thud and then a little final click. While the door was open I could hear the street sounds too, horses' hoofs and delivery wagons and people in the streets and big trucks and motor cars screaming on the asphalt.

I had been dreaming. At night I dreamt and woke up in the morning trembling, but not remembering the dream, except that in the dream I had been running. I could not remember when the dream—or dreams—had started; it had been long ago. For long periods maybe, I would have no dreams at all. And then they would come back, every night, I would try not to go to bed, I would go to sleep frightened and wake up frightened and have another day to get through with the nightmare at my shoulder. Now I was back from Chicago, busted, living off my friends in a dirty furnished room downtown. The show I had been with had folded in Chicago. It hadn't been much of a part—or much of a show either, to tell the truth. I played a kind of intellectual Uncle Tom, a young college student working for his race. The playwright had wanted to prove he was a liberal, I guess. But, as I say, the show had folded and here I was, back in New York and hating it. I knew that I should be getting another job, making the rounds, pounding the pavement. But I didn't. I couldn't face it.

It was summer. I seemed to be fagged out. And every day I hated myself more. Acting's a rough life, even if you're white. I'm not tall and I'm not good looking and I can't sing or dance and I'm not white; so even at the best of times I wasn't in much demand.

The room I lived in was heavy ceilinged, perfectly square, with walls the color of chipped dry blood. Jules Weissman, a Jewboy, had got the room for me. It's a room to sleep in, he said, or maybe to die in but God knows it wasn't meant to live in. Perhaps because the room was so hideous it had a fantastic array of light fixtures: one on the ceiling, one on the left wall, two on the right wall, and a lamp on the table beside my bed. My bed was in front of the window through which nothing ever blew but dust. It was a furnished room and they'd thrown enough stuff in it to furnish three rooms its size. Two easy chairs and a desk, the bed, the table, a straight-backed chair, a bookcase, a cardboard wardrobe; and my books and my suitcase, both unpacked; and my dirty clothes flung in a corner. It was the kind of room that defeated you. It had a fireplace, too, and a heavy marble mantelpiece and a great gray mirror above the mantelpiece. It was hard to see anything in the mirror very clearly—which was perhaps just as well—and it would have been worth your life to have started a fire in the fireplace.

"Well, you won't have to stay here long," Jules told me the night I came. Jules smuggled me in, sort of, after dark, when everyone had gone to bed.

"Christ, I hope not."

"I'll be moving to a big place soon," Jules said. "You can move in with me." He turned all the lights on. "Think it'll be all right for a while?" He sounded apologetic, as though he had designed the room himself.

"Oh, sure. D'you think I'll have any trouble?"

"I don't think so. The rent's paid. She can't put you out."

I didn't say anything to that.

"Sort of stay undercover," Jules said. "You know."

"Roger," I said.

I had been living there for three days, timing it so I left after everyone else had gone, coming back late at night when everyone else was asleep. But I knew it wouldn't work. A couple of the tenants had seen me on the stairs, a woman had surprised me coming out of the john. Every morning I waited for the landlady to come banging on the door. I didn't know what would happen. It might be all right. It might not be. But the waiting was getting me.

The sweat on my body was turning cold. Downstairs a radio was tuned in to the Breakfast Symphony. They were playing Beethoven. I sat up and lit a cigarette. "Peter," I said, "don't let them scare you to death. You're a man, too." I listened to Ludwig and I watched the smoke rise to the dirty ceiling. Under Ludwig's drums and horns I listened to hear footsteps on the stairs.

I'd done a lot of traveling in my time. I'd knocked about through St. Louis, Frisco, Seattle, Detroit, New Orleans, worked at just about everything. I'd run away from my old lady when I was about sixteen. She'd never been able to handle me. You'll never be nothin' *but* a bum, she'd say. We lived in an old shack in a town in New Jersey in the nigger part of town, the kind of houses colored people live in all over the U.S. I hated my mother for living there. I hated all the people in my neighborhood. They went to church and they got drunk. They were nice to the white people. When the landlord came around they paid him and took his crap.

The first time I was ever called nigger I was seven years old. It was a little white girl with long black curls. I used to leave the front of my house and go wandering by myself through town. This little girl was playing ball alone and as I passed her the ball rolled out of her hands into the gutter.

I threw it back to her.

"Let's play catch," I said.

But she held the ball and made a face at me.

"My mother don't let me play with niggers," she told me.

I did not know what the word meant. But my skin grew warm. I stuck my tongue out at her.

"I don't care. Keep your old ball." I started down the street.

She screamed after me: "Nigger, nigger, nigger!"

I screamed back: "Your mother was a nigger!"

I asked my mother what a nigger was.

"Who called you that?"

"I heard somebody say it."

"Who?"

"Just somebody."

"Go wash your face," she said. "You dirty as sin. Your supper's on the table."

I went to the bathroom and splashed water on my face and wiped my face and hands on the towel.

"You call that clean?" my mother cried. "Come here, boy!"

She dragged me back to the bathroom and began to soap my face and neck.

"You run around dirty like you do all the time, everybody'll call you a little nigger, you hear?" She rinsed my face and looked at my hands and dried me. "Now, go on and eat your supper."

I didn't say anything. I went to the kitchen and sat down at the table. I remember I wanted to cry. My mother sat down across from me.

"Mama," I said. She looked at me. I started to cry.

She came around to my side of the table and took me in her arms.

"Baby, don't fret. Next time somebody calls you nigger you

tell them you'd rather be your color than be lowdown and
nasty like some white folks is."

We formed gangs when I was older, my friends and I. We
met white boys and their friends on the opposite sides of
fences and we threw rocks and tin cans at each other.

I'd come home bleeding. My mother would slap me and
scold me and cry.

"Boy, you wanna get killed? You wanna end up like your
father?"

My father was a bum and I had never seen him. I was
named for him: Peter.

I was always in trouble: truant officers, welfare workers,
everybody else in town.

"You ain't never gonna be nothin' *but* a bum," my mother
said.

By and by older kids I knew finished school and got jobs and
got married and settled down. They were going to settle down
and bring more black babies into the world and pay the same
rents for the same old shacks and it would go on and on—

When I was sixteen I ran away. I left a note and told Mama
not to worry, I'd come back one day and I'd be all right. But
when I was twenty-two she died. I came back and put my
mother in the ground. Everything was like it had been. Our
house had not been painted and the porch floor sagged and
there was somebody's raincoat stuffed in the broken window.
Another family was moving in.

Their furniture was stacked along the walls and their children were running through the house and laughing and somebody was frying pork chops in the kitchen. The oldest boy was
tacking up a mirror.

Last year Ida took me driving in her big car and we passed
through a couple of towns upstate. We passed some crumbling

houses on the left. The clothes on the line were flying in the wind.

"Are people living there?" asked Ida.

"Just darkies," I said.

Ida passed the car ahead, banging angrily on the horn. "D'you know you're becoming paranoiac, Peter?"

"All right. All right. I know a lot of white people are starving too."

"You're damn right they are. I know a little about poverty myself."

Ida had come from the kind of family called shanty Irish. She was raised in Boston. She's a very beautiful woman who married young and married for money—so now I can afford to support attractive young men, she'd giggle. Her husband was a ballet dancer who was forever on the road. Ida suspected that he went with boys. Not that I give a damn, she said, as long as he leaves me alone. When we met last year she was thirty and I was twenty-five. We had a pretty stormy relationship but we stuck. Whenever I got to town I called her; whenever I was stranded out of town I'd let her know. We never let it get too serious. She went her way and I went mine.

In all this running around I'd learned a few things. Like a prizefighter learns to take a blow or a dancer learns to fall, I'd learned how to get by. I'd learned never to be belligerent with policemen, for instance. No matter who was right, I was certain to be wrong. What might be accepted as just good old American independence in someone else would be insufferable arrogance in me. After the first few times I realized that I had to play smart, to act out the role I was expected to play. I only had one head and it was too easy to get it broken. When I faced a policeman I acted like I didn't know a thing. I let my jaw drop and I let my eyes get big. I didn't give him any smart answers, none of the crap about my rights. I figured out what answers he wanted and I gave them to him. I never let him

think he wasn't king. If it was more than routine, if I was
picked up on suspicion of robbery or murder in the neighborhood, I looked as humble as I could and kept my mouth shut
and prayed. I took a couple of beatings but I stayed out of
prison and I stayed off chain gangs. That was also due to luck,
Ida pointed out once. "Maybe it would've been better for you
if you'd been a little less lucky. Worse things have happened
than chain gangs. Some of them have happened to you."

There was something in her voice. "What are you talking
about?" I asked.

"Don't lose your temper. I said maybe."

"You mean you think I'm a coward?"

"I didn't say that, Peter."

"But you meant that. Didn't you?"

"No. I didn't mean that. I didn't mean anything. Let's not
fight."

There are times and places when a Negro can use his color
like a shield. He can trade on the subterranean Anglo-Saxon
guilt and get what he wants that way; or some of what he
wants. He can trade on his nuisance value, his value as forbidden fruit; he can use it like a knife, he can twist it and get his
vengeance that way. I knew these things long before I realized
that I knew them and in the beginning I used them, not knowing what I was doing. Then when I began to see it, I felt betrayed. I felt beaten as a person. I had no honest place to stand.

This was the year before I met Ida. I'd been acting in stock
companies and little theaters; sometimes fairly good parts.
People were nice to me. They told me I had talent. They said
it sadly, as though they were thinking, What a pity, he'll never
get anywhere. I had got to the point where I resented praise
and I resented pity and I wondered what people were thinking
when they shook my hand. In New York I met some pretty fine
people; easygoing, hard-drinking, flotsam and jetsam; and they
liked me; and I wondered if I trusted them; if I was able any

longer to trust anybody. Not on top, where all the world could see, but underneath where everybody lives.

Soon I would have to get up. I listened to Ludwig. He shook the little room like the footsteps of a giant marching miles away. On summer evenings (and maybe we would go this summer) Jules and Ida and I would go up to the Stadium and sit beneath the pillars on the cold stone steps. There is seemed to me the sky was far away; and I was not myself, I was high and lifted up. We never talked, the three of us. We sat and watched the blue smoke curl in the air and watched the orange tips of cigarettes. Every once in a while the boys who sold popcorn and soda pop and ice cream climbed the steep steps chattering; and Ida shifted slightly and touched her blue-black hair; and Jules scowled. I sat with my knee up, watching the lighted half-moon below, the black-coated, straining conductor, the faceless men beneath him moving together in a rhythm like the sea. There were pauses in the music for the rushing, calling, halting piano. Everything would stop except the climbing soloist; he would reach a height and everything would join him, the violins first and then the horns; and then the deep blue bass and the flute and the bitter trampling drums; beating, beating and mounting together and stopping with a crash like daybreak. When I first heard the *Messiah* I was alone; my blood bubbled like fire and wine; I cried; like an infant crying for its mother's milk; or a sinner running to meet Jesus.

Now below the music I heard footsteps on the stairs. I put out my cigarette. My heart was beating so hard I thought it would tear my chest apart. Someone knocked on the door.

I thought: Don't answer. Maybe she'll go away.

But the knocking came again, harder this time.

Just a minute, I said. I sat on the edge of the bed and put on my bathrobe. I was trembling like a fool. For Christ's sake, Peter, you've been through this before. What's the worst thing that can happen? You won't have a room. The world's full of rooms.

When I opened the door the landlady stood there, red-and-whitefaced and hysterical.

"Who are you? I didn't rent this room to you."

My mouth was dry. I started to say something.

"I can't have no colored people here," she said. "All my tenants are complainin'. Women afraid to come home nights."

"They ain't gotta be afraid of me," I said. I couldn't get my voice up; it rasped and rattled in my throat; and I began to be angry. I wanted to kill her. "My friend rented this room for me," I said.

"Well, I'm sorry, he didn't have no right to do that, I don't have nothin' against you, but you gotta get out."

Her glasses blinked, opaque in the light on the landing. She was frightened to death. She was afraid of me but she was more afraid of losing her tenants. Her face was mottled with rage and fear, her breath came rushed and little bits of spittle gathered at the edges of her mouth; her breath smelled bad, like rotting hamburger on a July day.

"You can't put me out," I said. "This room was rented in my name." I started to close the door, as though the matter was finished: "I live here, see, this is my room, you can't put me out."

"You get outa my house!" she screamed. "I got the right to know who's in my house! This is a white neighborhood, I don't rent to colored people. Why don't you go on uptown, like you belong?"

"I can't stand niggers," I told her. I started to close the door again but she moved and stuck her foot in the way. I wanted to kill her, I watched her stupid, wrinkled frightened white face and I wanted to take a club, a hatchet, and bring it down with all my weight, splitting her skull down the middle where she parted her iron-grey hair.

"Get out of the door," I said. "I want to get dressed."

But I knew that she had won, that I was already on my way. We stared at each other. Neither of us moved. From her came an emanation of fear and fury and something else. You maggot-eaten bitch, I thought. I said evilly, "You wanna come in and watch me?" Her face didn't change, she didn't take her foot away. My skin prickled, tiny hot needles punctured my flesh. I was aware of my body under the bathrobe; and it was as though I had done something wrong, something monstrous, years ago, which no one had forgotten and for which I would be killed.

"If you don't get out," she said, "I'll get a policeman to put you out."

I grabbed the door to keep from touching her. "All right. All right. You can have the goddamn room. Now get out and let me dress."

She turned away. I slammed the door. I heard her going down the stairs. I threw stuff into my suitcase. I tried to take as long as possible but I cut myself while shaving because I was afraid she would come back upstairs with a policeman.

Jules was making coffee when I walked in.

"Good morning, good morning! What happened to you?"

"No room at the inn," I said. "Pour a cup of coffee for the notorious son of man. I sat down and dropped my suitcase on the floor."

Jules looked at me. "Oh. Well. Coffee coming up."

He got out the coffee cups. I lit a cigarette and sat there. I couldn't think of anything to say. I knew that Jules felt bad and I wanted to tell him that it wasn't his fault.

He pushed coffee in front of me and sugar and cream.

"Cheer up, baby. The world's wide and life—life, she is very long."

"Shut up. I don't want to hear any of your bad philosophy."

"Sorry."

"I mean, let's not talk about the good, the true, and the beautiful."

"All right. But don't sit there holding onto your table manners. Scream if you want to."

"Screaming won't do any good. Besides I'm a big boy now."

I stirred my coffee. "Did you give her a fight?" Jules asked.

I shook my head. "No."

"Why the hell not?"

I shrugged; a little ashamed now. I couldn't have won it. What the hell.

"You might have won it. You might have given her a couple of bad moments."

"Goddamit to hell, I'm sick of it. Can't I get a place to sleep without dragging it through the courts? I'm goddamn tired of battling every Tom, Dick, and Harry for what everybody else takes for granted. I'm tired, man, tired! Have you ever been sick to death of something? Well, I'm sick to death. And I'm scared. I've been fighting so goddamn long I'm not a person any more. I'm not Booker T. Washington. I've got no vision of emancipating anybody. I want to emancipate myself. If this goes on much longer, they'll send me to Bellevue, I'll blow my top, I'll break somebody's head. I'm not worried about that miserable little room. I'm worried about what's happening to me, *to me*, inside. I don't walk the streets, I crawl. I've never been like this before. Now when I go to a strange place I wonder what will happen, will I be accepted, if I'm accepted, can I accept?—"

"Take it easy," Jules said.

"Jules, I'm beaten."

"I don't think you are. Drink your coffee."

"Oh," I cried, "I know you think I'm making it dramatic, that I'm paranoiac and just inventing trouble! Maybe I think so sometimes, how can I tell? You get so used to being hit you find you're always waiting for it. Oh, I know, you're Jewish, you get kicked around, too, but you can walk into a bar and nobody *knows* you're Jewish and if you go looking for a job you'll get a better job than mine! How can I say what it feels like? I don't know. I know everybody's in trouble and nothing is easy, but how can I explain to you what it feels like to be black when I don't understand it and don't want to and spend all my time trying to forget it? I don't want to hate anybody— but now maybe, I can't love anybody either—are we friends? Can we be really friends?"

"We're friends," Jules said, "don't worry about it." He scowled. "If I wasn't Jewish I'd ask you why you don't live in Harlem." I looked at him. He raised his hand and smiled— "But I'm Jewish, so I didn't ask you. Ah Peter," he said, "I can't help you—take a walk, get drunk, we're all in this together."

I stood up. "I'll be around later. I'm sorry."

"Don't be sorry. I'll leave my door open. Bunk here for awhile."

"Thanks," I said.

I felt that I was drowning; that hatred had corrupted me like cancer in the bone.

I saw Ida for dinner. We met in a restaurant in the Village, an Italian place in a gloomy cellar with candles on the tables.

It was not a busy night, for which I was grateful. When I came in there were only two other couples on the other side of the room. No one looked at me. I sat down in a corner booth and ordered a Scotch old-fashioned. Ida was late and I had three of them before she came.

She was very fine in black, a high-necked dress with a pearl choker; and her hair was combed page-boy style, falling just below her ears.

"You look real sweet, baby."

"Thank you. It took fifteen extra minutes but I hoped it would be worth it."

"It was worth it. What're you drinking?"

"Oh—what're you drinking?"

"Old-fashioneds."

She sniffed and looked at me. "How many?"

I laughed. "Three."

"Well," she said, "I suppose you had to do something." The waiter came over. We decided on one Manhattan and one lasagna and one spaghetti with clam sauce and another old-fashioned for me.

"Did you have a constructive day, sweetheart? Find a job?"

"Not today," I said. I lit her cigarette. "Metro offered me a fortune to come to the coast and do the lead in *Native Son* but I turned it down. Type casting, you know. It's so difficult to find a decent part."

"Well, if they don't come up with a decent offer soon tell them you'll go back to Selznick. *He'll* find you a part with guts—the very *idea* of offering you *Native Son!* I wouldn't stand for it."

"You ain't gotta tell me. I told them if they didn't find me a decent script in two weeks I was through, that's all."

"Now that's talking, Peter my lad."

The drinks came and we sat in silence for a minute or two. I finished half of my drink at a swallow and played with the toothpicks on the table. I felt Ida watching me.

"Peter, you're going to be awfully drunk."

"Honeychile, the first thing a southern gentleman learns is how to hold his liquor."

"That myth is older than the rock of ages. And anyway you come from Jersey."

I finished my drink and snarled at her: "That's just as good as the South."

Across the table from me I could see that she was readying herself for trouble: her mouth tightened slightly, setting her chin so that the faint cleft showed: "What happened to you today?"

I resented her concern; I resented my need. "Nothing worth talking about," I muttered, "just a mood."

And I tried to smile at her, to wipe away the bitterness.

"Now I know something's the matter. Please tell me."

It sounded trivial as hell: "You know the room Jules found for me? Well, the landlady kicked me out of it today."

"God save the American republic," Ida said. "D'you want to waste some of my husband's money? We can sue her."

"Forget it. I'll end up with lawsuits in every state in the union."

"Still, as a gesture—"

"The devil with the gesture. I'll get by."

The food came. I didn't want to eat. The first mouthful hit my belly like a gong. Ida began cutting up lasagna.

"Peter," she said, "try not to feel so badly. We're all in this together the whole world. Don't let it throw you. What can't be helped you have to learn to live with."

"That's easy for you to say, " I told her.

She looked at me quickly and looked away. "I'm not pretending that it's easy to do," she said.

I didn't believe that she could really understand it; and there was nothing I could say. I sat like a child being scolded, looking down at my plate, not eating, not saying anything. I wanted her to stop talking, to stop being intelligent about it, to stop being calm and grown-up about it; good Lord, none of us has ever grown up, we never will.

"It's no better anywhere else," she was saying. "In all of Europe there's famine and disease, in France and England they hate the Jews—nothing's going to change, baby, people are too empty-headed, too empty-hearted—it's always been like that, people always try to destroy what they don't understand—and they hate almost everything because they understand so little—"

I began to sweat in my side of the booth. I wanted to stop her voice. I wanted her to eat and be quiet and leave me alone. I looked around for the waiter so I could order another drink. But he was on the far side of the restaurant, waiting on some people who had just come in; a lot of people had come in since we had been sitting there.

"Peter," Ida said, "Peter please don't look like that."

I grinned: the painted grin of the professional clown. "Don't worry, baby, I'm all right. I know what I'm going to do. I'm gonna go back to my people where I belong and find me a nice, black nigger wench and raise me a flock of babies."

Ida had an old maternal trick; the grin tricked her into using it now. She raised her fork and rapped me with it across the knuckles. "Now, stop that. You're too old for that."

I screamed and stood up screaming and knocked the candle over: "Don't *do* that, you bitch, don't *ever* do that!"

She grabbed the candle and set it up and glared at me. Her face had turned perfectly white: "Sit down! Sit *down!*"

I fell back into my seat. My stomach felt like water. Everyone was looking at us. I turned cold, seeing what they were seeing: a black boy and a white woman, alone together. I knew it would take nothing to have them at my throat.

"I'm sorry," I muttered, "I'm sorry, I'm sorry."

The waiter was at my elbow. "Is everything all right, miss?"

"Yes, quite, thank you." She sounded like a princess dismissing a slave. I didn't look up. The shadow of the waiter moved away from me.

"Baby," Ida said, "forgive me, please forgive me."

I stared at the tablecloth. She put her hand on mine, brightness and blackness.

"Let's go," I said, "I'm terribly sorry."

She motioned for the check. When it came she handed the waiter a ten dollar bill without looking. She picked up her bag.

"Shall we go to a nightclub or a movie or something?"

"No, honey, not tonight." I looked at her. "I'm tired, I think I'll go on over to Jules's place. I'm gonna sleep on his floor for a while. Don't worry about me. I'm all right."

She looked at me steadily. She said: "I'll come see you tomorrow?"

"Yes, baby, please."

The waiter brought the change and she tipped him. We stood up; as we passed the tables (not looking at the people) the ground under me seemed falling, the doorway seemed impossibly far away. All my muscles tensed; I seemed ready to spring; I was waiting for the blow.

I put my hands in my pockets and we walked to the end of the block. The lights were green and red, the lights from the theater across the street exploded blue and yellow, off and on.

"Peter?"

"Yes?"

"I'll see you tomorrow?"

"Yeah. Come by Jules's. I'll wait for you."

"Goodnight, darling."

"Goodnight."

I started to walk away. I felt her eyes on my back. I kicked a bottle-top on the sidewalk.

God save the American republic.

I dropped into the subway and got on an uptown train, not knowing where it was going and not caring. Anonymous, is-landed people surrounded me, behind newspapers, behind make-up, fat, fleshy masks and flat eyes. I watched the empty faces. (No one looked at me.) I looked at the ads, unreal women and pink-cheeked men selling cigarettes, candy, shaving cream, nightgowns, chewing gum, movies, sex; sex without organs, drier than sand and more secret than death. The train stopped. A white boy and a white girl got on. She was nice, short, svelte. Nice legs. She was hanging on his arm. He was the football type, blond, ruddy. They were dressed in summer clothes. The wind from the doors blew her print dress. She squealed, holding the dress at the knees and giggled and looked at him. He said something I didn't catch and she looked at me and the smile died. She stood so that she faced him and had her back to me. I looked back at the ads. Then I hated them. I wanted to do something to make them hurt, something that would crack the pink-cheeked mask. The white boy and I did not look at each other again. They got off at the next stop.

I wanted to keep on drinking. I got off in Harlem and went to a rundown bar on Seventh Avenue. My people, my people. Sharpies stood on the corner, waiting. Women in summer dresses pranced by on wavering heels. Click clack. Click clack. There were white mounted policemen in the streets. On every block there was another policeman on foot. I saw a black cop.

God save the American republic.

The juke box was letting loose with "Hamps' Boogie." The place was jumping, I walked over to the man.

"Rye," I said.

I was standing next to somebody's grandmother. "Hello, papa. What you puttin' down?"

"Baby, you can't pick it up," I told her. "My rye came and I drank."

"Nigger," she said, "you must think you's somebody."

I didn't answer. She turned away, back to her beer, keeping time to the juke box, her face sullen and heavy and aggrieved. I watched her out of the side of my eye. She had been good looking once, pretty even, before she hit the bottle and started crawling into too many beds. She was flabby now, flesh heaved all over in her thin dress. I wondered what she'd be like in

bed; then I realized that I was a little excited by her; I laughed
and set my glass down.

"The same," I said. "And a beer chaser."

The juke box was playing something else now, something
brassy and commercial which I didn't like. I kept on drinking,
listening to the voices of my people, watching the faces of my
people. (God pity us, the terrified republic.) Now I was sorry
to have angered the woman who still sat next to me, now deep
in conversation with another, younger woman. I longed for
some opening, some sign, something to make me part of the
life around me. But there was nothing except my color. A
white outsider coming in would have seen a young Negro
drinking in a Negro bar, perfectly in his element, in his place,
as the saying goes. But the people here knew differently, as I
did. I didn't seem to have a place.

So I kept on drinking by myself, saying to myself after each
drink, Now I'll go. But I was afraid; I didn't want to sleep on
Jules's floor; I didn't want to go to sleep. I kept on drinking
and listening to the juke box. They were playing Ella Fitz-
gerald, "Cow-Cow Boogie."

"Let me buy you a drink," I said to the woman.

She looked at me, startled, suspicious, ready to blow her top.

"On the level," I said. I tried to smile. "Both of you."

"I'll take a beer," the young one said.

I was shaking like a baby. I finished my drink.

"Fine," I said. I turned to the bar.

"Baby," said the old one, "what's your story?"

The man put three beers on the counter.

"I got no story, Ma," I said.

TWIN FLAMES

VINTAGE AND CONTEMPORARY CLOTHES POP-UP

The Forks Market (beside McNally), November 17th and 18th from 10am to 6pm.

 @SHOPTWINFLAMES

Sonny's Blues

I READ ABOUT IT in the the paper, in the subway, on my way to work. I read it, and I couldn't believe it, and I read it again. Then perhaps I just stared at it, at the newsprint spelling out his name, spelling out the story. I stared at it in the swinging lights of the subway car, and in the faces and bodies of the people, and in my own face, trapped in the darkness which roared outside.

It was not to be believed and I kept telling myself that, as I walked from the subway station to the high school. And at the same time I couldn't doubt it. I was scared, scared for Sonny. He became real to me again. A great block of ice got settled in my belly and kept melting there slowly all day long, while I taught my classes algebra. It was a special kind of ice. It kept melting, sending trickles of ice water all up and down my veins, but it never got less. Sometimes it hardened and seemed to expand until I felt my guts were going to come spilling out or that I was going to choke or scream. This would always be at a moment when I was remembering some specific thing Sonny had once said or done.

When he was about as old as the boys in my classes his face had been bright and open, there was a lot of copper in it; and he'd had wonderfully direct brown eyes, and great gentleness and privacy. I wondered what he looked like now. He had been picked up, the evening before, in a raid on an apartment downtown, for peddling and using heroin.

I couldn't believe it: but what I mean by that is that I couldn't find any room for it anywhere inside me. I had kept it outside me for a long time. I hadn't wanted to know. I had had suspicions, but I didn't name them, I kept putting them away. I told myself that Sonny was wild, but he wasn't crazy. And he'd always been a good boy, he hadn't ever turned hard or evil or disrespectful, the way kids can, so quick, so quick, especially in Harlem. I didn't want to believe that I'd ever see my brother going down, coming to nothing, all that light in his face gone out, in the condition I'd already seen so many others. Yet it had happened and here I was, talking about algebra to a lot of boys who might, every one of them for all I knew, be popping off needles every time they went to the head. Maybe it did more for them than algebra could.

I was sure that the first time Sonny had ever had horse, he couldn't have been much older than these boys were now. These boys, now, were living as we'd been living then, they were growing up with a rush and their heads bumped abruptly against the low ceiling of their actual possibilities. They were filled with rage. All they really knew were two darknesses, the darkness of their lives, which was now closing in on them, and the darkness of the movies, which had blinded them to that other darkness, and in which they now, vindictively, dreamed, at once more together than they were at any other time, and more alone.

When the last bell rang, the last class ended, I let out my breath. It seemed I'd been holding it for all that time. My clothes were wet—I may have looked as though I'd been sitting in a steam bath, all dressed up, all afternoon. I sat alone in the classroom a long time. I listened to the boys outside, downstairs, shouting and cursing and laughing. Their laughter struck me for perhaps the first time. It was not the joyous laughter which—God knows why—one associates with children. It was mocking and insular, its intent was to denigrate. It was disenchanted, and in this, also, lay the authority of their curses. Perhaps I was listening to them because I was thinking about my brother and in them I heard my brother. And myself.

One boy was whistling a tune, at once very complicated and very simple, it seemed to be pouring out of him as though he were a bird, and it sounded very cool and moving through all that harsh, bright air, only just holding its own through all those other sounds."

I stood up and walked over to the window and looked down into the courtyard. It was the beginning of the spring and the sap was rising in the boys. A teacher passed through them every now and again, quickly, as though he or she couldn't wait to get out of that courtyard, to get those boys out of their sight and off their minds. I started collecting my stuff. I thought I'd better get home and talk to Isabel.

The courtyard was almost deserted by the time I got downstairs. I saw this boy standing in the shadow of a doorway, looking just like Sonny. I almost called his name. Then I saw that it wasn't Sonny, but somebody we used to know, a boy from around our block. He'd been Sonny's friend. He'd never been mine, having been too young for me, and, anyway, I'd never liked him. And now, even though he was a grown-up man, he still hung around that block, still spent hours on the street corners, was always high and raggy. I used to run into him from time to time and he'd often work around to asking me for a quarter or fifty cents. He always had some real good excuse, too, and I always gave it to him, I don't know why.

But now, abruptly, I hated him. I couldn't stand the way he looked at me, partly like a dog, partly like a cunning child. I wanted to ask him what the hell he was doing in the school courtyard.

He sort of shuffled over to me, and he said, "I see you got the papers. So you already know about it."

"You mean about Sonny? Yes, I already know about it. How come they didn't get you?"

He grinned. It made him repulsive and it also brought to mind what he'd looked like as a kid. "I wasn't there. I stay away from them people."

"Good for you." I offered him a cigarette and I watched him through the smoke. "You come all the way down here just to tell me about Sonny?"

"That's right." He was sort of shaking his head and his eyes looked strange, as though they were about to cross. The bright sun deadened his damp dark brown skin and it made his eyes look yellow and showed up the dirt in his kinked hair. He smelled funky. I moved a little away from him and I said, "Well, thanks. But I already know about it and I got to get home."

"I'll walk you a little ways," he said. We started walking. There were a couple of kids still loitering in the courtyard and one of them said goodnight to me and looked strangely at the boy beside me.

"What're you going to do?" he asked me. "I mean, about Sonny?"

"Look. I haven't seen Sonny for over a year, I'm not sure I'm going to do anything. Anyway, what the hell *can* I do?"

"That's right," he said quickly, "ain't nothing you can do. Can't much help old Sonny no more, I guess."

It was what I was thinking and so it seemed to me he had no right to say it.

"I'm surprised at Sonny, though," he went on—he had a funny way of talking, he looked straight ahead as though he were talking to himself—"I thought Sonny was a smart boy, I thought he was too smart to get hung."

"I guess he thought so too," I said sharply, "and that's how he got hung. And now about you? You're pretty goddamn smart, I bet."

Then he looked directly at me, just for a minute. "I ain't smart," he said. "If I was smart, I'd have reached for a pistol a long time ago."

"Look. Don't tell *me* your sad story, if it was up to me, I'd give you one." Then I felt guilty—guilty, probably, for never having supposed that the poor bastard *had* a story of his own, much less a sad one, and I asked, quickly, "What's going to happen to him now?"

He didn't answer this. He was off by himself some place. "Funny thing," he said, and from his tone we might have been

discussing the quickest way to get to Brooklyn, "when I saw
the papers this morning, the first thing I asked myself was if I
had anything to do with it. I felt sort of responsible."

I began to listen more carefully. The subway station was
on the corner, just before us, and I stopped. He stopped, too.
We were in front of a bar and he ducked slightly, peering in,
but whoever he was looking for didn't seem to be there. The
juke box was blasting away with something black and bouncy
and I half watched the barmaid as she danced her way from
the juke box to her place behind the bar. And I watched her
face as she laughingly responded to something someone said to
her, still keeping time to the music. When she smiled one saw
the little girl, one sensed the doomed, still-struggling woman
beneath the battered face of the semi-whore.

"I never *give* Sonny nothing," the boy said finally, "but a
long time ago I come to school high and Sonny asked me how
it felt." He paused, I couldn't bear to watch him, I watched the
barmaid, and I listened to the music which seemed to be causing the pavement to shake. "I told him it felt great." The music
stopped, the barmaid paused and watched the juke box until
the music began again. "It did."

All this was carrying me some place I didn't want to go. I
certainly didn't want to know how it felt. It filled everything,
the people, the houses, the music, the dark, quicksilver barmaid, with menace; and this menace was their reality.

"What's going to happen to him now?" I asked again.

"They'll send him away some place and they'll try to cure
him." He shook his head. "Maybe he'll even think he's kicked
the habit. Then they'll let him loose"—he gestured, throwing
his cigarette into the gutter. "That's all."

"What do you mean, that's *all?*"

But I knew what he meant.

"I *mean*, that's *all.*" He turned his head and looked at me, pulling down the corners of his mouth. "Don't you know what I mean?" he asked, softly.

"How the hell *would* I know what you mean?" I almost whispered it, I don't know why.

"That's right," he said to the air, "how would *he* know what I mean?" He turned toward me again, patient and calm, and yet I somehow felt him shaking, shaking as though he were going to fall apart. I felt that ice in my guts again, the dread I'd felt all afternoon; and again I watched the barmaid, moving about the bar, washing glasses, and singing. "Listen. They'll let him out and then it'll just start all over again. That's what I mean."

"You mean—they'll let him out. And then he'll just start working his way back in again. You mean he'll never kick the habit. Is that what you mean?"

"That's right," he said, cheerfully. "*You* see what I mean."

"Tell me," I said it last, "why does he want to die? He must want to die, he's killing himself, why does he want to die?"

He looked at me in surprise. He licked his lips. "He don't want to die. He wants to live. Don't nobody want to die, ever."

Then I wanted to ask him—too many things. He could not have answered, or if he had, I could not have borne the answers. I started walking. "Well, I guess it's none of my business."

"It's going to be rough on old Sonny," he said. We reached the subway station. "This is your station?" he asked. I nodded. I took one step down. "Damn!" he said, suddenly. I looked up at him. He grinned again. "Damn it if I didn't leave all my money home. You ain't got a dollar on you, have you? Just for a couple of days, is all."

All at once something inside gave and threatened to come pouring out of me. I didn't hate him any more. I felt that in another moment I'd start crying like a child.

"Sure," I said. "Don't sweat." I looked in my wallet and didn't have a dollar, I only had a five. "Here," I said. "That hold you?"

He didn't look at it—he didn't want to look at it. A terrible, closed look came over his face, as though he were keeping the number on the bill a secret from him and me. "Thanks," he said, and now he was dying to see me go. "Don't worry about Sonny. Maybe I'll write him or something."

"Sure," I said. "You do that. So long."

"Be seeing you," he said. I went on down the steps.

And I didn't write Sonny or send him anything for a long time. When I finally did, it was just after my little girl died, he wrote me back a letter which made me feel like a bastard.

Here's what he said:

> Dear brother,
> You don't know how much I needed to hear from you. I wanted to write you many a time but I dug how much I must have hurt you and so I didn't write. But now I feel like a man who's been trying to climb up out of some deep, real deep and funky hole and just saw the sun up there, outside. I got to get outside.
> I can't tell you much about how I got here. I mean I don't know how to tell you. I guess I was afraid of something or I was trying to escape from something and you know I have never been very strong in the head (smile). I'm glad Mama and Daddy are dead and can't see what's happened to their son and I swear if I'd known what I was doing I would never have hurt you so, you and a lot of other fine people who were nice to me and who believed in me.
> I don't want you to think it had anything to do with me being a musician. It's more than that. Or maybe less than that. I can't get anything straight in my head down here and

I try not to think about what's going to happen to me when I get outside again. Sometime I think I'm going to flip and *never* get outside and sometime I think I'll come straight back. I tell you one thing, though, I'd rather blow my brains out than go through this again. But that's what they all say, so they tell me. If I tell you when I'm coming to New York and if you could meet me, I sure would appreciate it. Give my love to Isabel and the kids and I was sure sorry to hear about little Gracie. I wish I could be like Mama and say the Lord's will be done, but I don't know it seems to me that trouble is the one thing that never does get stopped and I don't know what good it does to blame it on the Lord. But maybe it does some good if you believe it.

Your brother,
Sonny

Then I kept in constant touch with him and I sent him whatever I could and I went to meet him when he came back to New York. When I saw him many things I thought I had forgotten came flooding back to me. This was because I had begun, finally, to wonder about Sonny, about the life that Sonny lived inside. This life, whatever it was, had made him older and thinner and it had deepened the distant stillness in which he had always moved. He looked very unlike my baby brother. Yet, when he smiled, when we shook hands, the baby brother I'd never known looked out from the depths of his private life, like an animal waiting to be coaxed into the light.

"How you been keeping?" he asked me.

"All right. And you?"

"Just fine." He was smiling all over his face. "It's good to see you again."

"It's good to see you."

The seven years' difference in our ages lay between us like a chasm: I wondered if these years would ever operate between us as a bridge. I was remembering, and it made it hard to catch my breath, that I had been there when he was born; and I had heard the first words he had ever spoken. When he started to walk, he walked from our mother straight to me. I caught him just before he fell when he took the first steps he ever took in this world.

"How's Isabel?"

"Just fine. She's dying to see you."

"And the boys?"

"They're fine, too. They're anxious to see their uncle."

"Oh, come on. You know they don't remember me."

"Are you kidding? Of course they remember you."

He grinned again. We got into a taxi. We had a lot to say to each other, far too much to know how to begin.

As the taxi began to move, I asked, "You still want to go to India?"

He laughed. "You still remember that. Hell, no. This place is Indian enough for me."

"It used to belong to them," I said.

And he laughed again. "They damn sure knew what they were doing when they got rid of it."

Years ago, when he was around fourteen, he'd been all hipped on the idea of going to India. He read books about people sitting on rocks, naked, in all kinds of weather, but mostly bad, naturally, and walking barefoot through hot coals and arriving at wisdom. I used to say that it sounded to me as though they were getting away from wisdom as fast as they could. I think he sort of looked down on me for that.

"Do you mind," he asked, "if we have the driver drive alongside the park? On the west side—I haven't seen the city in so long."

"Of course not," I said. I was afraid that I might sound as though I were humoring him, but I hoped he wouldn't take it that way.

So we drove along, between the green of the park and the

stony, lifeless elegance of hotels and apartment buildings, toward the vivid, killing streets of our childhood. These streets hadn't changed, though housing projects jutted up out of them now like rocks in the middle of a boiling sea. Most of the houses in which we had grown up had vanished, as had the stores from which we had stolen, the basements in which we had first tried sex, the rooftops from which we had hurled tin cans and bricks. But houses exactly like the houses of our past yet dominated the landscape, boys exactly like the boys we once had been found themselves smothering in these houses, came down into the streets for light and air and found themselves encircled by disaster. Some escaped the trap, most didn't. Those who got out always left something of themselves behind, as some animals amputate a leg and leave it in the trap. It might be said, perhaps, that I had escaped, after all, I was a school teacher; or that Sonny had, he hadn't lived in Harlem for years. Yet, as the cab moved uptown through streets which seemed, with a rush, to darken with dark people, and as I covertly studied Sonny's face, it came to me that what we both were seeking through our separate cab windows was that part of ourselves which had been left behind. It's always at the hour of trouble and confrontation that the missing member aches.

We hit 110th Street and started rolling up Lenox Avenue. And I'd known this avenue all my life, but it seemed to me again, as it had seemed on the day I'd first heard about Sonny's trouble, filled with a hidden menace which was its very breath of life.

"We almost there," said Sonny.

"Almost." We were both too nervous to say anything more.

We live in a housing project. It hasn't been up long. A few days after it was up it seemed uninhabitably new, now, of course, it's already rundown. It looks like a parody of the good, clean, faceless life—God knows the people who live in it do

their best to make it a parody. The beat-looking grass lying
around isn't enough to make their lives green, the hedges will
never hold out the streets, and they know it. The big windows
fool no one, they aren't big enough to make space out of no
space. They don't bother with the windows, they watch the TV
screen instead. The playground is most popular with the children who don't play at jacks, or skip rope, or roller skate, or
swing, and they can be found in it after dark. We moved in
partly because it's not too far from where I teach, and partly
for the kids; but it's really just like the houses in which Sonny
and I grew up. The same things happen, they'll have the same
things to remember. The moment Sonny and I started into the
house I had the feeling that I was simply bringing him back
into the danger he had almost died trying to escape.

Sonny has never been talkative. So I don't know why I was
sure he'd be dying to talk to me when supper was over the first
night. Everything went fine, the oldest boy remembered him,
and the youngest boy liked him, and Sonny had remembered
to bring something for each of them; and Isabel, who is really
much nicer than I am, more open and giving, had gone to a lot
of trouble about dinner and was genuinely glad to see him.
And she's always been able to tease Sonny in a way that I
haven't. It was nice to see her face so vivid again and to hear
her laugh and watch her make Sonny laugh. She wasn't, or,
anyway, she didn't seem to be, at all uneasy or embarrassed.
She chatted as though there were no subject which had to be
avoided and she got Sonny past his first, faint stiffness. And
thank God she was there, for I was filled with that icy dread
again. Everything I did seemed awkward to me, and everything I said sounded freighted with hidden meaning. I was
trying to remember everything I'd heard about dope addiction
and I couldn't help watching Sonny for signs. I wasn't doing it
out of malice. I was trying to find out something about my
brother. I was dying to hear him tell me he was safe.

"Safe!" my father grunted, whenever Mama suggested trying to move to a neighborhood which might be safer for children. "Safe, hell! Ain't no place safe for kids, nor nobody."

He always went on like this, but he wasn't, ever, really as bad as he sounded, not even on weekends, when he got drunk. As a matter of fact, he was always on the lookout for "something a little better," but he died before he found it. He died suddenly, during a drunken weekend in the middle of the war, when Sonny was fifteen. He and Sonny hadn't ever got on too well. And this was partly because Sonny was the apple of his father's eye. It was because he loved Sonny so much and was frightened for him, that he was always fighting with him. It doesn't do any good to fight with Sonny. Sonny just moves back, inside himself, where he can't be reached. But the principal reason that they never hit it off is that they were so much alike. Daddy was big and rough and loud-talking, just the opposite of Sonny, but they both had—that same privacy.

Mama tried to tell me something about this, just after Daddy died. I was home on leave from the army.

This was the last time I ever saw my mother alive. Just the same, this picture gets all mixed up in my mind with pictures I had of her when she was younger. The way I always see her is the way she used to be on a Sunday afternoon, say, when the old folks were talking after the big Sunday dinner. I always see her wearing pale blue. She'd be sitting on the sofa. And my father would be sitting in the easy chair, not far from her. And the living room would be full of church folks and relatives. There they sit, in chairs all around the living room, and the night is creeping up outside, but nobody knows it yet. You can see the darkness growing against the windowpanes and you hear the street noises every now and again, or maybe the jangling beat of a tambourine from one of the churches close by, but it's real quiet in the room. For a moment nobody's talking, but every face looks darkening, like the sky outside.

And my mother rocks a little from the waist, and my father's eyes are closed. Everyone is looking at something a child can't see. For a minute they've forgotten the children. Maybe a kid is lying on the rug, half asleep. Maybe somebody's got a kid in his lap and is absent-mindedly stroking the kid's head. Maybe there's a kid, quiet and big-eyed, curled up in a big chair in the corner. The silence, the darkness coming, and the darkness in the faces frightens the child obscurely. He hopes that the hand which strokes his forehead will never stop—will never die. He hopes that there will never come a time when the old folks won't be sitting around the living room, talking about where they've come from, and what they've seen, and what's happened to them and their kinfolk.

But something deep and watchful in the child knows that this is bound to end, is already ending. In a moment someone will get up and turn on the light. Then the old folks will remember the children and they won't talk any more that day. And when light fills the room, the child is filled with darkness. He knows that every time this happens he's moved just a little closer to that darkness outside. The darkness outside is what the old folks have been talking about. It's what they've come from. It's what they endure. The child knows that they won't talk any more because if he knows too much about what's happened to *them*, he'll know too much too soon, about what's going to happen to *him*.

The last time I talked to my mother, I remember I was restless. I wanted to get out and see Isabel. We weren't married then and we had a lot to straighten out between us.

There Mama sat, in black, by the window. She was humming an old church song, *Lord, you brought me from a long ways off*. Sonny was out somewhere. Mama kept watching the streets.

"I don't know," she said, "if I'll ever see you again, after you go off from here. But I hope you'll remember the things I tried to teach you."

"Don't talk like that," I said, and smiled. "You'll be here a long time yet."

She smiled, too, but she said nothing. She was quiet for a long time. And I said, "Mama, don't you worry about nothing. I'll be writing all the time, and you be getting the checks. . . ."

"I want to talk to you about your brother," she said, suddenly. "If anything happens to me he ain't going to have nobody to look out for him."

"Mama," I said, "ain't nothing going to happen to you *or* Sonny. Sonny's all right. He's a good boy and he's got good sense."

"It ain't a question of his being a good boy," Mama said, "nor of his having good sense. It ain't only the bad ones, nor yet the dumb ones that gets sucked under." She stopped, looking at me. "Your Daddy once had a brother," she said, and she smiled in a way that made me feel she was in pain. "You didn't never know that, did you?"

"No," I said, "I never knew that," and I watched her face.

"Oh, yes," she said, "your Daddy had a brother." She looked out of the window again. "I know you never saw your Daddy cry. But *I* did—many a time, through all these years."

I asked her, "What happened to his brother? How come nobody's ever talked about him?"

This was the first time I ever saw my mother look old.

"His brother got killed," she said, "when he was just a little younger than you are now. I knew him. He was a fine boy. He was maybe a little full of the devil, but he didn't mean nobody no harm."

Then she stopped and the room was silent, exactly as it had sometimes been on those Sunday afternoons. Mama kept looking out into the streets.

"He used to have a job in the mill," she said, "and, like all young folks, he just liked to perform on Saturday nights. Sat-

urday nights, him and your father would drift around to
different place, go to dances and things like that, or just sit
around with people they knew, and your father's brother
would sing, he had a fine voice, and play along with himself on
his guitar. Well, this particular Saturday night, him and your
father was coming home from some place, and they were both
a little drunk and there was a moon that night, it was bright
like day. Your father's brother was feeling kind of good, and he
was whistling to himself, and he had his guitar slung over his
shoulder. They was coming down a hill and beneath them was
a road that turned off from the highway. Well, your father's
brother, being always kind of frisky, decided to run down this
hill, and he did, with that guitar banging and clanging behind
him, and he ran across the road, and he was making water
behind a tree. And your father was sort of amused at him and
he was still coming down the hill, kind of slow. Then he heard
a car motor and that same minute his brother stepped from
behind the tree, into the road, in the moonlight. And he started
to cross the road. And your father started to run down the hill,
he says he don't know why. This car was full of white men.
They was all drunk, and when they seen your father's brother
they let out a great whoop and holler and they aimed the car
straight at him. They was having fun, they just wanted to scare
him, the way they do sometimes, you know. But they was
drunk. And I guess the boy, being drunk, too, and scared, kind
of lost his head. By the time he jumped it was too late. Your
father says he heard his brother scream when the car rolled
over him, and he heard the wood of that guitar when it give,
and he heard them strings go flying, and he heard them white
men shouting, and the car kept on a-going and it ain't stopped
till this day. And, time your father got down the hill, his
brother weren't nothing but blood and pulp."

Tears were gleaming on my mother's face. There wasn't anything I could say.

"He never mentioned it," she said, "because I never let him

mention it before you children. Your Daddy was like a crazy man that night and for many a night thereafter. He says he never in his life seen anything as dark as that road after the lights of that car had gone away. Weren't nothing, weren't nobody on that road, just your Daddy and his brother and that busted guitar. Oh, yes. Your Daddy never did really get right again. Till the day he died he weren't sure but that every white man he saw was the man that killed his brother."

She stopped and took out her handkerchief and dried her eyes and looked at me.

"I ain't telling you all this," she said, "to make you scared or bitter or to make you hate nobody. I'm telling you this because you got a brother. And the world ain't changed."

I guess I didn't want to believe this. I guess she saw this in my face. She turned away from me, toward the window again, searching those streets.

"But I praise my Redeemer," she said at last, "that He called your Daddy home before me. I ain't saying it to throw no flowers at myself, but, I declare, it keeps me from feeling too cast down to know I helped your father get safely through this world. Your father always acted like he was the roughest, strongest man on earth. And everybody took him to be like that. But if he hadn't had *me* there—to see his tears!"

She was crying again. Still, I couldn't move. I said, "Lord, Lord, Mama, I didn't know it was like that."

"Oh, honey," she said, "there's a lot that you don't know. But you are going to find it out." She stood up from the window and came over to me. "You got to hold on to your brother," she said, "and don't let him fall, no matter what it looks like is happening to him and no matter how evil you gets with him. You going to be evil with him many a time. But don't you forget what I told you, you hear?"

"I won't forget," I said. "Don't you worry, I won't forget. I won't let nothing happen to Sonny."

My mother smiled as though she were amused at something she saw in my face. Then, "You may not be able to stop nothing from happening. But you got to let him know you's *there*."

Two days later I was married, and then I was gone. And I had a lot of things on my mind and I pretty well forgot my promise to Mama until I got shipped home on a special furlough for her funeral.

And, after the funeral, with just Sonny and me alone in the empty kitchen, I tried to find out something about him.

"What do you want to do?" I asked him.

"I'm going to be a musician," he said.

For he had graduated, in the time I had been away, from dancing to the juke box to finding out who was playing what, and what they were doing with it, and he had bought himself a set of drums.

"You mean, you want to be a drummer?" I somehow had the feeling that being a drummer might be all right for other people but not for my brother Sonny.

"I don't think," he said, looking at me very gravely, "that I'll ever be a good drummer. But I think I can play a piano."

I frowned. I'd never played the role of the older brother quite so seriously before, had scarcely ever, in fact, *asked* Sonny a damn thing. I sensed myself in the presence of something I didn't really know how to handle, didn't understand. So I made my frown a little deeper as I asked: "What kind of musician do you want to be?"

He grinned. "How many kinds do you think there are?"

"Be *serious*," I said.

He laughed, throwing his head back, and then looked at me. "I *am* serious."

"Well, then, for Christ's sake, stop kidding around and answer a serious question. I mean, do you want to be a concert pianist, you want to play classical music and all that, or—or what?" Long before I finished he was laughing again. "For Christ's *sake*, Sonny!"

He sobered, but with difficulty. "I'm sorry. But you sound so—*scared!*" and he was off again.

"Well, you may think it's funny now, baby, but it's not going to be so funny when you have to make your living at it, let me tell you *that*." I was furious because I knew he was laughing at me and I didn't know why.

"No," he said, very sober now, and afraid, perhaps, that he'd hurt me, "I don't want to be a classical pianist. That isn't what interests me. I mean"—he paused, looking hard at me, as though his eyes would help me to understand, and then gestured helplessly, as though perhaps his hand would help—"I mean, I'll have a lot of studying to do, and I'll have to study *everything*, but, I mean, I want to play *with*—jazz musicians." He stopped. "I want to play jazz," he said.

Well, the word had never before sounded as heavy, as real, as it sounded that afternoon in Sonny's mouth. I just looked at him and I was probably frowning a real frown by this time. I simply couldn't see why on earth he'd want to spend his time hanging around nightclubs, clowning around on bandstands, while people pushed each other around a dance floor. It seemed—beneath him, somehow. I had never thought about it before, had never been forced to, but I suppose I had always put jazz musicians in a class with what Daddy called "good-time people."

"Are you *serious?*"

"Hell, *yes*, I'm serious."

He looked more helpless than ever, and annoyed, and deeply hurt.

I suggested, helpfully: "You mean—like Louis Armstrong?"

His face closed as though I'd struck him. "No. I'm not talking about none of that old-time, down home crap."

"Well, look, Sonny, I'm sorry, don't get mad. I just don't

altogether get it, that's all. Name somebody—you know, a jazz musician you admire."

"Bird."

"Who?"

"Bird! Charlie Parker! Don't they teach you nothing in the goddamn army?"

I lit a cigarette. I was surprised and then a little amused to discover that I was trembling. "I've been out of touch," I said. "You'll have to be patient with me. Now. Who's this Parker character?"

"He's just one of the greatest jazz musicians alive," said Sonny, sullenly, his hands in his pockets, his back to me. "Maybe *the* greatest," he added, bitterly, "that's probably why *you* never heard of him."

"All right," I said, "I'm ignorant. I'm sorry. I'll go out and buy all the cat's records right away, all right?"

"It don't," said Sonny, with dignity, "make any difference to me. I don't care what you listen to. Don't do me no favors."

I was beginning to realize that I'd never seen him so upset before. With another part of my mind I was thinking that this would probably turn out to be one of those things kids go through and that I shouldn't make it seem important by pushing it too hard. Still, I didn't think it would do any harm to ask: "Doesn't all this take a lot of time? Can you make a living at it?"

He turned back to me and half leaned, half sat, on the kitchen table. "Everything takes time," he said, "and—well, yes, sure, I can make a living at it. But what I don't seem to be able to make you understand is that it's the only thing I want to do."

"Well, Sonny," I said, gently, "you know people can't always do exactly what they *want* to do—"

"*No*, I don't know that," said Sonny, surprising me. "I think people *ought* to do what they want to do, what else are they alive for?"

"You getting to be a big boy," I said desperately, "it's time you started thinking about your future."

"I'm thinking about my future," said Sonny, grimly. "I think about it all the time."

I gave up. I decided, if he didn't change his mind, that we could always talk about it later. "In the meantime," I said, "you got to finish school." We had already decided that he'd have to move in with Isabel and her folks. I knew this wasn't the ideal arrangement because Isabel's folks are inclined to be dicty and they hadn't especially wanted Isabel to marry me. But I didn't know what else to do. "And we have to get you fixed up at Isabel's."

There was a long silence. He moved from the kitchen table to the window. "That's a terrible idea. You know it yourself."

"Do you have a *better* idea?"

He just walked up and down the kitchen for a minute. He was as tall as I was. He had started to shave. I suddenly had the feeling that I didn't know him at all.

He stopped at the kitchen table and picked up my cigarettes. Looking at me with a kind of mocking, amused defiance, he put one between his lips. "You mind?"

"You smoking already?"

He lit the cigarette and nodded, watching me through the smoke. "I just wanted to see if I'd have the courage to smoke in front of you." He grinned and blew a great cloud of smoke to the ceiling. "It was easy." He looked at my face. "Come on, now. I bet you was smoking at my age, tell the truth."

I didn't say anything but the truth was on my face, and he laughed. But now there was something very strained in his laugh. "Sure. And I bet that ain't all you was doing."

He was frightening me a little. "Cut the crap," I said. "We already decided that you was going to go and live at Isabel's. Now what's got into you all of a sudden?"

"*You* decided it," he pointed out. "*I* didn't decide nothing."
He stopped in front of me, leaning against the stove, arms
loosely folded. "Look, brother. I don't want to stay in Harlem
no more, I really don't." He was very earnest. He looked at me,
then over toward the kitchen window. There was something in
his eyes I'd never seen before, some thoughtfulness, some
worry all his own. He rubbed the muscle of one arm. "It's time
I was getting out of here."

"Where do you want to *go*, Sonny?"

"I want to join the army. Or the navy, I don't care. If I say
I'm old enough, they'll believe me."

Then I got mad. It was because I was so scared. "You must
be crazy. You goddamn fool, what the hell do you want to go
and join the *army* for?"

"I just told you. To get out of Harlem."

"Sonny, you haven't even finished *school*. And if you really
want to be a musician, how do you expect to study if you're in
the *army?*"

He looked at me, trapped, and in anguish. "There's ways. I
might be able to work out some kind of deal. Anyway, I'll have
the G.I. Bill when I come out."

"*If* you come out." We stared at each other. "Sonny, please.
Be reasonable. I know the setup is far from perfect. But we got
to do the best we can."

"I ain't learning nothing in school," he said. "Even when I
go." He turned away from me and opened the window and
threw his cigarette out into the narrow alley. I watched his
back. "At least, I ain't learning nothing you'd want me to
learn." He slammed the window so hard I thought the glass
would fly out, and turned back to me. "And I'm sick of the
stink of these garbage cans!"

"Sonny," I said, "I know how you feel. But if you don't finish
school now, you're going to be sorry later that you didn't." I
grabbed him by the shoulders. "And you only got another year.
It ain't so bad. And I'll come back and I swear I'll help you do

whatever you want to do. Just try to put up with it till I come
back. Will you please do that? For me?"

He didn't answer and he wouldn't look at me.

"Sonny. You hear me?"

He pulled away. "I hear you. But you never hear anything *I*
say."

I didn't know what to say to that. He looked out of the
window and then back at me. "OK," he said, and sighed. "I'll
try."

Then I said, trying to cheer him up a little, "They got a
piano at Isabel's. You can practice on it."

And as a matter of fact, it did cheer him up for a minute.
"That's right," he said to himself. "I forgot that." His face
relaxed a little. But the worry, the thoughtfulness, played on it
still, the way shadows play on a face which is staring into the
fire.

But I thought I'd never hear the end of that piano. At first,
Isabel would write me, saying how nice it was that Sonny was
so serious about his music and how, as soon as he came in from
school, or wherever he had been when he was supposed to be
at school, he went straight to that piano and stayed there until
suppertime. And, after supper, he went back to that piano and
stayed there until everybody went to bed. He was at the piano
all day Saturday and all day Sunday. Then he bought a record
player and started playing records. He'd play one record over
and over again, all day long sometimes, and he'd improvise
along with it on the piano. Or he'd play one section of the record, one chord, one change, one progression, then he'd do it
on the piano. Then back to the record. Then back to the piano.

Well, I really don't know how they stood it. Isabel finally
confessed that it wasn't like living with a person at all, it was
like living with sound. And the sound didn't make any sense to
her, didn't make any sense to any of them—naturally. They
began, in a way, to be afflicted by this presence that was living

in their home. It was as though Sonny were some sort of god, or monster. He moved in an atmosphere which wasn't like theirs at all. They fed him and he ate, he washed himself, he walked in and out of their door; he certainly wasn't nasty or unpleasant or rude, Sonny isn't any of those things; but it was as though he were all wrapped up in some cloud, some fire, some vision all his own; and there wasn't any way to reach him.

At the same time, he wasn't really a man yet, he was still a child, and they had to watch out for him in all kinds of ways. They certainly couldn't throw him out. Neither did they dare to make a great scene about that piano because even they dimly sensed, as I sensed, from so many thousands of miles away, that Sonny was at that piano playing for his life.

But he hadn't been going to school. One day a letter came from the school board and Isabel's mother got it—there had, apparently, been other letters but Sonny had torn them up. This day, when Sonny came in, Isabel's mother showed him the letter and asked where he'd been spending his time. And she finally got it out of him that he'd been down in Greenwich Village, with musicians and other characters, in a white girl's apartment. And this scared her and she started to scream at him and what came up, once she began—though she denies it to this day—was what sacrifices they were making to give Sonny a decent home and how little he appreciated it.

Sonny didn't play the piano that day. By evening, Isabel's mother had calmed down but then there was the old man to deal with, and Isabel herself. Isabel says she did her best to be calm but she broke down and started crying. She says she just watched Sonny's face. She could tell, by watching him, what was happening with him. And what was happening was that they penetrated his cloud, they had reached him. Even if their fingers had been a thousand times more gentle than human fingers ever are, he could hardly help feeling that they had stripped him naked and were spitting on that nakedness. For he also had to see that his presence, that music, which was life or death to him, had been torture for them and that they had endured it, not at all for his sake, but only for mine. And Sonny couldn't take that. He can take it a little better today than he could then but he's still not very good at it and, frankly, I don't know anybody who is.

The silence of the next few days must have been louder than the sound of all the music ever played since time began. One morning, before she went to work, Isabel was in his room for something and she suddenly realized that all of his records were gone. And she knew for certain that he was gone. And he was. He went as far as the navy would carry him. He finally sent me a postcard from some place in Greece and that was the first I knew that Sonny was still alive. I didn't see him any more until we were both back in New York and the war had long been over.

He was a man by then, of course, but I wasn't willing to see it. He came by the house from time to time, but we fought almost every time we met. I didn't like the way he carried himself, loose and dreamlike all the time, and I didn't like his friends, and his music seemed to be merely an excuse for the life he led. It sounded just that weird and disordered.

Then we had a fight, a pretty awful fight, and I didn't see him for months. By and by I looked him up, where he was living, in a furnished room in the Village, and I tried to make it up. But there were lots of other people in the room and Sonny just lay on his bed, and he wouldn't come downstairs with me, and he treated these other people as though they were his family and I weren't. So I got mad and then he got mad, and then I told him that he might just as well be dead as live the way he was living. Then he stood up and he told me not to worry about him any more in life, that he *was* dead as far as I was concerned. Then he pushed me to the door and the other people looked on as though nothing were happening, and he

slammed the door behind me. I stood in the hallway, staring at
the door. I heard somebody laugh in the room and then the
tears came to my eyes. I started down the steps, whistling to
keep from crying, I kept whistling to myself, *You going to
need me, baby, one of these cold, rainy days.*

I read about Sonny's trouble in the spring. Little Grace died
in the fall. She was a beautiful little girl. But she only lived a
little over two years. She died of polio and she suffered. She
had a slight fever for a couple of days, but it didn't seem like
anything and we just kept her in bed. And we would certainly
have called the doctor, but the fever dropped, she seemed to
be all right. So we thought it had just been a cold. Then, one
day, she was up, playing, Isabel was in the kitchen fixing lunch
for the two boys when they'd come in from school, and she
heard Grace fall down in the living room. When you have a lot
of children you don't always start running when one of them
falls, unless they start screaming or something. And, this time,
Grace was quiet. Yet, Isabel says that when she heard that
thump and then that silence, something happened in her to
make her afraid. And she ran to the living room and there was
little Grace on the floor, all twisted up, and the reason she
hadn't screamed was that she couldn't get her breath. And
when she did scream, it was the worst sound, Isabel says, that
she'd ever heard in all her life, and she still hears it sometimes
in her dreams. Isabel will sometimes wake me up with a low,
moaning, strangled sound and I have to be quick to awaken
her and hold her to me and where Isabel is weeping against
me seems a mortal wound.

I think I may have written Sonny the very day that little
Grace was buried. I was sitting in the living room in the dark,
by myself, and I suddenly thought of Sonny. My trouble made
his real.

One Saturday afternoon, when Sonny had been living with us, or, anyway, been in our house, for nearly two weeks, I found myself wandering aimlessly about the living room, drinking from a can of beer, and trying to work up the courage to search Sonny's room. He was out, he was usually out whenever I was home, and Isabel had taken the children to see their grandparents. Suddenly I was standing still in front of the living room window, watching Seventh Avenue. The idea of searching Sonny's room made me still. I scarcely dared to admit to myself what I'd be searching for. I didn't know what I'd do if I found it. Or if I didn't.

On the sidewalk across from me, near the entrance to a barbecue joint, some people were holding an old-fashioned revival meeting. The barbecue cook, wearing a dirty white apron, his conked hair reddish and metallic in the pale sun, and a cigarette between his lips, stood in the doorway, watching them. Kids and older people paused in their errands and stood there, along with some older men and a couple of very tough-looking women who watched everything that happened on the avenue, as though they owned it, or were maybe owned by it. Well, they were watching this, too. The revival was being carried on by three sisters in black, and a brother. All they had were their voices and their Bibles and a tambourine. The brother was testifying and while he testified two of the sisters stood together, seeming to say, amen, and the third sister walked around with the tambourine outstretched and a couple of people dropped coins into it. Then the brother's testimony ended and the sister who had been taking up the collection dumped the coins into her palm and transferred them to the pocket of her long black robe. Then she raised both hands, striking the tambourine against the air, and then against one hand, and she started to sing. And the two other sisters and the brother joined in.

It was strange, suddenly, to watch, though I had been seeing these street meetings all my life. So, of course, had everybody else down there. Yet, they paused and watched and listened and I stood still at the window. *"Tis the old ship of Zion,"* they sang, and the sister with the tambourine kept a steady, jangling beat, *"it has rescued many a thousand!"* Not a soul under the sound of their voices was hearing this song for the first time, not one of them had been rescued. Nor had they seen much in the way of rescue work being done around them. Neither did they especially believe in the holiness of the three sisters and the brother, they knew too much about them, knew where they lived, and how. The woman with the tambourine, whose voice dominated the air, whose face was bright with joy, was divided by very little from the woman who stood watching her, a cigarette between her heavy, chapped lips, her hair a cuckoo's nest, her face scarred and swollen from many beatings, and her black eyes glittering like coal. Perhaps they both knew this, which was why, when, as rarely, they addressed each other, they addressed each other as Sister. As the singing filled the air the watching, listening faces underwent a change, the eyes focusing on something within; the music seemed to soothe a poison out of them; and time seemed, nearly, to fall away from the sullen, belligerent, battered faces, as though they were fleeing back to their first condition, while dreaming of their last. The barbecue cook half shook his head and smiled, and dropped his cigarette and disappeared into his joint. A man fumbled in his pockets for change and stood holding it in his hand impatiently, as though he had just remembered a pressing appointment further up the avenue. He looked furious. Then I saw Sonny, standing on the edge of the crowd. He was carrying a wide, flat notebook with a green cover, and it made him look, from where I was standing, almost like a schoolboy. The coppery sun brought out the copper in his skin, he was very faintly smiling, standing very still. Then the singing stopped, the tambourine turned into a collection plate again. The furious man dropped in his coins and vanished, so did a couple of the women, and Sonny dropped some change in the plate, looking directly at the woman with a little smile. He started across the avenue, toward the house. He has a slow, loping walk, something like the way Harlem hipsters walk, only he's imposed on this his own half-beat. I had never really noticed it before.

I stayed at the window, both relieved and apprehensive. As Sonny disappeared from my sight, they began singing again. And they were still singing when his key turned in the lock.

"Hey," he said.

"Hey, yourself. You want some beer?"

"No. Well, maybe." But he came up to the window and stood beside me, looking out. "What a warm voice," he said.

They were singing *If I could only hear my mother pray again!*

"Yes," I said, "and she can sure beat that tambourine."

"But what a terrible song," he said, and laughed. He dropped his notebook on the sofa and disappeared into the kitchen. "Where's Isabel and the kids?"

"I think they went to see their grandparents. You hungry?"

"No." He came back into the living room with his can of beer. "You want to come some place with me tonight?"

I sensed, I don't know how, that I couldn't possibly say no. "Sure. Where?"

He sat down on the sofa and picked up his notebook and started leafing through it. "I'm going to sit in with some fellows in a joint in the Village."

"You mean, you're going to play, tonight?"

"That's right." He took a swallow of his beer and moved back to the window. He gave me a sidelong look. "If you can stand it."

"I'll try," I said.

He smiled to himself and we both watched as the meeting

across the way broke up. The three sisters and the brother, heads bowed, were singing *God be with you till we meet again*. The faces around them were very quiet. Then the song ended. The small crowd dispersed. We watched the three women and the lone man walk slowly up the avenue.

"When she was singing before," said Sonny, abruptly, "her voice reminded me for a minute of what heroin feels like some-times—when it's in your veins. It makes you feel sort of warm and cool at the same time. And distant. And—and sure." He sipped his beer, very deliberately not looking at me. I watched his face. "It makes you feel—in control. Sometimes you've got to have that feeling."

"Do you?" I sat down slowly in the easy chair.

"Sometimes." He went to the sofa and picked up his note-book again. "Some people do."

"In order," I asked, "to play?" And my voice was very ugly, full of contempt and anger.

"Well"—he looked at me with great, troubled eyes, as though, in fact, he hoped his eyes would tell me things he could never otherwise say—"they *think* so. And *if* they think so—!"

"And what do *you* think?" I asked.

He sat on the sofa and put his can of beer on the floor. "I don't know," he said, and I couldn't be sure if he were answer-ing my question or pursuing his thoughts. His face didn't tell me. "It's not so much to *play*. It's to *stand* it, to be able to make it at all. On any level." He frowned and smiled: "In order to keep from shaking to pieces."

"But these friends of yours," I said, "they seem to shake themselves to pieces pretty goddamn fast."

"Maybe." He played with the notebook. And something told me that I should curb my tongue, that Sonny was doing his best to talk, that I should listen. "But of course you only know the ones that've gone to pieces. Some don't—or at least they haven't *yet* and that's just about all *any* of us can say." He paused. "And then there are some who just live, really, in hell, and they know it and they see what's happening and they go right on. I don't know." He sighed, dropped the notebook, folded his arms. "Some guys, you can tell from the way they play, they on something *all* the time. And you can see that, well, it makes something real for them. But of course," he picked up his beer from the floor and sipped it and put the can down again, "they *want* to, too, you've got to see that. Even some of them that say they don't—*some*, not all."

"And what about you?" I asked—I couldn't help it. "What about you? Do *you* want to?"

He stood up and walked to the window and remained silent for a long time. Then he sighed. "Me," he said. Then: "While I was downstairs before, on my way here, listening to that woman sing, it struck me all of a sudden how much suffering she must have had to go through—to sing like that. It's *repulsive* to think you have to suffer that much."

I said: "But there's no way not to suffer—is there, Sonny?"

"I believe not," he said and smiled, "but that's never stopped anyone from trying." He looked at me. "Has it?" I realized, with this mocking look, that there stood between us, forever, beyond the power of time or forgiveness, the fact that I had held silence—so long!—when he had needed human speech to help him. He turned back to the window. "No, there's no way not to suffer. But you try all kinds of ways to keep from drowning in it, to keep on top of it, and to make it seem—well, like *you*. Like you did something, all right, and now you're suffering for it. You know?" I said nothing. "Well you know," he said, impatiently, "why *do* people suffer? Maybe it's better to do something to give it a reason, *any* reason."

"But we just agreed," I said, "that there's no way not to suffer. Isn't it better, then, just to—take it?"

"But nobody just takes it," Sonny cried, "that's what I'm

telling you! *Everybody* tries not to. You're just hung up on the
way some people try—it's not *your* way!"

The hair on my face began to itch, my face felt wet. "That's
not true," I said, "that's not true. I don't give a damn what
other people do, I don't even care how they suffer. I just care
how *you* suffer." And he looked at me. "Please believe me," I
said, "I don't want to see you—die—trying not to suffer."

"I won't," he said, flatly, "die trying not to suffer. At least,
not any faster than anybody else."

"But there's no need," I said, trying to laugh, "is there? in
killing yourself."

I wanted to say more, but I couldn't. I wanted to talk about
will power and how life could be—well, beautiful. I wanted to
say that it was all within; but was it? or, rather, wasn't that
exactly the trouble? And I wanted to promise that I would
never fail him again. But it would all have sounded—empty
words and lies.

So I made the promise to myself and prayed that I would
keep it.

"It's terrible sometimes, inside," he said, "that's what's the
trouble. You walk these streets, black and funky and cold, and
there's not really a living ass to talk to, and there's nothing
shaking, and there's no way of getting it out—that storm inside. You can't talk it and you can't make love with it, and
when you finally try to get with it and play it, you realize
nobody's listening. So you've got to listen. You got to find a
way to listen."

And then he walked away from the window and sat on the
sofa again, as though all the wind had suddenly been knocked
out of him. "Sometimes you'll do *anything* to play, even cut
your mother's throat." He laughed and looked at me. "Or your
brother's." Then he sobered. "Or your own." Then: "Don't
worry. I'm all right now and I think I'll *be* all right. But I can't

forget—where I've been. I don't mean just the physical place I've been, I mean where I've *been*. And *what* I've been."

"What have you been, Sonny?" I asked.

He smiled—but sat sideways on the sofa, his elbow resting on the back, his fingers playing with his mouth and chin, not looking at me. "I've been something I didn't recognize, didn't know I could be. Didn't know anybody could be." He stopped, looking inward, looking helplessly young, looking old. "I'm not talking about it now because I feel *guilty* or anything like that—maybe it would be better if I did, I don't know. Anyway, I can't really talk about it. Not to you, not to anybody," and now he turned and faced me. "Sometimes, you know, and it was actually when I was most *out* of the world, I felt that I was in it, that I was *with* it, really, and I could play or I didn't really have to *play*, it just came out of me, it was there. And I don't know how I played, thinking about it now, but I know I did awful things, those times, sometimes, to people. Or it wasn't that I *did* anything to them—it was that they weren't real." He picked up the beer can; it was empty; he rolled it between his palms: "And other times—well, I needed a fix, I needed to find a place to lean, I needed to clear a space to *listen*—and I couldn't find it, and I—went crazy, I did terrible things to *me*, I was terrible *for* me." He began pressing the beer can between his hands, I watched the metal begin to give. It glittered, as he played with it, like a knife, and I was afraid he would cut himself, but I said nothing. "Oh well. I can never tell you. I was all by myself at the bottom of something, stinking and sweating and crying and shaking, and I smelled it, you know? *my* stink, and I thought I'd die if I couldn't get away from it and yet, all the same, I knew that everything I was doing was just locking me in with it. And I didn't know," he paused, still flattening the beer can, "I didn't know, I still *don't* know, something kept telling me that maybe it was good to smell your own stink, but I didn't think that *that* was what I'd been trying to do—and—who can stand it?" and he abruptly dropped the ruined beer can, looking at me with a small, still smile, and then rose, walking to the window as though it were the lodestone rock. I watched his face, he watched the avenue. "I couldn't tell you when Mama died—but the reason I wanted to leave Harlem so bad was to get away from drugs. And then, when I ran away, that's what I was running from—really. When I came back, nothing had changed, *I* hadn't changed, I was just—older." And he stopped, drumming with his fingers on the windowpane. The sun had vanished, soon darkness would fall. I watched his face. "It can come again," he said, almost as though speaking to himself. Then he turned to me. "It can come again," he repeated. "I just want you to know that."

"All right," I said, at last. "So it can come again, All right."

He smiled, but the smile was sorrowful. "I had to try to tell you," he said.

"Yes," I said. "I understand that."

"You're my brother," he said, looking straight at me, and not smiling at all.

"Yes," I repeated, "yes. I understand that."

He turned back to the window, looking out. "All that hatred down there," he said, "all that hatred and misery and love. It's a wonder it doesn't blow the avenue apart."

We went to the only nightclub on a short, dark street, down-town. We squeezed through the narrow, chattering, jam-packed bar to the entrance of the big room, where the band-stand was. And we stood there for a moment, for the lights were very dim in this room and we couldn't see. Then, "Hello, boy," said a voice and an enormous black man, much older than Sonny or myself, erupted out of all that atmospheric light-ing and put an arm around Sonny's shoulder. "I been sitting right here," he said, "waiting for you."

He had a big voice, too, and heads in the darkness turned toward us.

Sonny grinned and pulled a little away, and said, "Creole, this is my brother. I told you about him."

Creole shook my hand. "I'm glad to meet you, son," he said, and it was clear that he was glad to meet me *there*, for Sonny's sake. And he smiled, "You got a real musician in *your* family," and he took his arm from Sonny's shoulder and slapped him, lightly, affectionately, with the back of his hand.

"Well. Now I've heard it all," said a voice behind us. This was another musician, and a friend of Sonny's, a coal-black, cheerful-looking man, built close to the ground. He immediately began confiding to me, at the top of his lungs, the most terrible things about Sonny, his teeth gleaming like a lighthouse and his laugh coming up out of him like the beginning of an earthquake. And it turned out that everyone at the bar knew Sonny, or almost everyone; some were musicians, working there, or nearby, or not working, some were simply hangers-on, and some were there to hear Sonny play. I was introduced to all of them and they were all very polite to me. Yet, it was clear that, for them, I was only Sonny's brother. Here, I was in Sonny's world. Or, rather: his kingdom. Here, it was not even a question that his veins bore royal blood.

They were going to play soon and Creole installed me, by myself, at a table in a dark corner. Then I watched them, Creole, and the little black man, and Sonny, and the others, while they horsed around, standing just below the bandstand. The light from the bandstand spilled just a little short of them and, watching them laughing and gesturing and moving about, I had the feeling that they, nevertheless, were being most careful not to step into that circle of light too suddenly: that if they moved into the light too suddenly, without thinking, they would perish in flame. Then, while I watched, one of them, the small, black man, moved into the light and crossed the bandstand and started fooling around with his drums. Then—being funny and being, also, extremely ceremonious—Creole took Sonny by the arm and led him to the piano. A woman's voice called Sonny's name and a few hands started clapping. And Sonny, also being funny and being ceremonious, and so touched, I think, that he could have cried, but neither hiding it nor showing it, riding it like a man, grinned, and put both hands to his heart and bowed from the waist.

Creole then went to the bass fiddle and a lean, very bright-skinned brown man jumped up on the bandstand and picked up his horn. So there they were, and the atmosphere on the bandstand and in the room began to change and tighten. Someone stepped up to the microphone and announced them. Then there were all kinds of murmurs. Some people at the bar shushed others. The waitress ran around, frantically getting in the last orders, guys and chicks got closer to each other, and the lights on the bandstand, on the quartet, turned to a kind of indigo. Then they all looked different there. Creole looked about him for the last time, as though he were making certain that all his chickens were in the coop, and then he—jumped and struck the fiddle. And there they were.

All I know about music is that not many people ever really hear it. And even then, on the rare occasions when something opens within, and the music enters, what we mainly hear, or hear corroborated, are personal, private, vanishing evocations. But the man who creates the music is hearing something else, is dealing with the roar rising from the void and imposing order on it as it hits the air. What is evoked in him, then, is of another order, more terrible because it has no words, and triumphant, too, for that same reason. And his triumph, when he triumphs, is ours. I just watched Sonny's face. His face was troubled, he was working hard, but he wasn't with it. And I had the feeling that, in a way, everyone on the bandstand was waiting for him, both waiting for him and pushing him along.

But as I began to watch Creole, I realized that it was Creole who held them all back. He had them on a short rein. Up there, keeping the beat with his whole body, wailing on the fiddle, with his eyes half closed, he was listening to everything, but he was listening to Sonny. He was having a dialogue with Sonny. He wanted Sonny to leave the shoreline and strike out for the deep water. He was Sonny's witness that deep water and drowning were not the same thing—he had been there, and he knew. And he wanted Sonny to know. He was waiting for Sonny to do the things on the keys which would let Creole know that Sonny was in the water.

And, while Creole listened, Sonny moved, deep within, exactly like someone in torment. I had never before thought of how awful the relationship must be between the musician and his instrument. He has to fill it, this instrument, with the breath of life, his own. He has to make it do what he wants it to do. And a piano is just a piano. It's made out of so much wood and wires and little hammers and big ones, and ivory. While there's only so much you can do with it, the only way to find this out is to try; to try and make it do everything.

And Sonny hadn't been near a piano for over a year. And he wasn't on much better terms with his life, not the life that stretched before him now. He and the piano stammered, started one way, got scared, stopped; started another way, panicked, marked time, started again; then seemed to have found a direction, panicked again, got stuck. And the face I saw on Sonny I'd never seen before. Everything had been burned out of it, and, at the same time, things usually hidden were being burned in, by the fire and fury of the battle which was occurring in him up there.

Yet, watching Creole's face as they neared the end of the first set, I had the feeling that something had happened, something I hadn't heard. Then they finished, there was scattered applause, and then, without an instant's warning, Creole

started into something else, it was almost sardonic, it was *Am I
Blue*. And, as though he commanded, Sonny began to play.
Something began to happen. And Creole let out the reins. The
dry, low, black man said something awful on the drums,
Creole answered, and the drums talked back. Then the horn
insisted, sweet and high, slightly detached perhaps, and Creole
listened, commenting now and then, dry, and driving, beautiful and calm and old. Then they all came together again, and
Sonny was part of the family again. I could tell this from his
face. He seemed to have found, right there beneath his fingers,
a damn brand-new piano. It seemed that he couldn't get over
it. Then, for awhile, just being happy with Sonny, they seemed
to be agreeing with him that brand-new pianos certainly were
a gas.

Then Creole stepped forward to remind them that what
they were playing was the blues. He hit something in all of
them, he hit something in me, myself, and the music tightened
and deepened, apprehension began to beat the air. Creole
began to tell us what the blues were all about. They were not
about anything very new. He and his boys up there were
keeping it new, at the risk of ruin, destruction, madness, and
death, in order to find new ways to make us listen. For, while
the tale of how we suffer, and how we are delighted, and how
we may triumph is never new, it always must be heard. There
isn't any other tale to tell, it's the only light we've got in all this
darkness.

And this tale, according to that face, that body, those strong
hands on those strings, has another aspect in every country,
and a new depth in every generation. Listen, Creole seemed to
be saying, listen. Now these are Sonny's blues. He made the
little black man on the drums know it, and the bright, brown
man on the horn. Creole wasn't trying any longer to get Sonny
in the water. He was wishing him Godspeed. Then he stepped

back, very slowly, filling the air with the immense suggestion that Sonny speak for himself.

Then they all gathered around Sonny and Sonny played. Every now and again one of them seemed to say, amen. Sonny's fingers filled the air with life, his life. But that life contained so many others. And Sonny went all the way back, he really began with the spare, flat statement of the opening phrase of the song. Then he began to make it his. It was very beautiful because it wasn't hurried and it was no longer a lament. I seemed to hear with what burning he had made it his, with what burning we had yet to make it ours, how we could cease lamenting. Freedom lurked around us and I understood, at last, that he could help us to be free if we would listen, that he would never be free until we did. Yet, there was no battle in his face now. I heard what he had gone through, and would continue to go through until he came to rest in earth. He had made it his: that long line, of which we knew only Mama and Daddy. And he was giving it back, as everything must be given back, so that, passing through death, it can live forever. I saw my mother's face again, and felt, for the first time, how the stones of the road she had walked on must have bruised her feet. I saw the moonlit road where my father's brother died. And it brought something else back to me, and carried me past it, I saw my little girl again and felt Isabel's tears again, and I felt my own tears begin to rise. And I was yet aware that this was only a moment, that the world waited outside, as hungry as a tiger, and that trouble stretched above us, longer than the sky.

Then it was over. Creole and Sonny let out their breath, both soaking wet, and grinning. There was a lot of applause and some of it was real. In the dark, the girl came by and I asked her to take drinks to the bandstand. There was a long pause, while they talked up there in the indigo light and after awhile I saw the girl put a Scotch and milk on top of the piano for Sonny. He didn't seem to notice it, but just before they started playing again, he sipped from it and looked toward me, and nodded. Then he put it back on top of the piano. For me, then, as they began to play again, it glowed and shook above my brother's head like the very cup of trembling.

This Morning,
This Evening, So Soon

"YOU ARE FULL of nightmares," Harriet tells me. She is in her dressing gown and has cream all over her face. She and my older sister, Louisa, are going out to be girls together. I suppose they have many things to talk about—they have *me* to talk about, certainly—and they do not want my presence. I have been given a bachelor's evening. The director of the film which has brought us such incredible and troubling riches will be along later to take me out to dinner.

I watch her face. I know that it is quite impossible for her to be as untroubled as she seems. Her self-control is mainly for my benefit—my benefit, and Paul's. Harriet comes from orderly and progressive Sweden and has reacted against all the advanced doctrines to which she has been exposed by becoming steadily and beautifully old-fashioned. We never fought in front of Paul, not even when he was a baby. Harriet does not so much believe in protecting children as she does in helping them to build a foundation on which they can build and build again, each time life's high-flying steel ball knocks down everything they have built.

Whenever I become upset, Harriet becomes very cheerful and composed. I think she began to learn how to do this over eight years ago, when I returned from my only visit to America. Now, perhaps, it has become something she could not control if she wished to. This morning, at breakfast, when I yelled at Paul, she averted Paul's tears and my own guilt by looking up and saying, "My God, your father is cranky this morning, isn't he?"

Paul's attention was immediately distracted from his wounds, and the unjust inflicter of those wounds, to his mother's laughter. He watched her.

"It is because he is afraid they will not like his songs in New York. Your father is an *artiste, mon chou,* and they are very mysterious people, *les artistes*. Millions of people are waiting for him in New York, they are begging him to come, and they will give him a *lot* of money, but he is afraid they will not like him. Tell him he is wrong."

She succeeded in rekindling Paul's excitement about places he has never seen. I was also, at once, reinvested with all my glamour. I think it is sometimes extremely difficult for Paul to realize that the face he sees on record sleeves and in the newspapers and on the screen is nothing more or less than the face of his father—who sometimes yells at him. Of course, since he is only seven—going on eight, he will be eight years old this winter—he cannot know that I am baffled, too.

"Of course, you are wrong, you are silly," he said with passion—and caused me to smile. His English is strongly accented and is not, in fact, as good as his French, for he speaks French all day at school. French is really his first language, the first he ever heard. "You are the greatest singer in France"—sounding exactly as he must sound when he makes this pronouncement to his schoolmates—"the greatest *American* singer"—this concession was so gracefully made that it was not a concession at all, it added inches to my stature, America being only a glamorous word for Paul. It is the place from which his father came, and to which he now is going, a place which very few people have ever seen. But his aunt is one of them and he looked over at her. "Mme. Dumont says so, and she says he is a *great actor, too.*" Louisa nodded, smiling. "And she has seen *Les Fauves Nous Attendent*—five times!" This clinched it, of course. Mme. Dumont is our concierge and she has known Paul all his life. I suppose he will not begin to doubt anything she says until he begins to doubt everything.

He looked over at me again. "So you are wrong to be afraid."

"I was wrong to yell at you, too. I won't yell at you any more today."

"All right." He was very grave.

Louisa poured more coffee. "He's going to knock them dead in New York. You'll see."

"*Mais bien sûr*," said Paul, doubtfully. He does not quite know what "knock them dead" means, though he was sure, from her tone, that she must have been agreeing with him. He does not quite understand this aunt, whom he met for the first time two months ago, when she arrived to spend the summer with us. Her accent is entirely different from anything he has ever heard. He does not really understand why, since she is my sister and his aunt, she should be unable to speak French.

Harriet, Louisa, and I looked at each other and smiled. "Knock them dead," said Harriet, "means *d'avoir un succès fou*. But you will soon pick up all the American expressions." She looked at me and laughed. "So will I."

"That's what he's afraid of." Louisa grinned. "We have *got* some expressions, believe me. Don't let anybody ever tell you America hasn't got a culture. Our culture is as thick as clabber milk."

"Ah," Harriet answered, "I know. I know."

"I'm going to be practicing later," I told Paul.

His face lit up. "*Bon.*" This meant that, later, he would come into my study and lie on the floor with his papers and crayons while I worked out with the piano and the tape recorder. He knew that I was offering this as an olive branch. All things considered, we get on pretty well, my son and I.

He looked over at Louisa again. She held a coffee cup in one hand and a cigarette in the other; and something about her baffled him. It was early, so she had not yet put on her face. Her short, thick, graying hair was rougher than usual, almost as rough as my own—later, she would be going to the hairdresser's; she is fairer than I, and better-looking; Louisa, in fact, caught all the looks in the family. Paul knows that she is my older sister and that she helped to raise me, though he does not, of course, know what this means. He knows that she is a schoolteacher in the *American* South, which is not, for some reason, the same place as South America. I could see him trying to fit all these exotic details together into a pattern which would explain her strangeness—strangeness of accent, strangeness of manner. In comparison with the people he has always known, Louisa must seem, for all her generosity and laughter and affection, peculiarly uncertain of herself, peculiarly hostile and embattled.

I wondered what he would think of his Uncle Norman, older and much blacker than I, who lives near the Alabama town in which we were born. Norman will meet us at the boat.

Now Harriet repeats, "Nightmares, nightmares. Nothing ever turns out as badly as you think it will—in fact," she adds laughing, "I am happy to say that that would scarcely be possible."

Her eyes seek mine in the mirror—dark-blue eyes, pale skin, black hair. I had always thought of Sweden as being populated entirely by blondes, and I thought that Harriet was abnormally dark for a Swedish girl. But when we visited Sweden, I found out differently. "It is all a great racial salad, Europe, that is why I am sure that I will never understand your country," Harriet said. That was in the days when we never imagined that we would be going to it.

I wonder what she is really thinking. Still, she is right, in two days we will be on a boat, and there is simply no point in carrying around my load of apprehension. I sit down on the bed, watching her fix her face. I realize that I am going to miss this old-fashioned bedroom. For years, we've talked about throwing out the old junk which came with the apartment and replacing it with less massive, modern furniture. But we never have.

"Oh, everything will probably work out," I say. "I've been in a bad mood all day long. I just can't sing any more." We both laugh. She reaches for a wad of tissues and begins wiping off the cream. "I wonder how Paul will like it, if he'll make friends —that's all."

"Paul will like any place where you are, where we are. Don't worry about Paul."

Paul has never been called any names, so far. Only, once he asked us what the word *métis* meant and Harriet explained to him that it meant mixed blood, adding that the blood of just about everybody in the world was mixed by now. Mme. Dumont contributed bawdy and detailed corroboration from her own family tree, the roots of which were somewhere in Corsica; the moral of the story, as she told it, was that women were weak, men incorrigible, and *le bon Dieu* appallingly clever. Mme. Dumont's version is the version I prefer, but it may not be, for Paul, the most utilitarian.

Harriet rises from the dressing table and comes over to sit in my lap. I fall back with her on the bed, and she smiles down into my face.

"Now, don't worry," she tells me, "please try not to worry. Whatever is coming, we will manage it all very well, you will see. We have each other and we have our son and we know what we want. So, we are luckier than most people."

I kiss her on the chin. "I'm luckier than most men."

"I'm a very lucky woman, too."

And for a moment we are silent, alone in our room, which we have shared so long. The slight rise and fall of Harriet's breathing creates an intermittent pressure against my chest, and I think how, if I had never left America, I would never have met her and would never have established a life of my own, would never have entered my own life. For everyone's life begins on a level where races, armies, and churches stop. And yet everyone's life is always shaped by races, churches, and armies; races, churches, armies menace, and have taken, many lives. If Harriet had been born in America, it would have taken her a long time, perhaps forever, to look on me as a man like other men; if I had met her in America, I would never have been able to look on her as a woman like all other women. The habits of public rage and power would also have been our private compulsions, and would have blinded our eyes. We would never have been able to love each other. And Paul would never have been born.

Perhaps, if I had stayed in America, I would have found another woman and had another son. But that other woman, that other son are in the limbo of vanished possibilities. I might also have become something else, instead of an actor-singer, perhaps a lawyer, like my brother, or a teacher, like my sister. But no, I am what I have become and this woman beside me is my wife, and I love her. All the sons I might have had mean nothing, since I *have* a son, I named him, Paul, for my father, and I love him.

I think of all the things I have seen destroyed in America, all the things that I have lost there, all the threats it holds for me and mine.

I grin up at Harriet. "Do you love me?"

"Of course not. I simply have been madly plotting to get to America all these years."

"What a patient wench you are."

"The Swedes are very patient."

She kisses me again and stands up. Louisa comes in, also in a dressing gown.

"I hope you two aren't sitting in here yakking about the *subject*." She looks at me. "My, you are the sorriest-looking celebrity I've ever seen. I've always wondered why people like you hired press agents. Now I know." She goes to Harriet's dressing table. "Honey, do you mind if I borrow some of that *mad* nail polish?"

Harriet goes over to the dressing table. "I'm not sure I know *which* mad nail polish you mean."

Harriet and Louisa, somewhat to my surprise, get on very
well. Each seems to find the other full of the weirdest and most
delightful surprises. Harriet has been teaching Louisa French
and Swedish expressions, and Louisa has been teaching Harriet some of the saltier expressions of the black South. Whenever one of them is not playing straight man to the other's
accent, they become involved in long speculations as to how a
language reveals the history and the attitudes of a people.
They discovered that all the European languages contain a
phrase equivalent to "to work like a nigger." ("Of course," says
Louisa, "they've had black men working for them for a long
time.") "Language is experience and language is power," says
Louisa, after regretting that she does not know any of the
African dialects. "That's what I keep trying to tell those dicty
bastards down South. They get their own experience into the
language, we'll have a great language. But, no, they all want to
talk like white folks." Then she leans forward, grasping Harriet
by the knee. "I tell them, honey, white folks ain't saying *nothing*. Not a thing are they saying—and *some* of them know it,
they *need* what you got, the whole world needs it." Then she
leans back, in disgust. "You think they listen to me? Indeed
they do not. They just go right on, trying to talk like white
folks." She leans forward again, in tremendous indignation.
"You know some of them folks are *ashamed* of Mahalia Jackson? *Ashamed* of her, one of the greatest singers alive! They
think she's common." Then she looks about the room as though
she held a bottle in her hand and were looking for a skull to
crack.

I think it is because Louisa has never been able to talk like
this to any white person before. All the white people she has
ever met needed, in one way or another, to be reassured, con-
soled, to have their consciences pricked but not blasted; could
not, could not afford to hear a truth which would shatter,
irrevocably, their image of themselves. It is astonishing the

lengths to which a person, or a people, will go in order to avoid a truthful mirror. But Harriet's necessity is precisely the opposite: it is of the utmost importance that she learn everything that Louisa can tell her, and then learn more, much more. Harriet is really trying to learn from Louisa how best to protect her husband and her son. This is why they are going out alone tonight. They will have, tonight, as it were, a final council of war. I may be moody, but they, thank God, are practical.

Now Louisa turns to me while Harriet rummages about on the dressing table. "What time is Vidal coming for you?"

"Oh, around seven-thirty, eight o'clock. He says he's reserved tables for us in some very chic place, but he won't say where." Louisa wriggles her shoulders, raises her eyebrows, and does a tiny bump and grind. I laugh. "That's right. And then I guess we'll go out and get drunk."

"I hope to God you do. You've been about as cheerful as a cemetery these last few days. And, that way, your hangover will keep you from bugging us tomorrow."

"What about *your* hangovers? I know the way you girls drink."

"Well, we'll be paying for our own drinks," says Harriet, "so I don't think we'll have that problem. But *you're* going to be feted, like an international movie star."

"You sure you don't want to change your mind and come out with Vidal and me?"

"We're sure," Louisa says. She looks down at me and gives a small, amused grunt. "An international movie star. And I used to change your diapers. I'll be damned." She is grave for a moment. "Mama'd be proud of you, you know that?" We look at each other and the air between us is charged with secrets which not even Harriet will ever know. "Now, get the hell out of here, so we can get dressed."

"I'll take Paul on down to Mme. Dumont's."

Paul is to have supper with her children and spend the night there.

"For the last time," says Mme. Dumont and she rubs her hand over Paul's violently curly black hair. *"Tu vas nous manquer, tu sais?"* Then she looks up at me and laughs. "He doesn't care. He is only interested in seeing the big ship and all the wonders of New York. Children are never sad to make journeys."

"I would be very sad to go," says Paul, politely, "but my father must go to New York to work and he wants me to come with him."

Over his head, Mme. Dumont and I smile at each other. *"Il est malin, ton gosse!"* She looks down at him again. "And do you think, my little diplomat, that you will like New York?"

"We aren't only going to New York," Paul answers, "we are going to California, too."

"Well, do you think you will like California?"

Paul looks at me. "I don't know. If we don't like it, we'll come back."

"So simple. Just like that," says Mme. Dumont. She looks at me. "It is the best way to look at life. Do come back. You know, we feel that you belong to us, too, here in France."

"I hope you do," I say. "I hope you do. I have always felt—always felt at home here." I bend down and Paul and I kiss each other on the cheek. We have always done so—but will we be able to do so in America? American fathers never kiss American sons. I straighten, my hand on Paul's shoulder. "You be good. I'll pick you up for breakfast, or, if you get up first you come and pick me up and we can hang out together tomorrow, while your *Maman* and your Aunt Louisa finish packing. They won't want two men hanging around the house."

"*D'accord.* Where shall we hang out?" On the last two words he stumbles a little and imitates me.

"Maybe we can go to the zoo, I don't know. And I'll take you to lunch at the Eiffel Tower, would you like that?"

"Oh, yes," he says, "I'd love that." When he is pleased, he seems to glow. All the energy of his small, tough, concentrated being charges an unseen battery and adds an incredible luster to his eyes, which are large and dark brown—like mine—and to his skin, which always reminds me of the colors of honey and the fires of the sun.

"OK, then." I shake hands with Mme. Dumont. "*Bonsoir, Madame,*" I ring for the elevator, staring at Paul. "*Ciao, Pauli.*"

"*Bonsoir, Papa.*"

And Mme. Dumont takes him inside.

Upstairs, Harriet and Louisa are finally powdered, perfumed, and jeweled, and ready to go: dry martinis at the Ritz, supper, "in some *very* expensive little place," says Harriet, and perhaps the Folies Bergère afterwards. "A real cornball, tourist evening," says Louisa. "I'm working on the theory that if I can get Harriet to act like an American now, she won't have so much trouble later."

"I very much doubt," Harriet says, "that I will be able to endure the Folies Bergère for three solid hours."

"Oh, then we'll duck across town to Harry's New York bar and drink mint juleps," says Louisa.

I realize that, quite apart from everything else, Louisa is having as much fun as she has ever had in her life. Perhaps she, too, will be sad to leave Paris, even though she has only known it for such a short time.

"Do people drink those in New York?" Harriet asks. I think she is making a list of the things people do or do not do in New York.

"*Some* people do." Louisa winks at me. "Do you realize that this Swedish chick's picked up an Alabama drawl?"

We laugh together. The elevator chugs to a landing.

"We'll stop and say goodnight to Paul," Harriet says. She kisses me. "Give our best to Vidal."

"Right. Have a good time. Don't let any Frenchmen run off with Louisa."

"I did not come to Paris to be protected, and if I had, this wild chick *you* married couldn't do it. I just *might* upset everybody and come home with a French count." She presses the elevator button and the cage goes down.

I walk back into our dismantled apartment. It stinks of departure. There are bags and crates in the hall which will be taken away tomorrow, there are no books in the bookcases, the kitchen looks as though we never cooked a meal there, never dawdled there, in the early morning or late at night, over coffee. Presently, I must shower and shave but now I pour myself a drink and light a cigarette and step out on our balcony. It is dusk, the brilliant light of Paris is beginning to fade, and the green of the trees is darkening.

I have lived in this city for twelve years. This apartment is on the top floor of a corner building. We look out over the trees and the roof tops to the Champ de Mars, where the Eiffel Tower stands. Beyond this field is the river, which I have crossed so often, in so many states of mind. I have crossed every bridge in Paris, I have walked along every *quai*. I know the river as one finally knows a friend, know it when it is black, guarding all the lights of Paris in its depths, and seeming, in its vast silence, to be communing with the dead who lie beneath it; when it is yellow, evil, and roaring, giving a rough time to tugboats and barges, and causing people to remember that it has been known to rise, it has been known to kill; when it is peaceful, a slick, dark, dirty green, playing host to rowboats and *les bateaux mouches* and throwing up from time to time an extremely unhealthy fish. The men who stand along the *quais* all summer with their fishing lines gratefully accept the slimy object and throw it in a rusty can. I have always wondered who eats those fish.

And I walk up and down, up and down, glad to be alone.

It is August, the month when all Parisians desert Paris and one has to walk miles to find a barbershop or a laundry open in some tree-shadowed, silent side street. There is a single person on the avenue, a paratrooper walking toward École Militaire. He is also walking, almost certainly, and rather sooner than later, toward Algeria. I have a friend, a good-natured boy who was always hanging around the clubs in which I worked in the old days, who has just returned from Algeria, with a recurring, debilitating fever, and minus one eye. The government has set his pension at the sum, arbitrary if not occult, of fifty-three thousand francs every three months. Of course, it is quite impossible to live on this amount of money without working—but who will hire a half-blind invalid? This boy has been spoiled forever, long before his thirtieth birthday, and there are thousands like him all over France.

And there are fewer Algerians to be found on the streets of Paris now. The rug sellers, the peanut vendors, the postcard peddlers and money-changers have vanished. The boys I used to know during my first years in Paris are scattered—or corralled—the Lord knows where.

Most of them had no money. They lived three and four together in rooms with a single skylight, a single hard cot, or in buildings that seemed abandoned, with cardboard in the windows, with erratic plumbing in a wet, cobblestoned yard, in dark, dead-end alleys, or on the outer, chilling heights of Paris.

The Arab cafés are closed—those dark, acrid cafés in which I used to meet with them to drink tea, to get high on hashish, to listen to the obsessive, stringed music which has no relation to any beat, any time, that I have ever known. I once thought of the North Africans as my brothers and that is why I went to their cafés. They were very friendly to me, perhaps one or two of them remained really fond of me even after I could no longer afford to smoke Lucky Strikes and after my collection of American sport shirts had vanished—mostly into their ward-robes. They seemed to feel that they had every right to them, since I could only have wrested these things from the world by cunning—it meant nothing to say that I had had no choice in the matter; perhaps I had wrested these things from the world by treason, by refusing to be identified with the misery of my people. Perhaps, indeed, I identified myself with those who were responsible for this misery.

And this was true. Their rage, the only note in all their music which I could not fail to recognize, to which I responded, yet had the effect of setting us more than ever at a division. They were perfectly prepared to drive all Frenchmen into the sea, and to level the city of Paris. But I could not hate the French, because they left me alone. And I love Paris, I will always love it, it is the city which saved my life. It saved my life by allowing me to find out who I am.

It was on a bridge, one tremendous, April morning, that I knew I had fallen in love. Harriet and I were walking hand in hand. The bridge was the Pont Royal, just before us was the great *horloge*, high and lifted up, saying ten to ten; beyond this, the golden statue of Joan of Arc, with her sword uplifted. Harriet and I were silent, for we had been quarreling about something. Now, when I look back, I think we had reached that state when an affair must either end or become something more than an affair.

I looked sideways at Harriet's face, which was still. Her dark-blue eyes were narrowed against the sun, and her full, pink lips were still slightly sulky, like a child's. In those days, she hardly ever wore make-up. I was in my shirt sleeves. Her face made me want to laugh and run my hand over her short dark hair. I wanted to pull her to me and say, *Baby, don't be mad at me*, and at that moment something tugged at my heart and made me catch my breath. There were millions of people all around us, but I was alone with Harriet. She was alone with me. Never, in all my life, until that moment, had I been alone with anyone. The world had always been with us, between us, defeating the quarrel we could not achieve, and making love impossible. During all the years of my life, until that moment, I had carried the menacing, the hostile, killing world with me everywhere. No matter what I was doing or saying or feeling, one eye had always been on the world—that world which I had learned to distrust almost as soon as I learned my name, that world on which I knew one could never turn one's back, the white man's world. And for the first time in my life I was free of it; it had not existed for me; I had been quarreling with my girl. It was our quarrel, it was entirely between us, it had nothing to do with anyone else in the world. For the first time in my life I had not been afraid of the patriotism of the mindless, in uniform or out, who would beat me up and treat the woman who was with me as though she were the lowest of untouchables. For the first time in my life I felt that no force jeopardized my right, my power, to possess and to protect a woman; for the first time, the first time, felt that the woman was not, in her own eyes or in the eyes of the world, degraded by my presence.

The sun fell over everything, like a blessing, people were moving all about us, I will never forget the feeling of Harriet's small hand in mine, dry and trusting, and I turned to her, slowing our pace. She looked up at me with her enormous, blue eyes, and she seemed to wait. I said, "Harriet. Harriet. *Tu sais, il y a quelque chose de très grave qui m'est arrivé. Fe t'aime. Fe t'aime. Tu me comprends*, or shall I say it in English?"

This was eight years ago, shortly before my first and only visit home.

That was when my mother died. I stayed in America for three months. When I came back, Harriet thought that the change in me was due to my grief—I was very silent, very thin. But it had not been my mother's death which accounted for the change. I had known that my mother was going to die. I had not known what America would be like for me after nearly four years away.

I remember standing at the rail and watching the distance between myself and LeHavre increase. Hands fell, ceasing to wave, handkerchiefs ceased to flutter, people turned away, they mounted their bicycles or got into their cars and rode off. Soon, Le Havre was nothing but a blur. I thought of Harriet, already miles from me in Paris, and I pressed my lips tightly together in order not to cry.

Then, as Europe dropped below the water, as the days passed and passed, as we left behind us the skies of Europe and the eyes of everyone on the ship began, so to speak, to refocus, waiting for the first glimpse of America, my apprehension began to give way to a secret joy, a checked anticipation. I thought of such details as showers, which are rare in Paris, and I thought of such things as rich, cold, American milk and heavy, chocolate cake. I wondered about my friends, wondered if I had any left, and wondered if they would be glad to see me.

The Americans on the boat did not seem to be so bad, but I was fascinated, after such a long absence from it, by the nature of their friendliness. It was a friendliness which did not suggest, and was not intended to suggest, any possibility of friendship. Unlike Europeans, they dropped titles and used first names almost at once, leaving themselves, unlike the Europeans, with nowhere thereafter to go. Once one had become "Pete" or "Jane" or "Bill" all that could decently be known was known and any suggestion that there might be further depths, a person, so to speak, behind the name, was taken as a violation of that privacy which did not, paradoxically, since they trusted it so little, seem to exist among Americans. They apparently equated privacy with the unspeakable things they did in the bathroom or the bedroom, which they related only to the analyst, and then read about in the pages of best sellers. There was an eerie and unnerving irreality about everything they said and did, as though they were all members of the same team and were acting on orders from some invincibly cheerful and tirelessly inventive coach. I was fascinated by it. I found it oddly moving, but I cannot say that I was displeased. It had not occurred to me before that Americans, who had never treated me with any respect, had no respect for each other.

On the last night but one, there was a gala in the big ballroom and I sang. It had been a long time since I had sung before so many Americans. My audience had mainly been penniless French students, in the weird, Left Bank bistros I worked in those days. Still, I was a great hit with them and by this time I had become enough of a drawing card, in the Latin Quarter and in St. Germain des Prés, to have attracted a couple of critics, to have had my picture in *France-soir*, and to have acquired a legal work permit which allowed me to make a little more money. Just the same, no matter how industrious and brilliant some of the musicians had been, or how devoted my audience, they did not know, they could not know, what my songs came out of. They did not know what was funny about it. It was impossible to translate: It damn well better be funny, or Laughing to keep from crying, or What did *I* do to be so black and blue?

The moment I stepped out on the floor, they began to smile, something opened in them, they were ready to be pleased. I found in their faces, as they watched me, smiling, waiting, an artless relief, a profound reassurance. Nothing was more familiar to them than the sight of a dark boy, singing, and there were few things on earth more necessary. It was under cover of darkness, my own darkness, that I could sing for them of the joys, passions, and terrors they smuggled about with them like steadily depreciating contraband. Under cover of the midnight fiction that I was unlike them because I was black, they could stealthily gaze at those treasures which they had been mysteriously forbidden to possess and were never permitted to declare.

I sang *I'm Coming, Virginia,* and *Take This Hammer, and Precious Lord.* They wouldn't let me go and I came back and sang a couple of the oldest blues I knew. Then someone asked me to sing *Swanee River,* and I did, astonished that I could, astonished that this song, which I had put down long ago, should have the power to move me. Then, if only, perhaps, to make the record complete, I wanted to sing *Strange Fruit,* but, on this number, no one can surpass the great, tormented Billie Holiday. So I finished with *Great Getting-Up Morning* and I guess I can say that if I didn't stop the show I certainly ended it. I got a big hand and I drank at a few tables and I danced with a few girls.

After one more day and one more night, the boat landed in New York. I woke up, I was bright awake at once, and I thought, *We're here.* I turned on all the lights in my small cabin and I stared into the mirror as though I were committing my face to memory. I took a shower and I took a long time shaving and I dressed myself very carefully. I walked the long ship corridors to the dining room, looking at the luggage piled high before the elevators and beside the steps. The dining room was nearly half empty and full of a quick and joyous excitement which depressed me even more. People ate quickly, chattering to each other, anxious to get upstairs and go on deck. Was it my imagination or was it true that they seemed to avoid my eyes? A few people waved and smiled, but let me pass; perhaps it would have made them uncomfortable, this morning, to try to share their excitement with me; perhaps they did not want to know whether or not it was possible for me to share it. I walked to my table and sat down. I munched toast as dry as paper and drank a pot of coffee. Then I tipped my waiter, who bowed and smiled and called me "sir" and said that he hoped to see me on the boat again. "I hope so, too," I said.

And was it true, or was it my imagination, that a flash of wondering comprehension, a flicker of wry sympathy, then appeared in the waiter's eyes? I walked upstairs to the deck.

There was a breeze from the water but the sun was hot and made me remember how ugly New York summers could be. All of the deck chairs had been taken away and people milled about in the space where the deck chairs had been, moved from one side of the ship to the other, clambered up and down the steps, crowded the rails, and they were busy taking photographs—of the harbor, of each other, of the sea, of the gulls. I walked slowly along the deck, and an impulse stronger than myself drove me to the rail. There it was, the great, unfinished city, with all its towers blazing in the sun. It came toward us slowly and patiently, like some enormous, cunning, and murderous beast, ready to devour, impossible to escape. I watched it come closer and I listened to the people around me, to their excitement and their pleasure. There was no doubt that it was real. I watched their shining faces and wondered if I were mad. For a moment I longed, with all my heart, to be able to feel whatever they were feeling, if only to know what such a feeling was like. As the boat moved slowly into the harbor, they were being moved into safety. It was only I who was being floated into danger. I turned my head, looking for Europe, but all that stretched behind me was the sky, thick with gulls. I moved away from the rail. A big, sandy-haired man held his daughter on his shoulders, showing her the Statue of Liberty. I would never know what this statue meant to others, she had always been an ugly joke for me. And the American flag was flying from the top of the ship, above my head. I had seen the French flag drive the French into the most unspeakable frenzies, I had seen the flag which was nominally mine used to dignify the vilest purposes: now I would never, as long as I lived, know what others saw when they saw a flag. "There's no place like home," said a voice close by, and I thought, *There damn sure isn't.* I decided to go back to my cabin and have a drink.

There was a cablegram from Harriet in my cabin. It said: Be good. Be quick. I'm waiting. I folded it carefully and put it in my breast pocket. Then I wondered if I would ever get back to her. How long would it take me to earn the money to get out of this land? Sweat broke out on my forehead and I poured myself some whiskey from my nearly empty bottle. I paced the tiny cabin. It was silent. There was no one down in the cabins now.

I was not sober when I faced the uniforms in the first-class lounge. There were two of them; they were not unfriendly. They looked at my passport, they looked at me. "You've been away a long time," said one of them.

"Yes," I said, "it's been a while."

"What did you do over there all that time?"—with a grin meant to hide more than it revealed, which hideously revealed more than it could hide.

I said, "I'm a singer," and the room seemed to rock around me. I held on to what I hoped was a calm, open smile. I had not had to deal with these faces in so long that I had forgotten how to do it. I had once known how to pitch my voice precisely between curtness and servility, and known what razor's edge of a pickaninny's smile would turn away wrath. But I had forgotten all the tricks on which my life had once depended. Once I had been an expert at baffling these people, at setting their teeth on edge, and dancing just outside the trap laid for me. But I was not an expert now. These faces were no longer merely the faces of two white men, who were my enemies. They were the faces of two white people whom I did not understand, and I could no longer plan my moves in accordance with what I knew of their cowardice and their needs and their strategy. That moment on the bridge had undone me forever.

"That's right," said one of them, "that's what it says, right here on the passport. Never heard of you, though." They looked up at me. "Did you do a lot of singing over there?"

"Some."

"What kind—concerts?"

"No." I wondered what I looked like, sounded like. I could tell nothing from their eyes. "I worked a few nightclubs."

"Nightclubs, eh? I guess they liked you over there."

"Yes," I said, "they seemed to like me all right."

"Well"—and my passport was stamped and handed back to me—"let's hope they like you over here."

"Thanks." They laughed—was it at me, or was it my imagination? and I picked up the one bag I was carrying and threw my trench coat over one shoulder and walked out of the first-class lounge. I stood in the slow-moving, murmuring line which led to the gangplank. I looked straight ahead and watched heads, smiling faces, step up to the shadow of the gangplank awning and then swiftly descend out of sight. I put my passport back in my breast pocket—*Be quick. I'm waiting* —and I held my landing card in my hand. Then, suddenly, there I was, standing on the edge of the boat, staring down the long ramp to the ground. At the end of the plank, on the ground, stood a heavy man in a uniform. His cap was pushed back from his gray hair and his face was red and wet. He looked up at me. This was the face I remembered, the face of my nightmares; perhaps hatred had caused me to know this face better than I would ever know the face of any lover. "Come on, boy," he cried, "come on, come on!"

And I almost smiled. I was home. I touched my breast pocket. I thought of a song I sometimes sang, *When will I ever get to be a man?* I came down the gangplank, stumbling a little, and gave the man my landing card.

Much later in the day, a customs inspector checked my baggage and waved me away. I picked up my bags and started walking down the long stretch which led to the gate, to the city.

And I heard someone call my name.

I looked up and saw Louisa running toward me. I dropped my bags and grabbed her in my arms and tears came to my eyes and rolled down my face. I did not know whether the tears were for joy at seeing her, or from rage, or both.

"How are you? How are you? You look wonderful, but, oh, haven't you lost weight? It's wonderful to see you again."

I wiped my eyes. "It's wonderful to see you, too, I bet you thought I was never coming back."

Louisa laughed. "I wouldn't have blamed you if you hadn't. These people are just as corny as ever, I swear I don't believe there's any hope for them. How's your French? Lord, when I think that it was I who studied French and now I can't speak a word. And you never went near it and you probably speak it like a native."

I grinned. *"Pas mal. Te me défends pas mal."* We started down the wide steps into the street. "My God," I said. "New York." I was not aware of its towers now. We were in the shadow of the elevated highway but the thing which most struck me was neither light nor shade, but noise. It came from a million things at once, from trucks and tires and clutches and brakes and doors; from machines shuttling and stamping and rolling and cutting and pressing; from the building of tunnels, the checking of gas mains, the laying of wires, the digging of foundations; from the chattering of rivets, the scream of the pile driver, the clanging of great shovels; from the battering down and the raising up of walls; from millions of radios and television sets and juke boxes. The human voices distinguished themselves from the roar only by their note of strain and hostility. Another fleshy man, uniformed and red faced, hailed a cab for us and touched his cap politely but could only manage a peremptory growl: "Right this way, miss. Step up, sir." He slammed the cab door behind us. Louisa directed the driver to the New Yorker Hotel.

"Do they take us there?"

She looked at me. "They got laws in New York, honey, it'd be the easiest thing in the world to spend all your time in court. But over at the New Yorker, I believe they've already got the message." She took my arm. "You see? In spite of all this chopping and booming, this place hasn't really changed very much. You still can't hear yourself talk."

And I thought to myself, Maybe that's the point.

Early the next morning we checked out of the hotel and took the plane for Alabama.

I am just stepping out of the shower when I hear the bell ring. I dry myself hurriedly and put on a bathrobe. It is Vidal, of course, and very elegant he is, too, with his bushy gray hair quite lustrous, his swarthy, cynical, gypsylike face shaved and lotioned. Usually he looks just any old way. But tonight his brief bulk is contained in a dark-blue suit and he has an ironical pearl stickpin in his blue tie.

"Come in, make yourself a drink. I'll be with you in a second."

"I am, *hélas!*, on time. I trust you will forgive me for my thoughtlessness."

But I am already back in the bathroom. Vidal puts on a record: Mahalia Jackson, singing *I'm Going to Live the Life I Sing About in My Song.*

When I am dressed, I find him sitting in a chair before the open window. The daylight is gone, but it is not exactly dark. The trees are black now against the darkening sky. The lights in windows and the lights of motorcars are yellow and ringed. The street lights have not yet been turned on. It is as though, out of deference to the departed day, Paris waited a decent interval before assigning her role to a more theatrical but inferior performer.

Vidal is drinking a whiskey and soda. I pour myself a drink. He watches me.

"Well. How are you, my friend? You are nearly gone. Are you happy to be leaving us?"

"No." I say this with more force than I had intended. Vidal raises his eyebrows, looking amused and distant. "I never really intended to go back there. I certainly never intended to raise my kid there—"

"*Mais, mon cher,*" Vidal says, calmly, "you are an intelligent man, you must have known that you would probably be returning one day." He pauses. "And, as for Pauli—did it never occur to you that he might wish one day to see the country in which his father and his father's fathers were born?"

"To do that, really, he'd have to go to Africa."

"America will always mean more to him than Africa, you know that."

"I don't know." I throw my drink down and pour myself another. "Why should he want to cross all that water just to be called a nigger? America never gave him anything."

"It gave him his father."

I look at him. "You mean, his father escaped."

Vidal throws back his head and laughs. If Vidal likes you, he is certain to laugh at you and his laughter can be very unnerving. But the look, the silence which follow this laughter can be very unnerving, too. And, now, in the silence, he asks me, "Do you really think that you have escaped anything? Come. I know you for a better man than that." He walks to the table which holds the liquor. "In that movie of ours which has made you so famous, and, as I now see, so troubled, what are you playing, after all? What is the tragedy of this half-breed troubadour if not, precisely, that he has taken all the possible roads to escape and that all these roads have failed him?" He pauses, with the bottle in one hand, and looks at me. "Do you remember the trouble I had to get a performance out of you? How you hated me, you sometimes looked as though you wanted to shoot me! And do you remember when the role of Chico began to come alive?" He pours his drink. "Think back, remember. I am a very great director, *mais pardon!* I could not have got such a performance out of anyone but you. And what were you thinking of, what was in your mind, what nightmare were you living with when you began, at last, to play the role—truthfully?" He walks back to his seat.

Chico, in the film, is the son of a Martinique woman and a French *colon* who hates both his mother and his father. He flees from the island to the capital, carrying his hatred with him. This hatred has now grown, naturally, to include all dark women and all white men, in a word, everyone. He descends into the underworld of Paris, where he dies. *Les fauves*—the wild beasts—refers to the life he has fled and to the life which engulfs him. When I agreed to do the role, I felt that I could probably achieve it by bearing in mind the North Africans I had watched in Paris for so long. But this did not please Vidal. The blowup came while we were rehearsing a fairly simple, straightforward scene. Chico goes into a sleazy Pigalle dance hall to beg the French owner for a particularly humiliating job. And this Frenchman reminds him of his father.

"You are playing this boy as though you thought of him as the noble savage," Vidal said, icily. "*Ca vient d'où*—all these ghastly mannerisms you are using all the time?"

Everyone fell silent, for Vidal rarely spoke this way. This silence told me that everyone, the actor with whom I was playing the scene and all the people in the "dance hall," shared Vidal's opinion of my performance and were relieved that he was going to do something about it. I was humiliated and too angry to speak; but perhaps I also felt, at the very bottom of my heart, a certain relief, an unwilling respect.

"You are doing it all wrong," he said, more gently. Then, "Come, let us have a drink together."

We walked into his office. He took a bottle and two glasses out of his desk. "Forgive me, but you put me in mind of some of those English *lady* actresses who love to play *putain* as long as it is always absolutely clear to the audience that they are really ladies. So perhaps they read a book, not usually, *hélas!*, *Fanny Hill*, and they have their chauffeurs drive them through Soho once or twice—and they come to the stage with a performance so absolutely loaded with detail, every bit of it meaningless, that there can be no doubt that they are acting. It is what the British call a triumph." He poured two cognacs. "That is what you are doing. Why? Who do you think this boy is, what do you think he is feeling, when he asks for this job?" He watched me carefully and I bitterly resented his look. "You come from America. The situation is not so pretty there for boys like you. I know you may not have been as poor as—as some—but is it really impossible for you to understand what a boy like Chico feels? Have you never, yourself, been in a similar position?"

I hated him for asking the question because I knew he knew the answer to it. "I would have had to be a very lucky black man not to have been in such a position."

"You would have had to be a very lucky *man*."

"Oh, God," I said, "please don't give me any of this equality-in-anguish business."

"It is perfectly possible," he said, sharply, "that there is not another kind."

Then he was silent. He sat down behind his desk. He cut a cigar and lit it, puffing up clouds of smoke, as though to prevent us from seeing each other too clearly. "Consider this," he said. "I am a French director who has never seen your country. I have never done you any harm, except, perhaps, historically —I mean, because I am white—but I cannot be blamed for that—"

"But *I* can be," I said, "and I am! I've never understood why, if *I* have to pay for the history written in the color of my skin, *you* should get off scot-free!" But I was surprised at my vehemence, I had not known I was going to say these things, and by the fact that I was trembling and from the way he looked at me I knew that, from a professional point of view anyway, I was playing into his hands.

"What makes you think I *do?*" His face looked weary and stern. "I am a Frenchman. Look at France. You think that I—we—are not paying for our history?" He walked to the window, staring out at the rather grim little town in which the studio was located. "If it is revenge that you want, well, then, let me tell you, you will have it. You will probably have it, whether you want it or not, our stupidity will make it inevitable." He turned back into the room. "But I beg you not to confuse me with the happy people of your country, who scarcely know that there is such a thing as history and so, naturally, imagine that they can escape, as you put it, scot-free. That is what you are doing, that is what I was about to say. I was about to say that I am a French director and I have never been in your country and I have never done you any harm— but you are not talking to that man, in this room, now. You are not talking to Jean Luc Vidal, but to some other white man, whom you remember, who has nothing to do with me." He paused and went back to his desk. "Oh, most of the time you are not like this, I know. But it is there all the time, it must be, because when you are upset, this is what comes out. So you are not playing Chico truthfully, you are lying about him, and I will not let you do it. When you go back, now, and play this scene again, I want you to remember what has just happened in this room. You brought your past into this room. That is what Chico does when he walks into the dance hall. The Frenchman whom he begs for a job is not merely a Frenchman —he is the father who disowned and betrayed him and all the Frenchmen whom he hates." He smiled and poured me another cognac. "Ah! If it were not for *my* history, I would not have so much trouble to get the truth out of you." He looked into my face, half smiling. "And you, you are angry—are you not?—that I *ask* you for the truth. You think I have no right to ask." Then he said something which he knew would enrage me. "Who are you then, and what good has it done you to come to France, and how will you raise your son? Will you teach him never to tell the truth to anyone?" And he moved behind his desk and looked at me, as though from behind a barricade.

"You have no right to talk to me this way."

"Oh, yes, I do," he said. "I have a film to make and a reputation to maintain and I am going to get a performance out of you." He looked at his watch. "Let us go back to work."

I watch him now, sitting quietly in my living room, tough, cynical, crafty old Frenchman, and I wonder if he knows that the nightmare at the bottom of my mind, as I played the role of Chico, was all the possible fates of Paul. This is but another way of saying that I relived the disasters which had nearly undone me; but, because I was thinking of Paul, I discovered that I did not want my son ever to feel toward me as I had felt toward my own father. He had died when I was eleven, but I had watched the humiliations he had to bear, and I had pitied him. But was there not, in that pity, however painfully and unwillingly, also some contempt? For how could I *know* what he had borne? I knew only that I was his son. However he had loved me, whatever he had borne, I, his son, was despised. Even had he lived, he could have done nothing to prevent it, nothing to protect me. The best that he could hope to do was to prepare me for it; and even at that he had failed. How can one be prepared for the spittle in the face, all the tireless ingenuity which goes into the spite and fear of small, unutterably miserable people, whose greatest terror is the singular identity, whose joy, whose safety, is entirely dependent on the humiliation and anguish of others?

But for Paul, I swore it, such a day would never come. I would throw my life and my work between Paul and the nightmare of the world. I would make it impossible for the world to treat Paul as it had treated my father and me.

Mahalia's record ends. Vidal rises to turn it over. "Well?" He looks at me very affectionately. "Your nightmares, please!"

"Oh, I was thinking of that summer I spent in Alabama, when my mother died." I stop. "You know, but when we finally filmed that bar scene, I was thinking of New York. I was scared in Alabama, but I almost went crazy in New York. I was sure I'd never make it back here—back here to Harriet. And I knew if I didn't, it was going to be the end of me." Now Mahalia is singing *When the Saints Go Marching In*. "I got a job in the town as an elevator boy, in the town's big department store. It was a special favor, one of my father's white friends got it for me. For a long time, in the South, we all—depended—on the—*kindness*—of white friends." I take out a handkerchief and wipe my face. "But this man didn't like me. I guess I didn't seem grateful enough, wasn't enough like my father, what he thought my father was. And I couldn't get used to the town again, I'd been away too long, I hated it. It's a terrible town, anyway, the whole thing looks as though it's been built around a jailhouse. There's a room in the courthouse, a room where they beat you up. Maybe you're walking

along the street one night, it's usually at night, but it happens
in the daytime, too. And the police car comes up behind you
and the cop says, 'Hey, boy. Come on over here.' So you go on
over. He says, 'Boy, I believe you're drunk.' And, you see, if
you say, 'No, no sir,' he'll beat you because you're calling him
a liar. And if you say anything else, unless it's something to
make him laugh, he'll take you in and beat you, just for fun.
The trick is to think of some way for them to have their fun
without beating you up."

The street lights of Paris click on and turn all the green
leaves silver. "Or to go along with the ways *they* dream up.
And they'll do anything, anything at all, to prove that you're
no better than a dog and to make you feel like one. And they
hated me because I'd been North and I'd been to Europe.
People kept saying, I hope you didn't bring no foreign notions
back here with you, boy. And I'd say, 'No sir,' or 'No ma'am,'
but I never said it right. And there was a time, all of them
remembered it, when I *had* said it right. But now they could
tell that I despised them—I guess, no matter what, I wanted
them to know that I despised them. But I didn't despise them
any more than everyone else did, only the others never let it
show. They knew how to keep the white folks happy, and it
was easy—you just had to keep them feeling like they were
God's favor to the universe. They'd walk around with great,
big, foolish grins on their faces and the colored folks loved to
see this, because they hated them so much. "Just look at So-
and-So," somebody'd say. "His white is *on* him today." And
when we didn't hate them, we pitied them. In America, that's
usually what it means to have a white friend. You pity the
poor bastard because he was born believing the world's a great
place to be, and you know it's not, and you can see that he's
going to have a terrible time getting used to this idea, if he
ever gets used to it."

Then I think of Paul again, those eyes which still imagine

that I can do anything, that skin, the color of honey and fire, his jet-black, curly hair. I look out at Paris again, and I listen to Mahalia. "Maybe it's better to have the terrible times first. I don't know. Maybe, then, you can have, *if* you live, a better life, a real life, because you had to fight so hard to get it away—you know?—from the mad dog who held it in his teeth. But then your life has all those tooth marks, too, all those tatters, and all that blood." I walk to the bottle and raise it. "One for the road?"

"Thank you," says Vidal.

I pour us a drink, and he watches me. I have never talked so much before, not about those things anyway. I know that Vidal has nightmares, because he knows so much about them, but he has never told me what his are. I think that he probably does not talk about his nightmares any more. I know that the war cost him his wife and his son, and that he was in prison in Germany. He very rarely refers to it. He has a married daughter who lives in England, and he rarely speaks of her. He is like a man who has learned to live on what is left of an enormous fortune.

We are silent for a moment.

"Please go on," he says, with a smile. "I am curious about the reality behind the reality of your performance."

"My sister, Louisa, never married," I say, abruptly, "because, once, years ago, she and the boy she was going with and two friends of theirs were out driving in a car and the police stopped them. The girl who was with them was very fair and the police pretended not to believe her when she said she was colored. They made her get out and stand in front of the headlights of the car and pull down her pants and raise her dress—they said that was the only way they could be sure. And you can imagine what they said, and what they did—and they were lucky, at that, that it didn't go any further. But none of the men could do anything about it. Louisa couldn't face that

boy again, and I guess he couldn't face her." Now it is really
growing dark in the room and I cross to the light switch. "You
know, I know what that boy felt, I've felt it. They want you
to feel that you're not a man, maybe that's the only way they
can feel like men, I don't know. I walked around New York
with Harriet's cablegram in my pocket as though it were
some atomic secret, in *code*, and they'd kill me if they ever
found out what it meant. You know, there's something wrong
with people like that. And thank God Harriet was here, she
proved that the world was bigger than the world they wanted
me to live in, I *had* to get back here, get to a place where
people were too busy with their own lives, *their private lives*,
to make fantasies about mine, to set up walls around mine."
I look at him. The light in the room has made the night outside blue-black and golden and the great searchlight of the
Eiffel Tower is turning in the sky. "That's what it's like in
America, for me, anyway. I always feel that I don't exist there,
except in someone else's—usually dirty—mind. I don't know if
you know what that means, but I do, and I don't want to put
Harriet through that and I don't want to raise Paul there."

"Well," he says at last, "you are not required to remain in
America forever, are you? You will sing in that elegant club
which apparently feels that it cannot, much longer, so much as
open its doors without you, and you will probably accept the
movie offer, you would be very foolish not to. You will make a
lot of money. Then, one day, you will remember that airlines
and steamship companies are still in business and that France
still exists. *That* will certainly be cause for astonishment."

Vidal was a Gaullist before de Gaulle came to power. But he
regrets the manner of de Gaulle's rise and he is worried about
de Gaulle's regime. "It is not the fault of *mon général*," he
sometimes says, sadly. "Perhaps it is history's fault. I *suppose* it
must be history which always arranges to bill a civilization at
the very instant it is least prepared to pay."

Now he rises and walks out on the balcony, as though to

reassure himself of the reality of Paris. Mahalia is singing
Didn't It Rain? I walk out and stand beside him.

"You are a good boy—Chico," he says. I laugh. "You believe
in love. You do not know all the things love cannot do, but"—
he smiles—"love will teach you that."

We go, after dinner, to a Left Bank discothèque which can
charge outrageous prices because Marlon Brando wandered in
there one night. By accident, according to Vidal. "Do you
know how many people in Paris are becoming rich—to say
nothing of those, *hélas!*, who are going broke—on the off
chance that Marlon Brando will lose his way again?"

He has not, presumably, lost his way tonight, but the
discothèque is crowded with those strangely faceless people
who are part of the night life of all great cities, and who
always arrive, moments, hours, or decades late, on the spot
made notorious by an event or a movement or a handful of
personalities. So here are American boys, anything but beard-
less, scratching around for Hemingway; American girls, titillat-
ing themselves with Frenchmen and existentialism, while waiting for the American boys to shave off their beards; French
painters, busily pursuing the revolution which ended thirty
years ago; and the young, bored, perverted, American
arrivistes who are buying their way into the art world via
flattery and liquor, and the production of canvases as arid as
their greedy little faces. Here are boys, of all nations, one step
above the pimp, who are occasionally walked across a stage or
trotted before a camera. And the girls, their enemies, whose
faces are sometimes seen in ads, one of whom will surely have
a tantrum before the evening is out.

In a corner, as usual, surrounded, as usual, by smiling young
men, sits the drunken blonde woman who was once the mis-
tress of a famous, dead painter. She is a figure of some importance in the art world, and so rarely has to pay for either her

drinks or her lovers. An older Frenchman, who was once a famous director, is playing *quatre cent ving-et-un* with the woman behind the cash register. He nods pleasantly to Vidal and me as we enter, but makes no move to join us, and I respect him for this. Vidal and I are obviously cast tonight in the role vacated by Brando: our entrance justifies the prices and sends a kind of shiver through the room. It is marvelous to watch the face of the waiter as he approaches, all smiles and deference and grace, not so much honored by our presence as achieving his reality from it; excellence, he seems to be saying, gravitates naturally toward excellence. We order two whiskey and sodas. I know why Vidal sometimes comes here. He is lonely. I do not think that he expects ever to love one woman again, and so he distracts himself with many.

Since this is a discothèque, jazz is blaring from the walls and record sleeves are scattered about with a devastating carelessness. Two of them are mine and no doubt, presently, someone will play the recording of the songs I sang in the film.

"I thought," says Vidal, with a malicious little smile, "that your farewell to Paris would not be complete without a brief exposure to the perils of fame. Perhaps it will help prepare you for America, where, I am told, the populace is yet more carnivorous than it is here."

I can see that one of the vacant models is preparing herself to come to our table and ask for an autograph, hoping, since she is pretty—she has, that is, the usual female equipment, dramatized in the usual, modern way—to be invited for a drink. Should the maneuver succeed, one of her boy friends or girl friends will contrive to come by the table, asking for a light or a pencil or a lipstick, and it will be extremely difficult not to invite this person to join us, too. Before the evening ends, we will be surrounded. I don't, now, know what I expected of fame, but I suppose it never occurred to me that the light could be just as dangerous, just as killing, as the dark.

"Well, let's make it brief," I tell him. "Sometimes I wish that you weren't quite so fond of me."

He laughs. "There are some very interesting people here tonight. Look."

Across the room from us, and now staring at our table, are a group of American Negro students, who are probably visiting Paris for the first time. There are four of them, two boys and two girls, and I suppose that they must be in their late teens or early twenties. One of the boys, a gleaming, curly-haired, golden-brown type—the color of his mother's fried chicken— is carrying a guitar. When they realize we have noticed them, they smile and wave—wave as though I were one of their possessions, as, indeed, I am. Golden-brown is a mime. He raises his guitar, drops his shoulders, and his face falls into the lugubrious lines of Chico's face as he approaches death. He strums a little of the film's theme music, and I laugh and the table laughs. It is as though we were all back home and had met for a moment, on a Sunday morning, say, before a church or a poolroom or a barbershop.

And they have created a sensation in the discothèque, natu- rally, having managed, with no effort whatever, to outwit all the gleaming boys and girls. Their table, which had been of no interest only a moment before, has now become the focus of a rather pathetic attention; their smiles have made it possible for the others to smile, and to nod in our direction.

"Oh," says Vidal, "he does that far better than you ever did, perhaps I will make him a star."

"Feel free, *m'sieu, le bon Dieu,* I got mine." But I can see that his attention has really been caught by one of the girls, slim, tense, and dark, who seems, though it is hard to know how one senses such things, to be treated by the others with a special respect. And, in fact, the table now seems to be having a council of war, to be demanding her opinion or her coopera- tion. She listens, frowning, laughing; the quality, the force of her intelligence causes her face to keep changing all the time, as though a light played on it. And, presently, with a gesture she might once have used to scatter feed to chickens, she scoops up from the floor one of those dangling rag bags women love to carry. She holds it loosely by the drawstrings, so that it is banging somewhere around her ankle, and walks over to our table. She has an honest, forthright walk, entirely unlike the calculated, pelvic workout by means of which most women get about. She is small, but sturdily, economically, put together.

As she reaches our table, Vidal and I rise, and this throws her for a second. (It has been a long time since I have seen such an attractive girl.)

Also, everyone, of course, is watching us. It is really a quite curious moment. They have put on the record of Chico singing a sad, angry Martinique ballad; my own voice is coming at us from the walls as the girl looks from Vidal to me, and smiles.

"I guess you know," she says, "we weren't *about* to let you get out of here without bugging you just a little bit. We've only been in Paris just a couple of days and we thought for sure that we wouldn't have a chance of running into you anywhere, because it's in all the papers that you're coming home."

"Yes," I say, "yes. I'm leaving the day after tomorrow."

"Oh!" She grins. "Then we really *are* lucky." I find that I have almost forgotten the urchin-like grin of a colored girl. "I guess, before I keep babbling on, I'd better introduce myself. My name is Ada Holmes."

We shake hands. "This is Monsieur Vidal, the director of the film."

"I'm very honored to meet you, sir."

"Will you join us for a moment? Won't you sit down?" And Vidal pulls a chair out for her.

But she frowns contritely. "I really ought to get back to my friends." She looks at me. "I really just came over to say, for myself and all the kids, that we've got your records and we've seen your movie, and it means so much to us"—and she laughs, breathlessly, nervously, it is somehow more moving than tears —"more than I can say. Much more. And we wanted to know if you and your friend"—she looks at Vidal—"your *director*, Monsieur Vidal, would allow us to buy you a drink? We'd be very honored if you would."

"It is we who are honored," says Vidal, promptly, "*and* grateful. We were getting terribly bored with one another, thank God you came along."

The three of us laugh, and we cross the room.

The three at the table rise, and Ada makes the introductions. The other girl, taller and paler than Ada, is named Ruth. One of the boys is named Talley—"short for Talliafero"—and Golden-brown's name is Pete. "Man," he tells me, "I dig you the most. Your tore me up, baby, tore me *up*."

"You tore up a lot of people," Talley says, cryptically, and he and Ruth laugh. Vidal does not know, but I do, that Talley is probably referring to white people.

They are from New Orleans and Tallahassee and North Carolina; are college students, and met on the boat. They have been in Europe all summer, in Italy and Spain, but are only just getting to Paris.

"We meant to come sooner," says Ada, "but we could never make up our minds to leave a place. I thought we'd never pry Ruth loose from Venice."

"I resigned myself," says Pete, "and just sat in the Piazza San Marco, drinking gin fizz and being photographed with the pigeons, while Ruth had herself driven *all* up and down the Grand Canal." He looks at Ruth. "Finally, thank heaven, it rained."

"She was working off her hostilities," says Ada, with a grin.

"We thought we might as well let her do it in Venice, the opportunities in North Carolina are really terribly limited."

"There are some very upset people walking around down there," Ruth says, "and a couple of tours around the Grand Canal might do them a world of good."

Pete laughs. "Can't you just see Ruth escorting them to the edge of the water?"

"I haven't lifted my hand in anger yet," Ruth says, "but, oh Lord," and she laughs, clenching and unclenching her fists.

"You haven't been back for a long time, have you?" Talley asks me.

"Eight years. I haven't really lived there for twelve years."

Pete whistles. "I fear you are in for some surprises, my friend. There have been some changes made." Then, "Are you afraid?"

"A little."

"We all are," says Ada, "that's why I was so glad to get away for a little while."

"Then you haven't been back since Black Monday," Talley says. He laughs. "That's how it's gone down in Confederate history." He turns to Vidal. "What do people think about it here?"

Vidal smiles, delighted. "It seems extraordinarily infantile behavior, even for Americans, from whom, I must say, I have never expected very much in the way of maturity." Everyone at the table laughs. Vidal goes on. "But I cannot really talk about it, I do not understand it. I have never really understood Americans; I am an old man now, and I suppose I never will. There is something very nice about them, something very winning, but they seem so ignorant—so ignorant of life. Perhaps it is strange, but the only people from your country with whom I have ever made contact are black people—like my good friend, my discovery, here," and he slaps me on the shoulder. "Perhaps it is because we, in Europe, whatever else we do not know, or have forgotten, know about suffering. We have suffered here. You have suffered, too. But most Americans do not yet know what anguish is. It is too bad, because the life of the West is in their hands." He turns to Ada. "I cannot help saying that I think it is a scandal—and we may all pay very dearly for it—that a civilized nation should elect to represent it a man who is so simple that he thinks the world is simple." And silence falls at the table and the four young faces stare at him.

"Well," says Pete, at last, turning to me, "you won't be bored, man, when you get back there."

"It's much too nice a night," I say, "to stay cooped up in this place, where all I can hear is my own records." We laugh. "Why don't we get out of here and find a sidewalk café?" I tap Pete's guitar. "Maybe we can find out if you've got any talent."

"Oh, talent I've got," says Pete, "but character, man, I'm lacking."

So, after some confusion about the bill, for which Vidal has already made himself responsible, we walk out into the Paris night. It is very strange to feel that, very soon now, these boulevards will not exist for me. People will be walking up and down, as they are tonight, and lovers will be murmuring in the black shadows of the plane trees, and there will be these same still figures on the benches or in the parks—but they will not exist for me, I will not be here. For a long while Paris will no longer exist for me, except in my mind; and only in the minds of some people will I exist any longer for Paris. After departure, only invisible things are left, perhaps the life of the world is held together by invisible chains of memory and loss and love. So many things, so many people, depart! And we can only repossess them in our minds. Perhaps this is what the old folks meant, what my mother and my father meant, when they counseled us to keep the faith.

We have taken a table at the Deux Magots and Pete strums on his guitar and begins to play this song:

> *Preach the word, preach the word, preach the word!*
> *If I never, never see you any more.*
> *Preach the word, preach the word.*
> *And I'll meet you on Canaan's shore.*

He has a strong, clear, boyish voice, like a young preacher's, and he is smiling as he sings his song. Ada and I look at each other and grin, and Vidal is smiling. The waiter looks a little worried, for we are already beginning to attract a crowd, but it is a summer night, the gendarmes on the corner do not seem to mind, and there will be time, anyway, to stop us.

Pete was not there, none of us were, the first time this song was needed; and no one now alive can imagine what that time was like. But the song has come down the bloodstained ages. I suppose this to mean that the song is still needed, still has its work to do.

The others are all, visibly, very proud of Pete; and we all join him, and people stop to listen:

> *Testify! Testify!*
> *If I never, never see you any more!*
> *Testify! Testify!*
> *I'll meet you on Canaan's shore!*

In the crowd that has gathered to listen to us, I see a face I know, the face of a North African prize fighter, who is no longer in the ring. I used to know him well in the old days, but have not seen him for a long time. He looks quite well, his face is shining, he is quite decently dressed. And something about the way he holds himself, not quite looking at our table, tells me that he has seen me, but does not want to risk a rebuff. So I call him. "Boona!"

And he turns, smiling, and comes loping over to our table, his hands in his pockets. Pete is still singing and Ada and Vidal have taken off on a conversation of their own. Ruth and Talley look curiously, expectantly, at Boona. Now that I have called him over, I feel somewhat uneasy. I realize that I do not know what he is doing now, or how he will get along with any of these people, and I can see in his eyes that he is delighted to be in the presence of two young girls. There are virtually no North African women in Paris, and not even the dirty, rat-faced girls who live, apparently, in cafés are willing to go with an Arab. So Boona is always looking for a girl, and because he is so deprived and because he is not Western, his techniques can be very unsettling. I know he is relieved that the girls are not French and not white. He looks briefly at Vidal and Ada. Vidal, also, though for different reasons, is always looking for a girl.

But Boona has always been very nice to me. Perhaps I am sorry that I called him over, but I did not want to snub him.

He claps one hand to the side of my nead, as is his habit. "*Comment vas-tu, mon frère?* I have not see you, oh, for long time." And he asks me, as in the old days, "You all right? Nobody bother you?" And he laughs. "Ah! *Tu as fait le chemin, toi!* Now you are *vedette*, big star—wonderful!" He looks around the table, made a little uncomfortable by the silence that has fallen, now that Pete has stopped singing. "I have seen you in the movies—you know?—and I tell every-body, I know *him!*" He points to me, and laughs, and Ruth and Talley laugh with him. "That's right, man, you make me real proud, you make me cry!"

"Boona, I want you to meet some friends of mine." And I go round the table: "Ruth, Talley, Ada, Pete"—and he bows and shakes hands, his dark eyes gleaming with pleasure—"*et Monsieur Vidal, le metteur en scène du film qui t'a arraché des larmes.*"

"*Enchanté.*" But his attitude toward Vidal is colder, more distrustful. "Of course I have heard of Monsieur Vidal. He is the director of many films, many of them made me cry." This last statement is utterly, even insolently, insincere.

But Vidal, I think, is relieved that I will now be forced to speak to Boona and will leave him alone with Ada.

"Sit down," I say, "have a drink with us, let me have your news. What's been happening with you, what are you doing with yourself these days?"

"Ah," he sits down, "nothing very brilliant, my brother." He looks at me quickly, with a little smile. "You know, we have been having hard times here."

"Where are you from?" Ada asks him.

His brilliant eyes take her in entirely, but she does not flinch. "I am from Tunis." He says it proudly, with a little smile.

"From Tunis. I have never been to Africa, I would love to go one day."

He laughs. "Africa is a big place. Very big. There are many countries in Africa, many"—he looks briefly at Vidal—"different kinds of people, many colonies."

"But Tunis," she continues, in her innocence, "is free? Freedom is happening all over Africa. That's why I would like to go there."

"I have not been back for a long time," says Boona, "but all the news I get from Tunis, from my people, is not good."

"Wouldn't you like to go back?" Ruth asks.

Again he looks at Vidal. "That is not so easy."

Vidal smiles. "You know what I would like to do? There's a wonderful Spanish place not far from here, where we can listen to live music and dance a little." He turns to Ada. "Would you like that?"

He is leaving it up to me to get rid of Boona, and it is, of course, precisely for this reason that I cannot do it. Besides, it is no longer so simple.

"Oh, I'd love that," says Ada, and she turns to Boona. "Won't you come, too?"

"Thank you, mam'selle," he says, softly, and his tongue flicks briefly over his lower lip, and he smiles. He is very moved, people are not often nice to him.

In the Spanish place there are indeed a couple of Spanish guitars, drums, castanets, and a piano, but the uses to which these are being put carry one back, as Pete puts it, to the levee. "These are the wailingest Spanish cats I ever heard," says Ruth. "They didn't learn how to do this in Spain, no, they didn't, they been rambling. You ever hear anything like this going on in Spain?" Talley takes her out on the dance floor, which is already crowded. A very handsome Frenchwoman is dancing with an enormous, handsome black man, who seems to be her lover, who seems to have taught her how to dance. Apparently, they are known to the musicians, who egg them on with small cries of *"Olé!"* It is a very good-natured crowd, mostly foreigners, Spaniards, Swedes, Greeks. Boona takes Ada out on the dance floor while Vidal is answering some questions put to him by Pete on the entertainment situation in France. Vidal looks a little put out, and I am amused.

We are there for perhaps an hour, dancing, talking, and I am, at last, a little drunk. In spite of Boona, who is a very good and tireless dancer, Vidal continues his pursuit of Ada, and I begin to wonder if he will make it and I begin to wonder if I want him to.

I am still puzzling out my reaction when Pete, who has disappeared, comes in through the front door, catches my eye, and signals to me. I leave the table and follow him into the streets.

He looks very upset. "I don't want to bug you, man," he says, "but I fear your boy has goofed."

I know he is not joking. I think he is probably angry at Vidal because of Ada, and I wonder what I can do about it and why he should be telling me.

I stare at him, gravely, and he says, "It looks like he stole some money."

"Stole *money*? Who, Vidal?"

And then, of course, I get it, in the split second before he says, impatiently, "No, are you kidding? Your friend, the Tunisian."

I do not know what to say or what to do, and so I temporize with questions. All the time I am wondering if this can be true and what I can do about it if it is. The trouble is, I know that Boona steals, he would probably not be alive if he didn't, but I cannot say so to these children, who probably still imagine that everyone who steals is a thief. But he has never, to my knowledge, stolen from a friend. It seems unlike him. I have always thought of him as being better than that, and smarter than that. And so I cannot believe it, but neither can I doubt it. I do not know anything about Boona's life, these days. This causes me to realize that I do not really know much about Boona.

"Who did he steal it from?"

"From Ada. Out of her bag."

"How much?"

"Ten dollars. It's not an awful lot of money, but"—he grimaces—"none of us *have* an awful lot of money."

"I know." The dark side street on which we stand is nearly empty. The only sound on the street is the muffled music of the Spanish club. "How do you know it was Boona?"

He anticipates my own unspoken rejoinder. "Who else could it be? Besides—somebody *saw* him do it."

"Somebody saw him?"

"Yes."

I do not ask him who this person is, for fear that he will say it is Vidal.

"Well," I say, "I'll try to get it back." I think that I will take Boona aside and then replace the money myself. "Was it in dollars or in francs?"

"In francs."

I have no dollars and this makes it easier. I do not know how I can possibly face Boona and accuse him of stealing money from my friends. I would rather give him the benefit of even the faintest doubt. But, "Who saw him?" I ask.

"Talley. But we didn't want to make a thing about it—"

"Does Ada know it's gone?"

"Yes." He looks at me helplessly. "I know this makes you feel pretty bad, but we thought we'd better tell you, rather than" —lamely—"anybody else."

Now, Ada comes out of the club, carrying her ridiculous handbag, and with her face all knotted and sad. "Oh," she says, "I hate to cause all this trouble, it's not worth it, not for ten lousy dollars." I am astonished to see that she has been weeping, and tears come to her eyes now.

I put my arm around her shoulder. "Come on, now. You're not causing anybody any trouble and, anyway, it's nothing to cry about."

"It isn't your fault, Ada," Pete says, miserably.

"Oh, I ought to get a sensible handbag," she says, "like you're always telling me to do," and she laughs a little, then looks at me. "Please don't try to do anything about it. Let's just forget it."

"What's happening inside?" I ask her.

"Nothing. They're just talking. I think Mr. Vidal is dancing with Ruth. He's a great dancer, that little Frenchman."

"He's a great talker, too," Pete says.

"Oh, he doesn't mean anything," says Ada, "he's just having fun. He probably doesn't get a chance to talk to many American girls."

"He certainly made up for lost time tonight."

"Look," I say, "if Talley and Boona are alone, maybe you better go back in. We'll be in in a minute. Let's try to keep this as quiet as we can."

"Yeah," he says, "okay. We're going soon anyway, okay?"

"Yes," she tells him, "right away."

But as he turns away, Boona and Talley step out into the street, and it is clear that Talley feels that he has Boona under arrest. I almost laugh, the whole thing is beginning to resemble one of those mad French farces with people flying in and out of doors; but Boona comes straight to me.

"They say I stole money, my friend. You know me, you are the only one here who knows me, you know I would not do such a thing."

I look at him and I do not know what to say. Ada looks at him with her eyes full of tears and looks away. I take Boona's arm.

"We'll be back in a minute," I say. We walk a few paces up the dark, silent street.

"She say I take her money," he says. He, too, looks as though he is about to weep—but I do not know for which reason. "You know me, you know me almost twelve years, you think I do such a thing?"

Talley saw you, I want to say, but I cannot say it. Perhaps Talley only thought he saw him. Perhaps it is easy to see a boy who looks like Boona with his hand in an American girl's purse.

"If you not believe me," he says, "search me. Search me!" And he opens his arms wide, theatrically, and now there are tears standing in his eyes.

I do not know what his tears mean, but I certainly cannot search him. I want to say, I know you steal, I know you have to steal. Perhaps you took the money out of this girl's purse in order to eat tomorrow, in order not to be thrown into the streets tonight, in order to stay out of jail. This girl means nothing to you, after all, she is only an American, an American like me. Perhaps, I suddenly think, no girl means anything to you, or ever will again, they have beaten you too hard and kept out in the gutter too long. And I also think, if you would steal from her, then of course you would lie to me, neither of us means anything to you; perhaps, in your eyes, we are simply luckier gangsters in a world which is run by gangsters. But I cannot say any of these things to Boona. I cannot say, Tell me the truth, nobody cares about the money any more.

So I say, "Of course I will not search you." And I realize that he knew I would not.

"I think it is that Frenchman who say I am a thief. They think we all are thieves." His eyes are bright and bitter. He looks over my shoulder. "They have all come out of the club now."

I look around and they are all there, in a little dark knot on the sidewalk.

"Don't worry," I say. "It doesn't matter."

"You believe me? My brother?" And his eyes look into mine with a terrible intensity.

"Yes," I force myself to say, "yes, of course, I believe you. Someone made a mistake, that's all."

"You know, the way American girls run around, they have their sack open all the time, she could lost the money anywhere. Why she blame me? Because I come from Africa?" Tears are glittering on his face. "Here she come now."

And Ada comes up the street with her straight, determined walk. She walks straight to Boona and takes his hand. "I am sorry," she says, "for everything that happened. Please believe me. It isn't worth all this fuss. I'm sure you're a very nice person, and"—she falters—"I must have lost the money, I'm sure I lost it." She looks at him. "It isn't worth hurting your feelings, and I'm terribly sorry about it."

"I no take your money," he says. "Really, truly, I no take it. Ask him"—pointing to me, grabbing me by the arm, shaking me—"he know me for years, he will tell you that I never, never steal!"

"I'm sure," she says. "I'm sure."

I take Boona by the arm again. "Let's forget it. Let's forget it all. We're all going home now, and one of these days we'll have a drink again and we'll forget all about it, all right?"

"Yes," says Ada, "let us forget it." And she holds out her hand.

Boona takes it, wonderingly. His eyes take her in again. "You are a very nice girl. Really. A very nice girl."

"I'm sure you're a nice person, too." She pauses. "Goodnight."

"Goodnight," he says, after a long silence.

Then he kisses me on both cheeks. *"Au revoir, mon frère."*

"Au revoir, Boona."

After a moment we turn and walk away, leaving him standing there.

"Did he take it?" asks Vidal.

"I tell you, I *saw* him," says Talley.

"Well," I say, "it doesn't matter now." I look back and see Boona's stocky figure disappearing down the street.

"No," says Ada, "it doesn't matter." She looks up. "It's almost morning."

"I would gladly," says Vidal, stammering, "gladly—"

But she is herself again. "I wouldn't think of it. We had a wonderful time tonight, a wonderful time, and I wouldn't think of it." She turns to me with that urchin-like grin. "It was wonderful meeting you. I hope you won't have too much trouble getting used to the States again."

"Oh, I don't think I will," I say. And then, "I hope you won't."

"No," she says, "I don't think anything they can do will surprise me any more."

"Which way are we all going?" asks Vidal. "I hope someone will share my taxi with me."

But he lives in the sixteenth arrondissement, which is not in anyone's direction. We walk him to the line of cabs standing under the clock at Odéon.

And we look each other in the face, in the growing morning light. His face looks weary and lined and lonely. He puts both hands on my shoulders and then puts one hand on the nape of my neck. "Do not forget me, Chico," he says. "You must come back and see us, one of these days. Many of us depend on you for many things."

"I'll be back," I say. "I'll never forget you."

He raises his eyebrows and smiles. "*Alors, Adieu.*"

"*Adieu, Vidal.*"

"I was happy to meet all of you," he says. He looks at Ada. "Perhaps we will meet again before you leave."

"Perhaps," she says. "Goodby, Monsieur Vidal."

"Goodby."

Vidal's cab drives away. "I also leave you now," I say. "I must go home and wake up my son and prepare for our journey."

I leave them standing on the corner, under the clock, which points to six. They look very strange and lost and determined, the four of them. Just before my cab turns off the boulevard, I wave to them and they wave back.

Mme. Dumont is in the hall, mopping the floor.

"Did all my family get home?" I ask. I feel very cheerful, I do not know why.

"Yes," she says, "they are all here. Paul is still sleeping."

"May I go in and get him?"

She looks at me in surprise. "Of course."

So I walk into her apartment and walk into the room where Paul lies sleeping. I stand over his bed for a long time.

Perhaps my thoughts traveled—travel through to him. He opens his eyes and smiles up at me. He puts a fist to his eyes and raises his arms. "*Bonjour, Papa.*"

I lift him up. "*Bonjour.* How do you feel today?"

"Oh, I don't know yet," he says.

I laugh. I put him on my shoulder and walk out into the hall. Mme. Dumont looks up at him with her radiant, aging face.

"Ah," she says, "you are going on a journey! How does it feel?"

"He doesn't know yet," I tell her. I walk to the elevator door and open it, dropping Paul down to the crook of my arm.

She laughs again. "He will know later. What a journey! *Fusqu'au nouveau monde!*"

I open the cage and we step inside. "Yes," I say, "all the way to the new world." I press the button and the cage, holding my son and me, goes up.

Come Out the Wilderness

PAUL did not yet feel her eyes on him. She watched him. He went to the window, peering out between the slats in the Venetian blinds. She could tell from his profile that it did not look like a pleasant day. In profile, all of the contradictions that so confounded her seemed to be revealed. He had a boy's long, rather thin neck but it supported a head that seemed even more massive than it actually was because of its plantation of thickly curling black hair, hair that was always a little too long or else, cruelly, much too short. His forehead was broad and high but this austerity was contradicted by a short, blunt, almost ludicrously upturned nose. And he had a large mouth and very heavy, sensual lips, which suggested a certain wry cruelty when turned down but looked like the mask of comedy when he laughed. His body was really excessively black with hair, which proved, she said, since Negroes were generally less hairy than whites, which race, in fact, had moved farthest from the ape. Other people did not see his beauty, which always mildly astonished her—it was like thinking that the sun was ordinary. He was sloppy about the way he stood and sat, that was true, and so his shoulders were already beginning to be round. And he was a poor man's son, a city boy, and so his body could not really remind anyone of a Michelangelo statue as she—"fantastically," he said—claimed; it did not have that luxury or that power. It was economically tense and hard and testified only to the agility of the poor, who are always dancing one step ahead of the devil.

He stepped away from the window, looking worried. Ruth closed her eyes. When she opened them he was disappearing away from her down the short, black hall that led to the bathroom. She wondered what time he had come in last night; she wondered if he had a hangover; she heard the water running. She thought that he had probably not been home long. She was very sensitive to his comings and goings and had often found herself abruptly upright and wide awake a moment after he, restless at two-thirty in the morning, had closed the door behind him. Then there was no more sleep for her. She lay there on a bed that inexorably became a bed of ashes and hot coals, while her imagination dwelt on every conceivable disaster, from his having forsaken her for another woman to his having, somehow, ended up in the morgue. And as the night faded from black to gray to daylight, the telephone began to seem another presence in the house, sitting not far from her like a great, malevolent black cat that might, at any moment, with one shrill cry, scatter her life like dismembered limbs all over this tiny room. There were places she could have called, but she would have died first. After all—he had only needed to point it out once, he would never have occasion to point it out again—they were not married. Often she had pulled herself out of bed, her loins cold and all her body trembling, and gotten dressed and had coffee and gone to work without seeing him. But he would call her in the office later in the day. She would have had several stiff drinks at lunch and so could be very offhand over the phone, pretending that she had only supposed him to have gotten up a little earlier than herself that morning. But the moment she put the receiver down she hated him. She made herself sick with fantasies of how she would be revenged. Then she hated herself; thinking into what an iron maiden of love and hatred he had placed her, she hated him even more. She could not help feeling that he treated her this way because of her color, because she was a colored girl. Then her past and her present threatened to engulf her. She knew she was being unfair; she could not help it; she thought of psychiatry; she saw herself transformed, at peace with the world, herself, her color, with the male of indeterminate color she would have found. Always, this journey round her skull ended with tears, resolutions, prayers, with Paul's face, which then had the power to reconcile her even to the lowest circle of hell.

After work, on the way home, she stopped for another drink, or two or three; bought Sen-Sen to muffle the odor; wore the most casually glowing of smiles as he casually kissed her when she came through the door.

She knew that he was going to leave her. It was in his walk, his talk, his eyes. He wanted to go. He had already moved back, crouching to leap. And she had no rival. He was not going to another woman. He simply wanted to go. It would happen today, tomorrow, three weeks from today; it was over, she could do nothing about it; neither could she save herself by jumping first. She had no place to go, she only wanted him. She had tried hard to want other men, and she was still young, only twenty-six, and there was no real lack of opportunity. But all she knew about other men was that they were not Paul.

Through the gloom of the hallway he came back into the room and, moving to the edge of the bed, lit a cigarette. She smiled at him.

"Good morning," she said. "Would you light one for me too?"

He looked down at her with a sleepy and slightly shame-faced grin. Without a word he offered her his freshly lit cigarette, lit another, and then got into bed, shivering slightly.

"Good morning," he said then. "Did you sleep well?"

"Very well," she said, lightly. "Did you? I didn't hear you come in."

"Ah, I was very quiet," he said teasingly, curling his great body toward her and putting his head on her breast. "I didn't want to wake you up. I was afraid you'd hit me with something."

She laughed. "What time *did* you come in?"

"Oh"—he raised his head, dragging on his cigarette, and half-frowned, half-smiled—"about an hour or so ago."

"What did you do? Find a new after-hours joint?"

"No. I ran into Cosmo. We went over to his place to look at

a couple new paintings he's done. He had a bottle, we sat around."

She knew Cosmo and distrusted him. He was about forty and he had had two wives; he did not think women were worth much. She was sure that Cosmo had been giving Paul advice as to how to be rid of her; she could imagine, or believed she could, how he had spoken about her, and she felt her skin tighten. At the same moment she became aware of the warmth of Paul's body.

"What did you talk about?" she asked.

"Oh. Painting. His paintings, my paintings, all God's chillun's paintings."

During the day, while she was at work, Paul painted in the back room of this cramped and criminally expensive Village apartment, where the light was bad and where there was not really room enough for him to step back and look at his canvas. Most of his paintings were stored with a friend. Still, there were enough, standing against the wall, piled on top of the closet and on the table, for a sizable one-man show. "If they were any good," said Paul, who worked very hard. She knew this, despite the fact that he said so rather too often. She knew by his face, his distance, his quality, frequently, of seeming to be like a spring, unutterably dangerous to touch. And by the exhaustion, different in kind from any other, with which he sometimes stretched out in bed.

She thought—of course—that his paintings were very good, but he did not take her judgment seriously. "You're sweet, funnyface," he sometimes said, "but, you know, you aren't really very bright." She was scarcely at all mollified by his adding. "Thank heaven. I hate bright women."

She remembered, now, how stupid she had felt about music all the time she had lived with Arthur, a man of her own color who had played a clarinet. She was still finding out today, so many years after their breakup, how much she had learned from him—not only about music, unluckily. If I stay on this

merry-go-round, she thought, I'm going to become very accomplished, just the sort of girl no man will every marry.

She moved closer to Paul, the fingers of one hand playing
with his hair. He lay still. It was very silent.

"Ruth," he said finally, "I've been thinking . . ."

At once she was all attention. She drew on her cigarette, her
fingers still drifting through his hair, as though she were playing with water.

"Yes?" she prompted.

She had always wondered, when the moment came, if she
would make things easy for him, or difficult. She still did not
know. He leaned up on one elbow, looking down at her. She
met his eyes, hoping that her own eyes reflected nothing but
calm curiosity. He continued to stare at her and put one hand
on her short, dark hair. Then, "You're a nice girl," he said,
irrelevantly, and leaned down and kissed her.

With a kiss! she thought.

"My father wouldn't think so," she said, "if he could see me
now. What is you've been thinking?"

He still said nothing but only looked down at her, an expression in his eyes that she could not read.

"I've been thinking," he said, "that it's about time I got
started on that portrait of you. I ought to get started right
away."

She felt, very sharply, that his nerve had failed him. But she
felt, too, that his decision, now, to do a portrait of her was a
means of moving far away enough from her to be able to tell
her the truth. Also, he had always said that he could do something wonderful with her on canvas—it would be foolish to let
the opportunity pass. Cosmo had probably told him this. She
had always been flattered by his desire to paint her but now
she hoped that he would suddenly go blind.

"Anytime," she said, and could not resist, "Am I to be part of
a gallery?"

"Yeah. I'll probably be able to sell you for a thousand bucks," he said, and kissed her again.

"That's not a very nice thing to say," she murmured.

"You're a funny girl. What's not nice about a thousand dollars?" He leaned over her to put out his cigarette in the ash tray near the bed; then took hers and put it out too. He fell back against her and put his hand on her breast.

She said, tentatively: "Well, I suppose if you do it often enough, I could stop working."

His arms tightened but she did not feel that this was due entirely to desire; it might be said that he was striving, now, to distract her. "If I do *what* enough?" he grinned.

"Now, now," she smiled, "you just said that I was a nice girl."

"You're one of the nicest girls I ever met," said Paul soberly. "Really you are. I often wonder . . ."

"You often wonder what?"

"What's going to become of you."

She felt like a river trying to run two ways at once: she felt herself shrinking from him, yet she flowed toward him too; she knew he felt it. "But as long as you're with me," she said, and she could not help herself, she felt she was about to cry; she held his face between her hands, pressing yet closer against him. "As long as you're with me." His face was white, his eyes glowed: there was a war in him too. Everything that divided them charged, for an instant, the tiny space between them. Then the veils of habit and desire covered both their eyes.

"Life is very long," said Paul at last. He kissed her. They both sighed. And slowly she surrendered, opening up before him like the dark continent, made mad and delirious and blind by the entry of a mortal as bright as the morning, as white as milk.

When she left the house he was sleeping. Because she was late for work and because it was raining, she dropped into a cab and was whirled out of the streets of the Village—which still suggested, at least, some faint memory of the individual life—into the grim publicities of midtown Manhattan. Blocks and squares and exclamation marks, stone and steel and glass as far as the eye could see; everything towering, lifting itself against though by no means into, heaven. The people, so surrounded by heights that they had lost any sense of what heights were, rather resembled, nevertheless, these gray rigidities and also resembled, in their frantic motion, people fleeing a burning town. Ruth, who was not so many years removed from trees and earth, had felt in the beginning that she would never be able to live on an island so eccentric; she had, for example, before she arrived, dreamed of herself as walking by the river. But apart from the difficulties of realizing this ambition, which were not inconsiderable, it turned out that a lone girl walking by the river was simply asking to be victimized by both the disturbers and the defenders of the public peace. She retreated into the interior and this dream was abandoned—along with others. For her as for most of Manhattan, trees and water ceased to be realities; the nervous, trusting landscape of the city began to be the landscape of her mind. And soon her mind, like life on the island, seemed to be incapable of flexibility, of moving outward, could only shriek upward into meaningless abstractions or drop downward into cruelty and confusion.

She worked for a life insurance company that had only recently become sufficiently progressive to hire Negroes. This meant that she worked in an atmosphere so positively electric with interracial good will that no one ever dreamed of telling the truth about anything. It would have seemed, and it quite possibly would have been, a spiteful act. The only other Negro there was male, a Mr. Davis, who was very highly placed. He

was an expert, it appeared, in some way about Negroes and
life insurance, from which Ruth had ungenerously concluded
that he was the company's expert on how to cheat more Negroes out of more money and not only remain within the law
but also be honored with a plaque for good race relations. She
often—but not always—took dictation from him. The other
girls, manifesting a rough, girl-scoutish camaraderie that made
the question of their sincerity archaic, found him "marvelous"
and wondered if he had a wife. Ruth found herself unable to
pursue these strangely overheated and yet eerily impersonal
speculations with anything like the indicated vehemence. Since
it was extremely unlikely that any of these girls would ever
even go dancing with Mr. Davis, it was impossible to believe
that they had any ambition to share his couch, matrimonial or
otherwise, and yet, lacking this ambition, it was impossible to
account for their avidity. But they were all incredibly innocent
and made her ashamed of her body. At the same time it demanded, during their maddening coffee breaks, a great deal of
will power not to take Paul's photograph out of her wallet and
wave it before them saying, *"You'll never lay a finger on Mr.
Davis. But look what I took from you!"* Her face at such moments allowed them to conclude that she was planning to
ensnare Mr. Davis herself. It was perhaps this assumption,
despite her phone calls from Paul, that allowed them to discuss
Mr. Davis so freely before her, and they also felt, in an in-
coherent way, that these discussions were proof of their de-
mocracy. She did not find Mr. Davis "marvelous," though she
thought him good-looking enough in a square, stocky, gleaming, black-boyish sort of way.

Near her office, visible from her window and having the air
of contraband in Caesar's market place, was a small gray
chapel. An ugly neon cross jutted out above the heads of
passers-by, proclaiming "Jesus Saves." Today, as the lunch
hour approached and she began, as always, to fidget, debating

whether she should telephone Paul or wait for Paul to telephone her, she found herself staring in some irritation at this
cross, thinking about her childhood. The telephone rang and
rang, but never for her; she began to feel the need of a drink.
She thought of Paul sleeping while she typed and became
outraged, then thought of his painting and became maternal;
thought of his arms and paused to light a cigarette, throwing
the most pitying of glances toward the girl who shared her
office, who still had a crush on Frank Sinatra. Nevertheless, the
sublimatory tube still burning, the smoke tickling her nostrils
and the typewriter bell clanging at brief intervals like signals
flashing by on a railroad track, she relapsed into bitterness,
confusion, fury: for she was trapped, Paul was a trap. She
wanted a man of her own and she wanted children and all she
could see for herself today was a lifetime of typing while Paul
slept or a lifetime of typing with no Paul. And she began
rather to envy the stocky girl with the crush on Frank Sinatra,
since she would settle one day, obviously, for a great deal less,
and probably turn out children as Detroit turned out cars and
never sigh for an instant for what she had missed, having
indeed never, and especially with a lifetime of moviegoing
behind her, missed anything.

"Jesus Saves." She began to think of the days of her innocence. These days had been spent in the South, where her
mother and father and older brother remained. She had an
older sister, married and with several children, in Oakland,
and a baby sister who had become a small-time nightclub
singer in New Orleans. There were relatives of her father's
living in Harlem and she was sure that they wrote to him often
complaining that she never visited them. They, like her father,
were earnest churchgoers, though, unlike her father, their religion was strongly mixed with an opportunistic respectability
and with ambitions to better society and their own place in it,

which her father would have scorned. Their ambitions vitiated
in them what her father called the "true" religion, and what
remained of this religion, which was principally vindictiveness,
prevented them from understanding anything whatever about
those concrete Northern realities that made them at once so
obsequious and so venomous.

Her innocence. It was many years ago. She remembered
their house, so poor and plain, standing by itself, apart from
other houses, as nude and fragile on the stony ground as an
upturned cardboard box. And it was nearly as dark inside as it
might have been beneath a box, it leaked when the rain fell,
froze when the wind blew, could scarcely be entered in July.
They tried to coax sustenance out of a soil that had long ago
gone out of the business. As time went on they grew to depend
less and less on the soil and more on the oyster boats, and on
the wages and leftovers brought home by their mother, and
then herself, from the white kitchens in town. And her mother
still struggled in these white kitchens, humming sweet hymns,
tiny, mild eyed and bent, her father still labored on the oyster
boats; after a lifetime of labor, should they drop dead tomorrow, there would not be a penny for their burial clothes. Her
brother, still unmarried, nearing thirty now, loitered through
the town with his dangeous reputation, drinking and living off
the women he murdered with his love-making. He made her
parents fearful but they reiterated in each letter that they had
placed him, and all of their children, in the hands of God.
Ruth opened each letter in guilt and fear, expecting each time
to be confronted with the catastrophe that had at last over-
taken her kin; anticipating too, with a selfish annoyance that
added to her guilt, the enforced and necessary journey back to
her home in mourning; the survivors gathered together to do
brief honor to the dead, whose death was certainly, in part,
attributable to the indifference of the living. She often wrote
her brother asking him to come North, and asked her sister in

Oakland to second her in this plea. But she knew that he would not come North—because of her. She had shamed him and embittered him, she was one of the reasons he drank.

Her mother's song, which she, doubtless, still hummed each evening as she walked the old streets homeward, began with the question, *How did you feel when you come out the wilderness?*

And she remembered her mother, half-humming, half-singing, with a steady, tense beat that would make any blues singer sit up and listen (though she thought it best not to say this to her mother:)

> *Come out the wilderness,*
> *Come out the wilderness.*
> *How did you feel when you come out the wilderness,*
> *Leaning on the Lord?*

And the answers were many: *Oh, my soul felt happy!* or, *I shouted hallelujah!* or, *I do thank God!*

Ruth finished her cigarette, looking out over the stone-cold, hideous New York streets, and thought with a strange new pain of her mother. Her mother had once been no older than she, Ruth, was today. She had probably been pretty, she had also wept and trembled and cried beneath the rude thrusting that was her master and her life, and children had knocked in her womb and split her as they came crying out. Out, and into the wilderness: she had placed them in the hands of God. She had known nothing but labor and sorrow, she had had to confront, every day of her life, the everlasting, nagging, infinitesimal details; it had clearly all come to nothing, how could she be singing still?

"Jesus Saves." She put out her cigarette and a sense of loss and disaster wavered through her like a mist. She wished, in that moment, from the bottom of her heart, that she had never left home. She wished that she had never met Paul. She wished that she had never been touched by his whiteness. She should have found a great, slow, black man, full of laughter and sighs and grace, a man at whose center there burned a steady, smokeless fire. She should have surrendered to him and been a woman, and had his children, and found, through being irreplaceable, despite whatever shadows life might cast, peace that would enable her to endure.

She had left home practically by accident; it had been partly due to her brother. He had grown too accustomed to thinking of her as his prized, adored little sister to recognize the changes that were occuring within her. This had had something to do with the fact that his own sexual coming of age had disturbed his peace with her—he would, in good faith, have denied this, which did not make it less true. When she was seventeen her brother had surprised her alone in a barn with a boy. Nothing had taken place between herself and this boy, though there was no saying what might not have happened if her brother had not come in. She, guilty though she was in everything but the act, could scarcely believe and had not, until today, ever quite forgiven his immediate leap to the obvious conclusion. She began screaming before he hit her, her father had had to come running to pull her brother off the boy. And she had shouted their innocence in a steadily blackening despair, for the boy was too badly beaten to be able to speak and it was clear that no one believed her. She bawled at last: "Goddamit, I wish I had, I wish I had, I might as well of done it!" Her father slapped her. Her brother gave her a look and said: "You dirty . . . you dirty . . . you black and dirty—" Then her mother had had to step between her father and her brother. She turned and ran and sat down for a long time in the darkness, on a hillside, by herself, shivering. And she felt dirty, she felt that nothing would ever make her clean.

After this she and her brother scarcely spoke. He had

wounded her so deeply she could not face his eyes. Her father dragged her to church to make her cry repentance but she was as stubborn as her father, she told him she had nothing to repent. And she avoided them all, which was exactly the most dangerous thing that could have happened, for when she met the musician, Arthur, who was more than twenty years older than she, she ran away to New York with him. She lived with him for more than four years. She did not love him all that time, she simply did not know how to escape his domination. He had never made the big-time himself and he therefore wanted her to become a singer; and perhaps she had ceased to love him when it became clear that she had no talent whatever. He was very disappointed, but he was also very proud, and he made her go to school to study shorthand and typing, and made her self-conscious about her accent and her grammar, and took great delight in dressing her. Through him, she got over feeling that she was black and unattractive and as soon as this happened she was able to leave him. In fleeing Harlem and her relatives there, she drifted downtown to the Village, where, eventually, she found employment as a waitress in one of those restaurants with candles on the tables. Here, after a year or so, and several increasingly disastrous and desperate liaisons, she met Paul.

The telephone rang several desks away from her and, at the same instant, she was informed that Mr. Davis wanted her in his office. She was sure that it was Paul telephoning but she picked up her pad and walked into Mr. Davis's cubbyhole. Someone picked up the receiver, cutting off the bell, and she closed the door of Mr. Davis's office behind her.

"Good morning," she said.

"Good morning," he answered. He looked out of his window. "Though, between you and me, I've seen better mornings. This morning ain't half trying."

They both laughed, self-consciously amused and relieved by his "ain't."

She sat down, her pencil poised, looking at him questioningly.

"How do you like your job?" he asked her.

She had not expected his question, which she immediately distrusted and resented, suspecting him, on no evidence whatever, of acting now as a company spy.

"It's quite pleasant," she said in a guarded, ladylike tone, and stared hypnotically at him as though she believed that he was about to do her mischief by magical means and she had to resist his spell.

"Are you intending to be a career girl?"

He was giving her more attention this morning than he ever had before, with the result that she found herself reciprocating. A tentative friendliness wavered in the air between them. She smiled. "I guess I ought to say that it depends on my luck."

He laughed—perhaps rather too uproariously, though, more probably, she had merely grown unaccustomed to his kind of laughter. Her brother bobbed briefly to the surface of her mind.

"Well," he said, "does your luck seem likely to take you out of this office anytime in the near future?"

"No," she said, "it certainly doesn't look that way," and they laughed again. But she wondered if he would be laughing if he knew about Paul.

"If you don't mind my saying so, then," he said, "*I'm* lucky." He quickly riffled some papers on his desk, putting on a business air as rakishly as she had seen him put on his hat. "There's going to be some changes made around here—I reckon you have heard that." He grinned. Then, briskly: "I'm going to be needing a secretary. Would you like it? You get a raise"—he coughed—"in salary, of course."

"Why, I'd love it," she heard herself saying before she had had time for the bitter reflection that this professional advance probably represented the absolute extent of her luck. And she was ashamed of the thought, which she could not repress, that Paul would probably hang on a little longer if he knew she was making more money.

She resolved not to tell him and wondered how many hours this resolution would last.

Mr. Davis looked at her with an intentness almost personal. There was a strained, brief silence. "Good," he said at last. "There are a few details to be worked out, like getting me more office space"—they both smiled—"but you'll be hearing directly in a few days. I only wanted to sound you out first." He rose and held out his hand. "I hope you're going to like working with me," he said. "I think I'm going to like working with you."

She rose and shook his hand, bewildered to find that something in his simplicity had touched her very deeply. "I'm sure I will," she said, gravely. "And thank you very much." She reached backward for the doorknob.

"Miss Bowman," he said sharply—and paused. "Well, if I were you I wouldn't mention it yet to"—he waved his hand uncomfortably—"the girls out there." Now he really did look rather boyish. "It looks better if it comes from the front office."

"I understand," she said quickly.

"Also, I didn't ask for you out of any—racial—considerations," he said. "You just seemed, the most *sensible* girl available."

"I understand," she repeated; they were both trying not to smile. "And thank you again." She closed the door of his office behind her.

"A man called you," said the stocky girl. "He said he'd call back."

"Thank you," Ruth said. She could see that the girl wanted to talk so she busily studied some papers on her desk and retired behind the noise of her typewriter.

The stocky girl had gone out to lunch and Ruth was reluctantly deciding that she might as well go too when Paul called again.

"Hello. How's it going up there?"

"Dull. How are things down there? Are you out of bed already?"

"What do you mean, already?" He sounded slightly nettled and was trying not to sound that way, the almost certain signal that a storm was coming. "It's nearly one o'clock. I got work to do too, you know."

"Yes. I know." But neither could she quite keep the sardonic edge out of her voice.

There was a silence.

"You coming straight home from work?"

"Yes. Will you be there?"

"Yeah. I got to go uptown with Cosmo this afternoon, talk to some gallery guy, Cosmo thinks he might like my stuff."

"Oh"—thinking *Damn Cosmo!*—"that's wonderful, Paul. I hope something comes of it."

Nothing whatever would come of it. The gallery owner would be evasive—*if* he existed, if they ever got to his gallery—and then Paul and Cosmo would get drunk. She would hear, while she ached to be free, to be anywhere else, *with* anyone else, from Paul, all about how stupid art dealers were, how incestuous the art world had become, how impossible it was to *do* anything—his eyes, meanwhile, focusing with a drunken intensity, his eyes at once arrogant and defensive.

Well. Most of what he said was true, and she knew it, it was not his fault.

Not his fault. "Yeah. I sure hope so. I thought I'd take up some of my water colors, some small sketches—you know, all the most *obvious* things I've got."

This policy did not, empirically, seem to be as foolproof as everyone believed but she did not know how to put her uncertain objections into words. "That sounds good. What time have you got to be there?"

"Around three. I'm meeting Cosmo now for lunch."

"Oh"—lightly—"why don't you two, just this once, order your lunch before you order your cocktails?"

He laughed too and was clearly no more amused than she. "Well, Cosmo'll be buying, he'll have to, so I guess I'll leave it up to him to order."

Touché. Her hand, holding the receiver, shook. "Well, I hope you two make it to the gallery without falling flat on your faces."

"Don't worry." Then, in a rush, she recognized the tone before she understood the words, it was his you-can't-say-I-haven't-been-honest-with-you tone: "Cosmos says the gallery owner's got a daughter."

I hope to God she marries you, she thought. I hope she marries you and takes you off to Istanbul forever, where I will never have to hear you again, so I can get a breath of air, so I can get out from under.

They both laughed, a laugh conspiratorial and sophisticated, like the whispered, whiskey laughter of a couple in a night-club. "Oh?" she said. "Is she pretty?"

"She's probably a pig. She's had two husbands already, both artists."

She laughed again. "Where has she buried the bodies?"

"Well"—really amused this time, but also rather grim—"one of them ended up in the booby hatch and the other turned into a fairy and was last seen dancing with some soldiers in Majorca."

Now they laughed together and the wires between them hummed, almost, with the stormless friendship they both hoped to feel for each other someday. "A powerful pig. Maybe you *better* have a few drinks."

"You see what I mean? But Cosmo says she's not such a fool about painting."

"She doesn't seem to have much luck with painters. Maybe you'll break the jinx."

"Maybe. Wish me luck. It sure would be nice to unload some of my stuff on somebody."

You're doing just fine, she thought. "Will you call me later?"

"Yeah. Around three-thirty, four o'clock, as soon as I get away from there."

"Right. Be good."

"You too. Goodby."

"Goodby."

She put down the receiver, still amused and still trembling. After all, he had called her. But he would probably not have called her if he were not actually nourishing the hope that the gallery owner's daughter might find him interesting; in that case he would have to tell Ruth about her and it was better to have the way prepared. Paul was always preparing the way for one unlikely exploit or flight or another, it was the reason he told Ruth "everything." To tell everything is a very effective means of keeping secrets. Secrets hidden at the heart of midnight are simply waiting to be dragged to the light, as, on some unlucky high noon, they always are. But secrets shrouded in the glare of candor are bound to defeat even the most determined and agile inspector for the light is always changing and proves that the eye cannot be trusted. So Ruth knew about Paul nearly all there was to know, knew him better than anyone else on earth ever had or probably ever would, only—she did not know him well enough to stop him from being Paul.

While she was waiting for the elevator she realized, with mild astonishment, that she was actually hoping that the gallery owner's daughter would take Paul away. This hope resembled the desperation of someone suffering from a toothache who, in order to bring the toothache to an end, was almost willing to jump out of a window. But she found herself wondering if love really ought to be like a toothache. Love ought—she stepped out of the elevator, really wondering for a moment which way to turn—to be a means of being released from guilt and terror. But Paul's touch would never release her. He had power over her not because she was free but because she was guilty. To enforce his power over her he had only to keep her guilt awake. This did not demand malice on his part, it scarcely demanded perception—it only demanded that he have, as, in fact, he overwhelmingly did have, an instinct for his own convenience. His touch, which should have raised her, lifted her roughly only to throw her down hard; whenever he touched her, she became blacker and dirtier than ever; the loneliest place under heaven was in Paul's arms.

And yet—she went into his arms with such eagerness and such hope. She had once thought herself happy. Was this because she had been proud that he was white? But—it was she who was insisting on these colors. Her blackness was not Paul's fault. Neither was her guilt. She was punishing herself for something, a crime she could not remember. *You dirty . . . you black and dirty . . .*

She bumped into someone as she passed the cigar stand in the lobby and, looking up to murmur, "Excuse me," recognized Mr. Davis. He was stuffing cigars into his breast pocket—though the gesture was rather like that of a small boy stuffing his pockets with cookies, she was immediately certain that they were among the most expensive cigars that could be bought. She wondered what he spent on his clothes—it looked like a great deal. From the crown of rakishly tilted, deafeningly conservative hat to the tips of his astutely dulled shoes, he glowed with a very nearly vindictive sharpness. There were no flies on Mr. Davis. He would always be the best-dressed man in *any*body's lobby.

He was just about the last person she wanted to see. But perhaps his lunch hour was over and he was coming in.

"Miss Bowman!" He gave her a delighted grin. "Are you just going to lunch?"

He made her want to laugh. There was something so incongruous about finding that grin behind all that manner and under all those clothes.

"Yes," she said. "I guess you've had your lunch?"

"*No.* I ain't had no lunch," he said. "I'm hungry, just like you." He paused. "I be delighted to have your company, Miss Bowman."

Very courtly, she thought, amused, and the smile is extremely wicked. Then she realized that she was pleased that a man was *being* courtly with her, even if only for an instant in a crowded lobby, and, at the same instant, made the discovery that what was so widely referred to as a "wicked" smile was really only the smile, scarcely ever to be encountered any more, of a man who was not afraid of women.

She thought it safe to demur. "Please don't think you have to be polite."

"I'm never polite about food," he told her. "Almost drove my mamma crazy." He took her arm. "I know a right nice place nearby." His stride and his accent made her think of home. She also realized that he, like many Negroes of his uneasily rising generation, kept in touch, so to speak, with himself by deliberately affecting, whenever possible, the illiterate speech of his youth. "We going to get on real well, you'll see. Time you get through being *my* secretary, you likely to end up with Alcoholics Anonymous."

The place "nearby" turned out to be a short taxi ride away, but it was, as he had said, "right nice." She doubted that Mr. Davis could possibly eat there every day, though it was clear that he was a man who liked to spend money.

She ordered a dry martini and he a bourbon on the rocks. He

professed himself astonished that she knew what a dry martini
was. "I thought you was a country girl."

"I *am* a country girl." she said.

"No, no," he said, "no more. You a country girl who came to
the city and that's the dangerous kind. Don't know if it's safe,
having you for my secretary."

Underneath all his chatter she felt him watching her, sizing
her up.

"Are you afraid your wife will object?" she asked.

"You ought to be able to look at me," he said, "and tell that I
ain't got a wife."

She laughed. "So you're *not* married. I wonder if I should
tell the girls in the office?"

"I don't care what you tell them," he said. Then: "How do
you get along with them?"

"We get along fine," she said. "We don't have much to talk
about except whether or not you're married but that'll probably last until you *do* get married and then we can talk about
your wife."

But thinking, For God's sake let's get off *this* subject, she
added, before he could say anything: "You called me a country
girl. Aren't you a country boy?"

"I am," he said, "but I didn't *change* my drinking habits
when I came North. If bourbon was good enough for me down
yonder, it's good enough for me up here."

"I didn't have any drinking habits to change, Mr. Davis," she
told him. "I was too young to be drinking when I left home."

His eyes were slightly questioning but he held his peace,
while she wished that she had held hers. She concentrated on
sipping her martini, suddenly remembering that she was sitting opposite a man who knew more about why girls left home
than could be learned from locker-room stories. She wondered
if he had a sister and tried to be amused at finding herself still

so incorrigibly old fashioned. But he did not, really, seem to be much like her brother. She met his eyes again.

"Where I come from," he said, with a smile, "*nobody* was too young to be drinking. Toughened them up for later life," and he laughed.

By the time lunch was over she had learned that he was from a small town in Alabama, was the youngest of three sons (but had no sisters), had gone to college in Tennessee, was a reserve officer in the Air Force. He was thirty-two. His mother was living, his father was dead. He had lived in New York for two years but was beginning, now, to like it less than he had in the beginning.

"At first," he said, "I thought it would be fun to live in a city where didn't nobody know you and you didn't know nobody and where, look like, you could just do anything you was big and black enough to do. But you get tired not knowing nobody and there ain't really that many things you want to do alone."

"Oh, but you must have friends," she said, "uptown."

"I don't live uptown. I live in Brooklyn. Ain't *nobody* in Brooklyn got friends."

She laughed with him, but distrusted the turn the conversation was taking. They were walking back to the office. He walked slowly, as though in deliberate opposition to the people around them, although they were already a little late—at least *she* was late, but, since she was with one of her superiors, it possibly didn't matter.

"Where do you live?" he asked her. "Do you live uptown?"

"No," she said, "I live downtown on Bank Street." And after a moment: "That's in the Village. Greenwich Village."

He grinned. "Don't tell me you studying to be a writer or a dancer or something?"

"No. I just found myself there. It used to be cheap."

He scowled. "Ain't nothing cheap in this town no more, not even the necessities."

His tone made clear to which necessities he referred and she would have loved to tease him a little, just to watch him laugh. But she was beginning, with every step they took, to be a little afraid of him. She was responding to him with parts of herself that had been buried so long she had forgotten they existed. In his office that morning, when he shook her hand, she had suddenly felt a warmth of affection, of nostalgia, of gratitude even—and again in the lobby—he had somehow made her feel safe. It was his friendliness that was so unsettling. She had grown used to unfriendly people.

Still, she did not *want* to be friends with him: still less did she desire that their friendship should ever become anything more. Sooner or later he would learn about Paul. He would look at her differently then. It would not be—so much— because of Paul as a man, perhaps not even Paul as a white man. But it would make him bitter, it would make her ashamed, for him to see how she was letting herself be wasted —for Paul, who did not love her.

This was the reason she was ashamed and wished to avoid the scrutiny of Mr. Davis. She was doing something to herself —out of shame?—that he would be right in finding indefensible. She was punishing herself. For what? She looked sideways at his black Sambo profile under the handsome lightweight Dobbs hat and wished that she could tell him about it, that he would turn his head, holding it slightly to one side, and watch her with those eyes that had seen and that had learned to hide so much. Eyes that had seen so many girls like her taken beyond the hope of rescue, while all the owner of the eyes could do—perhaps she wore Paul the way Mr. Davis wore his hat. And she looked away from him, half-smiling and yet near tears, over the furious streets on which, here and there, like a design, colored people also hurried, thinking, *And we were slaves here once.*

"Do you like music?" he asked her abruptly. "I don't necessarily mean Carnegie Hall."

Now was the time to stop him. She had only to say, "Mr.

Davis, I'm living with someone." It would not be necessary to say anything more than that.

She met his eyes. "Of course I like music," she said faintly.

"Well, I know a place I'd like to take you one of these evenings, after work. Not going to be easy, being *my* secretary."

His smile forced her to smile with him. But, "Mr. Davis," she said, and stopped. They were before the entrance to their office building.

"What's the matter?" he asked. "You forget something?"

"No." She looked down, feeling big, black and foolish. "Mr. Davis," she said, "you don't know anything about me."

"You don't know anything about me, either," he said.

"That's not what I mean," she said.

He sounded slightly angry. "I ain't asked you nothing yet," he said. "Why can't you wait till you're asked?"

"Well," she stammered, "it may be too late by then."

They stared hard at each other for a moment. "Well," he said, "if it turns out to be too late, won't be nobody to blame but me, will it?"

She stared at him again, almost hating him. She blindly felt that he had no right to do this to her, to cause her to feel such a leap of hope, if he was only, in the end, going to give her back all her shame.

"You know what they say down home," she said, slowly. "If you don't know what you doing, you better ask somebody." There were tears in her eyes.

He took her arm. "Come on in this house, girl," he said. "We got insurance to sell."

They said nothing to each other in the elevator on the way upstairs. She wanted to laugh and she wanted to cry. He, ostentatiously, did not watch her; he stood next to her, humming *Rocks in My Bed*.

She waited all afternoon for Paul to telephone, but although, perversely enough, the phone seemed never to cease ringing, it never rang for her. At five-fifteen, just before she left the office, she called the apartment. Paul was not there. She went downstairs to a nearby bar and ordered a drink and called again at a quarter to six. He was not there. She resolved to have one more drink and leave this bar, which she did, wandering a few blocks north to a bar frequented by theater people. She sat in a booth and ordered a drink and at a quarter to seven called again. He was not there.

She was in a reckless, desperate state, like flight. She knew that she could not possibly go home and cook supper and wait in the empty apartment until his key turned in the lock. He would come in, breathless and contrite—or else, truculently, *not* contrite—probably a little drunk, probably quite hungry. He would tell her where he had been and what he had been doing. Whatever he told her would probably be true—there are so many ways of telling the truth! And whether it was true or not did not matter and she would not be able to reproach him for the one thing that *did* matter: that he had left her sitting in the house alone. She could not make this reproach because, after all, leaving women sitting around in empty houses had been the specialty of all men for ages. And, for ages, when the men arrived, women bestirred themselves to cook supper—luckily, it was not yet common knowledge that many a woman had narrowly avoided committing murder by calmly breaking a few eggs.

She wondered where it had all gone to—the ease, the pleasure they had had together once. At one time their evenings together, sitting around the house, drinking beer or reading or simply laughing and talking, had been the best part of all their days. Paul, reading, or walking about with a can of beer in his hand, talking, gesturing, scratching his chest; Paul, stretched out on the sofa, staring at the ceiling; Paul, cheerful, with that lowdown, cavernous chuckle and that foolish grin; Paul, grim, with his mouth turned down and his eyes burning; Paul doing anything whatever, Paul with his eyelids sealed in sleep, drooling and snoring, Paul lighting her cigarette, touching her elbow, talking, talking, talking, in his million ways, to her, had been the light that lighted up her world. Now it was all gone, it would never come again, and that face which was like the heavens was darkening against her.

These present days, after supper, when the chatter each used as a cover began to show dangerous signs of growing thinner, there would be no choice but sleep. She might, indeed, have preferred a late movie, or a round of the bars, lights, noise, other people, but this would scarcely be Paul's desire, already tired from his day. Besides—after all, she had to face the office in the morning. Eventually, therefore, bed; perhaps he or she or both of them might read awhile; perhaps there would take place between them what had sometimes been described as the act of love. Then sleep, black and dreadful, like a drugged state, from which she would be rescued by the scream of the alarm clock or the realization that Paul was no longer in bed.

Ah. Her throat ached with tears of fury and despair. In the days before she had met Paul men had taken her out, she had laughed a lot, she had been young. She had not wished to spend her life protecting herself, with laughter, against men she cared nothing about; but she could not go on like this, either, drinking in random bars because she was afraid to go home; neither could she guess what life might bring her when Paul was gone.

She wished that she had never met him. She wished that he, or she, or both of them were dead. And for a moment she really wished it, with a violence that frightened her. Perhaps there was always murder at the very heart of love: the strong desire to murder the beloved, so that one could at last be assured of privacy and peace and be as safe and unchanging as the grave. Perhaps this was why disasters, thicker and more malevolent than bees, circled Paul's head whenever he was out of her sight. Perhaps in those moments when she had believed herself willing to lay down her life for him she had only been presenting herself with a metaphor for her peace, his death; death, which would be an inadequate revenge for the color of his skin, for his failure, by not loving her, to release her from the prison of her own.

The waitress passed her table and Ruth ordered another drink. After this drink she would go. The bar was beginning to fill up, mostly, as she judged, with theater people, some of them, possibly, on their way to work, most of them drawn here by habit and hope. For the past few moments, without realizing it, she had been watching a lean, pale boy at the bar, whose curly hair leaned electrically over his forehead like a living, awry crown. Something about him, his stance, his profile or his grin, prodded painfully at her attention. But it was not that he reminded her of Paul. He reminded her of a boy she had known, briefly, a few years ago, a very lonely boy who was now a merchant seaman, probably, wherever he might be on the globe at this moment, whoring his unbearably unrealized, mysteriously painful life away. She had been fond of him but loneliness in him had been like a cancer, it had really unfitted him for human intercourse, and she had not been sorry to see him go. She had not thought of him for years; yet, now, this stranger at the bar, whom she was beginning to recognize as an actor of brief but growing reputation, abruptly brought him back to her; brought him back encrusted, as it were, with the anguish of the intervening years. She remembered things she thought she had forgotten and wished that she had been wiser then—then she smiled at herself, wishing she were wiser now.

Once, when he had done something to hurt her, she had told him, trying to be calm but choked and trembling with rage: "Look. This is the twentieth century. We're not down on a plantation, you're not the master's son, and I'm not the black girl you can just sleep with when you want to and kick about as you please!"

His face, then, had held something, held many things—bitterness, amusement, fury; but the startling element was pain, his pain, with which she now invested the face of the actor at the bar. It made her wish that she had held her tongue.

"Well," he said at last. "I guess I'll get on back to the big house and leave you down here with the pickaninnies."

They had seen each other a few times thereafter but that was really the evening on which everything had ended between them.

She wondered if that boy had ever found a home.

The actor at the bar looked toward her briefly, but she knew he was not seeing her. He looked at his watch, frowned, she saw that he was not as young as he looked; he ordered another drink and looked downward, leaning both elbows on the bar. The dim lights played on his crown of hair. He moved his head slightly, with impatience, upward, his mouth slightly open, and in that instant, somehow, his profile was burned into her mind. He reminded her then of Paul, of the vanished boy, of others, of others she had seen and never touched, of an army of boys —boys forever!—an army she feared and hated and loved. In that gesture, that look upward, with the light so briefly on his face, she saw the bones that held his face together and the sorrow beginning to corrode his brow, the blood beating like butterfly wings against the cage of his heavy neck. But there was no name for something blind, cruel, lustful, lost, intolerably vulnerable in his eyes and mouth. She knew that in spite of everything, his color, his power or his coming fame, he was lost. He did not know what had happened to his life. And never would. This was the pain she had seen on the face of that boy so long ago, and it was this that had driven Paul into her arms, and now away. The sons of the masters were roaming the world, looking for arms to hold them. And the arms that might have held them—could not forgive.

A sound escaped her; she was astonished to realize it was a sob. The waitress looked at her sharply. Ruth put some money on the table and hurried out. It was dark now and the rain that had been falling intermittently all day spangled the air and glittered all over the streets. It fell against her face and mingled with her tears and she walked briskly through the crowds to hide from them and from herself the fact that she did not know where she was going.

Going to Meet the Man

"WHAT'S THE MATTER?" she asked.

"I don't know," he said, trying to laugh, "I guess I'm tired."

"You've been working too hard," she said. "I keep telling you."

"Well, goddammit, woman," he said, "it's not my fault!" He tried again; he wretchedly failed again. Then he just lay there, silent, angry, and helpless. Excitement filled him like a tooth-ache, but it refused to enter his flesh. He stroked her breast. This was his wife. He could not ask her to do just a little thing for him, just to help him out, just for a little while, the way he could ask a nigger girl to do it. He lay there, and he sighed. The image of a black girl caused a distant excitement in him, like a far-away light; but, again, the excitement was more like pain; instead of forcing him to act, it made action impossible.

"Go to sleep," she said, gently, "you got a hard day tomorrow."

"Yeah," he said, and rolled over on his side, facing her, one hand still on one breast. "Goddamn the niggers. The black stinking coons. You'd think they'd learn. Wouldn't you think they'd learn? I mean, *wouldn't* you?"

"They going to be out there tomorrow," she said, and took his hand away, "get some sleep."

He lay there, one hand between his legs, staring at the frail sanctuary of his wife. A faint light came from the shutters; the moon was full. Two dogs, far away, were barking at each other, back and forth, insistently, as though they were agreeing to make an appointment. He heard a car coming north on the road and he half sat up, his hand reaching for his holster, which was on a chair near the bed, on top of his pants. The lights hit the shutters and seemed to travel across the room and then went out. The sound of the car slipped away, he heard it

229

hit gravel, then heard it no more. Some liver-lipped students, probably, heading back to that college—but coming from where? His watch said it was two in the morning. They could be coming from anywhere, from out of state most likely, and they would be at the court-house tomorrow. The niggers were getting ready. Well, they would be ready, too.

He moaned. He wanted to let whatever was in him out; but it wouldn't come out. Goddamn! he said aloud, and turned again, on his side, away from Grace, staring at the shutters. He was a big, healthy man and he had never had any trouble sleeping. And he wasn't old enough yet to have any trouble getting it up—he was only forty-two. And he was a good man, a God-fearing man, he had tried to do his duty all his life, and he had been a deputy sheriff for several years. Nothing had ever bothered him before, certainly not getting it up. Sometimes, sure, like any other man, he knew that he wanted a little more spice than Grace could give him and he would drive over yonder and pick up a black piece or arrest her, it came to the same thing, but he couldn't do that now, no more. There was no telling what might happen once your ass was in the air. And they were low enough to kill a man then, too, everyone of them, or the girl herself might do it, right while she was making believe you made her feel so good. The niggers. What had the good Lord Almighty had in mind when he made the niggers? Well. They were pretty good at that, all right. Damn. Damn. Goddamn.

This wasn't helping him to sleep. He turned again, toward Grace again, and moved close to her warm body. He felt something he had never felt before. He felt that he would like to hold her, hold her, hold her, and be buried in her like a child and never have to get up in the morning again and go downtown to face those faces, good Christ, they were ugly! and never have to enter that jail house again and smell that smell and hear that singing; never again feel that filthy, kinky,

greasy hair under his hand, never again watch those black
breasts leap against the leaping cattle prod, never hear those
moans again or watch that blood run down or the fat lips split
or the sealed eyes struggle open. They were animals, they were
no better than animals, what could be done with people like
that? Here they had been in a civilized country for years and
they still lived like animals. Their houses were dark, with oil
cloth or cardboard in the windows, the smell was enough to
make you puke your guts out, and there they sat, a whole
tribe, pumping out kids, it looked like, every damn five minutes, and laughing and talking and playing music like they
didn't have a care in the world, and he reckoned they didn't,
neither, and coming to the door, into the sunlight, just standing there, just looking foolish, not thinking of anything but just
getting back to what they were doing, saying, Yes suh, Mr.
Jesse. I surely will, Mr. Jesse. Fine weather, Mr. Jesse. Why,
I thank you, Mr. Jesse. He had worked for a mail-order house
for a while and it had been his job to collect the payments for
the stuff they bought. They were too dumb to know that they
were being cheated blind, but that was no skin off his ass—he
was just supposed to do his job. They would be late—they
didn't have the sense to put money aside; but it was easy to
scare them, and he never really had any trouble. Hell, they all
liked him, the kids used to smile when he came to the door. He
gave them candy, sometimes, or chewing gum, and rubbed
their rough bullet heads—maybe the candy should have been
poisoned. Those kids were grown now. He had had trouble
with one of them today.

"There was this nigger today," he said; and stopped; his
voice sounded peculiar. He touched Grace. "You awake?" he
asked. She mumbled something, impatiently, she was probably
telling him to go to sleep. It was all right. He knew that he was
not alone.

"What a funny time," he said, "to be thinking about a thing

like that—you listening?" She mumbled something again. He
rolled over on his back. "This nigger's one of the ringleaders.
We had trouble with him before. We must have had him out
there at the work farm three or four times. Well, Big Jim C.
and some of the boys really had to whip that nigger's ass
today." He looked over at Grace; he could not tell whether she
was listening or not; and he was afraid to ask again. "They had
this line you know, to register"—he laughed, but she did not—
"and they wouldn't stay where Big Jim C. wanted them, no,
they had to start blocking traffic all around the court house so
couldn't nothing or nobody get through, and Big Jim C. told
them to disperse and they wouldn't move, they just kept up
that singing, and Big Jim C. figured that the others would move
if this nigger would move, him being the ring-leader, but he
wouldn't move and he wouldn't let the others move, so they
had to beat him and a couple of the others and they threw them
in the wagon—but *I* didn't see this nigger till I got to the jail.
They were still singing and I was supposed to make them stop.
Well, I couldn't make them stop for me but I knew he could
make them stop. He was lying on the ground jerking and
moaning, they had threw him in a cell by himself, and blood
was coming out his ears from where Big Jim C. and his boys
had whipped him. Wouldn't you think they'd learn? I put the
prod to him and he jerked some more and he kind of screamed
—but he didn't have much voice left. "You make them stop
that singing," I said to him, "you hear me? You make them stop
that singing." He acted like he didn't hear me and I put it to
him again, under his arms, and he just rolled around on the
floor and blood started coming from his mouth. He'd pissed his
pants already." He paused. His mouth felt dry and his throat
was as rough as sandpaper; as he talked, he began to hurt all
over with that peculiar excitement which refused to be released. "You all are going to stop your singing, I said to him,
and you are going to stop coming down to the court house and

disrupting traffic and molesting the people and keeping us from our duties and keeping doctors from getting to sick white women and getting all them Northerners in this town to give our town a bad name—!" As he said this, he kept prodding the boy, sweat pouring from beneath the helmet he had not yet taken off. The boy rolled around in his own dirt and water and blood and tried to scream again as the prod hit his testicles, but the scream did not come out, only a kind of rattle and a moan. He stopped. He was not supposed to kill the nigger. The cell was filled with a terrible odor. The boy was still. "You hear me?" he called. "You had enough?" The singing went on. "You had enough?" His foot leapt out, he had not known it was going to, and caught the boy flush on the jaw. *Jesus,* he thought, *this ain't no nigger, this is a goddamn bull,* and he screamed again, "You had enough? You going to make them stop that singing now?"

But the boy was out. And now he was shaking worse than the boy had been shaking. He was glad no one could see him. At the same time, he felt very close to a very peculiar, particular joy; something deep in him and deep in his memory was stirred, but whatever was in his memory eluded him. He took off his helmet. He walked to the cell door.

"White man," said the boy, from the floor, behind him.

He stopped. For some reason, he grabbed his privates.

"You remember Old Julia?"

The boy said, from the floor, with his mouth full of blood, and one eye, barely open, glaring like the eye of a cat in the dark, "My grandmother's name was Mrs. Julia Blossom. *Mrs. Julia Blossom.* You going to call our women by their right names yet.—And those kids ain't going to stop singing. We going to keep on singing until every one of you miserable white mothers go stark raving out of your minds." Then he closed the one eye; he spat blood; his head fell back against the floor.

He looked down at the boy, whom he had been seeing, off and on, for more than a year, and suddenly remembered him: Old Julia had been one of his mail-order customers, a nice old woman. He had not seen her for years, he supposed that she must be dead.

He had walked into the yard, the boy had been sitting in a swing. He had smiled at the boy, and asked, "Old Julia home?"

The boy looked at him for a long time before he answered. "Don't no Old Julia live here."

"This is her house. I know her. She's lived her for years."

The boy shook his head. "You might know a Old Julia someplace else, white man. But don't nobody by that name live here."

He watched the boy; the boy watched him. The boy certainly wasn't more than ten. *White man.* He didn't have time to be fooling around with some crazy kid. He yelled, "Hey! Old Julia!"

But only silence answered him. The expression on the boy's face did not change. The sun beat down on them both, still and silent; he had the feeling that he had been caught up in a nightmare, a nightmare dreamed by a child; perhaps one of the nightmares he himself had dreamed as a child. It had that feeling—everything familiar, without undergoing any other change, had been subtly and hideously displaced: the trees, the sun, the patches of grass in the yard, the leaning porch and the weary porch steps and the card-board in the windows and the black hole of the door which looked like the entrance to a cave, and the eyes of the pickaninny, all, all, were charged with malevolence. *White man.* He looked at the boy. "She's gone out?"

The boy said nothing.

"Well," he said, "tell her I passed by and I'll pass by next week." He started to go; he stopped. "You want some chewing gum?"

The boy got down from the swing and started for the house. He said, "I don't want nothing you got, white man." He walked into the house and closed the door behind him.

Now the boy looked as though he were dead. Jesse wanted to go over to him and pick him up and pistol whip him until the boy's head burst open like a melon. He began to tremble with what he believed was rage, sweat, both cold and hot, raced down his body, the singing filled him as though it were a weird, uncontrollable, monstrous howling rumbling up from the depths of his own belly, he felt an icy fear rise in him and raise him up, and he shouted, he howled, "You lucky we *pump* some white blood into you every once in a while—your women! Here's what I got for all the black bitches in the world—!" Then he was, abruptly, almost too weak to stand; to his bewilderment, his horror, beneath his own fingers, he felt himself violently stiffen—with no warning at all; he dropped his hands and he stared at the boy and he left the cell.

"All that singing they do," he said. "All that singing." He could not remember the first time he had heard it; he had been hearing it all his life. It was the sound with which he was most familiar—though it was also the sound of which he had been least conscious—and it had always contained an obscure comfort. They were singing to God. They were singing for mercy and they hoped to go to heaven, and he had even sometimes felt, when looking into the eyes of some of the old women, a few of the very old men, that they were singing for mercy for his soul, too. Of course he had never thought of their heaven or of what God was, or could be, for them; God was the same for everyone, he supposed, and heaven was where good people went—he supposed. He had never thought much about what it meant to be a good person. He tried to be a good person and treat everybody right: it wasn't his fault if the niggers had taken it into their heads to fight against God and go against the rules laid down in the Bible for everyone to read! Any preacher would tell you that. He was only doing his duty:

protecting white people from the niggers and the niggers from themselves. And there were still lots of good niggers around— he had to remember that; they weren't all like that boy this afternoon; and the good niggers must be mighty sad to see what was happening to their people. They would thank him when this was over. In that way they had, the best of them, not quite looking him in the eye, in a low voice, with a little smile: We surely thanks you, Mr. Jesse. From the bottom of our hearts, we thanks you. He smiled. They hadn't all gone crazy. This trouble would pass.—He knew that the young people had changed some of the words to the songs. He had scarcely listened to the words before and he did not listen to them now; but he knew that the words were different; he could hear that much. He did not know if the faces were different, he had never, before this trouble began, watched them as they sang, but he certainly did not like what he saw now. They hated him, and this hatred was blacker than their hearts, blacker than their skins, redder than their blood, and harder, by far, than his club. Each day, each night, he felt worn out, aching, with their smell in his nostrils and filling his lungs, as though he were drowning—drowning in niggers; and it was all to be done again when he awoke. It would never end. It would never end. Perhaps this was what the singing had meant all along. They had not been singing black folks into heaven, they had been singing white folks into hell.

Everyone felt this black suspicion in many ways, but no one knew how to express it. Men much older than he, who had been responsible for law and order much longer than he, were now much quieter than they had been, and the tone of their jokes, in a way that he could not quite put his finger on, had changed. These men were his models, they had been friends to his father, and they had taught him what it meant to be a man. He looked to them for courage now. It wasn't that he didn't know that what he was doing was right—he knew that, nobody had to tell him that; it was only that he missed the ease of former years. But they didn't have much time to hang out with each other these days. They tended to stay close to their families every free minute because nobody knew what might happen next. Explosions rocked the night of their tranquil town. Each time each man wondered silently if perhaps this time the dynamite had not fallen into the wrong hands. They thought that they knew where all the guns were; but they could not possibly know every move that was made in that secret place where the darkies lived. From time to time it was suggested that they form a posse and search the home of every nigger, but they hadn't done it yet. For one thing, this might have brought the bastards from the North down on their backs; for another, although the niggers were scattered throughout the town—down in the hollow near the railroad tracks, way west near the mills, up on the hill, the well-off ones, and some out near the college—nothing seemed to happen in one part of town without the niggers immediately knowing it in the other. This meant that they could not take them by surprise. They rarely mentioned it, but they *knew* that some of the niggers had guns. It stood to reason, as they said, since, after all, some of them had been in the Army. There were niggers in the Army right now and God knows they wouldn't have had any trouble stealing this half-assed government blind—the whole world was doing it, look at the European countries and all those countries in Africa. They made jokes about it—bitter jokes; and they cursed the government in Washington, which had betrayed them; but they had not yet formed a posse. Now, if their town had been laid out like some towns in the North, where all the niggers lived together in one locality, they could have gone down and set fire to the houses and brought about peace that way. If the niggers had all lived in one place, they could have kept the fire in one place. But the way this town was laid out, the fire

could hardly be controlled. It would spread all over town—
and the niggers would probably be helping it to spread. Still,
from time to time, they spoke of doing it, anyway; so that now
there was a real fear among them that somebody might go
crazy and light the match.

They rarely mentioned anything not directly related to the
war that they were fighting, but this had failed to establish
between them the unspoken communication of soldiers during
a war. Each man, in the thrilling silence which sped outward
from their exchanges, their laughter, and their anecdotes,
seemed wrestling, in various degrees of darkness, with a secret
which he could not articulate to himself, and which, however
directly it related to the war, related yet more surely to his
privacy and his past. They could no longer be sure, after all,
that they had all done the same things. They had never
dreamed that their privacy could contain any element of terror, could threaten, that is, to reveal itself, to the scrutiny of a
judgment day, while remaining unreadable and inaccessible to
themselves; nor had they dreamed that the past, while certainly refusing to be forgotten, could yet so stubbornly refuse
to be remembered. They felt themselves mysteriously set at
naught, as no longer entering into the real concerns of other
people—while here they were, out-numbered, fighting to save
the civilized world. They had thought that people would care
—people didn't care; not enough, anyway, to help them. It
would have been a help, really, or at least a relief, even to
have been forced to surrender. Thus they had lost, probably
forever, their old and easy connection with each other. They
were forced to depend on each other more and, at the same
time, to trust each other less. Who could tell when one of them
might not betray them all, for money, or for the ease of
confession? But no one dared imagine what there might be to
confess. They were soldiers fighting a war, but their relation-

ship to each other was that of accomplices in a crime. They all had to keep their mouths shut.

I stepped in the river at Jordan.

Out of the darkness of the room, out of nowhere, the line came flying up at him, with the melody and the beat. He turned wordlessly toward his sleeping wife. *I stepped in the river at Jordan.* Where had he heard that song?

"Grace," he whispered. "You awake?"

She did not answer. If she was awake, she wanted him to sleep. Her breathing was slow and easy, her body slowly rose and fell.

I stepped in the river at Jordan.
The water came to my knees.

He began to sweat. He felt an overwhelming fear, which yet contained a curious and dreadful pleasure.

I stepped in the river at Jordan.
The water came to my waist.

It had been night, as it was now, he was in the car between his mother and his father, sleepy, his head in his mother's lap, sleepy, and yet full of excitement. The singing came from far away, across the dark fields. There were no lights anywhere. They had said good-bye to all the others and turned off on this dark dirt road. They were almost home.

I stepped in the river at Jordan,
The water came over my head,
I looked way over to the other side,
He was making up my dying bed!

"I guess they singing for him," his father said, seeming very weary and subdued now. "Even when they're sad, they sound like they just about to go and tear off a piece." He yawned and leaned across the boy and slapped his wife lightly on the shoulder, allowing his hand to rest there for a moment. "Don't they?"

"Don't talk that way," she said.

"Well, that's what we going to do," he said, "you can make up your mind to that." He started whistling. "You see? When I begin to feel it, I gets kind of musical, too."

Oh, Lord! Come on and ease my troubling mind!

He had a black friend, his age, eight, who lived nearby. His name was Otis. They wrestled together in the dirt. Now the thought of Otis made him sick. He began to shiver. His mother put her arm around him.

"He's tired," she said.

"We'll be home soon," said his father. He began to whistle again.

"We didn't see Otis this morning," Jesse said. He did not know why he said this. His voice, in the darkness of the car, sounded small and accusing.

"You haven't seen Otis for a couple of mornings," his mother said.

That was true. But he was only concerned about *this* morning.

"No," said his father, "I reckon Otis's folks was afraid to let him show himself this morning."

"But Otis didn't do nothing!" Now his voice sounded questioning.

"Otis *can't* do nothing," said his father, "he's too little." The car lights picked up their wooden house, which now solemnly approached them, the lights falling around it like yellow dust. Their dog, chained to a tree, began to bark.

"We just want to make sure Otis *don't* do nothing," said his father, and stopped the car. He looked down at Jesse. "And you tell him what your Daddy said, you hear?"

"Yes sir," he said.

His father switched off the lights. The dog moaned and pranced, but they ignored him and went inside. He could not sleep. He lay awake, hearing the night sounds, the dog yawning and moaning outside, the sawing of the crickets, the cry of

the owl, dogs barking far away, then no sounds at all, just the
heavy, endless buzzing of the night. The darkness pressed on
his eyelids like a scratchy blanket. He turned, he turned again.
He wanted to call his mother, but he knew his father would
not like this. He was terribly afraid. Then he heard his
father's voice in the other room, low, with a joke in it; but this
did not help him, it frightened him more, he knew what was
going to happen. He put his head under the blanket, then
pushed his head out again, for fear, staring at the dark window. He heard his mother's moan, his father's sigh; he gritted
his teeth. Then their bed began to rock. His father's breathing
seemed to fill the world.

That morning, before the sun had gathered all its strength,
men and women, some flushed and some pale with excitement,
came with news. Jesse's father seemed to know what the news
was before the first jalopy stopped in the yard, and he ran out,
crying, "They got him, then? They got him?"

The first jalopy held eight people, three men and two
women and three children. The children were sitting on the
laps of the grown-ups. Jesse knew two of them, the two boys;
they shyly and uncomfortably greeted each other. He did not
know the girl.

"Yes, they got him," said one of the women, the older one,
who wore a wide hat and a fancy, faded blue dress. "They
found him early this morning."

"How far had he got?" Jesse's father asked.

"He hadn't got no further than Harkness," one of the men
said. "Look like he got lost up there in all them trees—or
maybe he just go so scared he couldn't move." They all
laughed.

"Yes, and you know it's near a graveyard, too," said the
younger woman, and they laughed again.

"Is that where they got him now?" asked Jesse's father.

By this time there were three cars piled behind the first one, with everyone looking excited and shining, and Jesse noticed that they were carrying food. It was like a Fourth of July picnic.

"Yeah, that's where he is," said one of the men, "declare, Jesse, you going to keep us here all day long, answering your damn fool questions. Come on, we ain't got no time to waste."

"Don't bother putting up no food," cried a woman from one of the other cars, "we got enough. Just come on."

"Why, thank you," said Jesse's father, "we be right along, then."

"I better get a sweater for the boy," said his mother, "in case it turns cold."

Jesse watched his mother's thin legs cross the yard. He knew that she also wanted to comb her hair a little and maybe put on a better dress, the dress she wore to church. His father guessed this, too, for he yelled behind her, "Now don't you go trying to turn yourself into no movie star. You just come on." But he laughed as he said this, and winked at the men; his wife was younger and prettier than most of the other women. He clapped Jesse on the head and started pulling him toward the car. "You all go on," he said, "I'll be right behind you. Jesse, you go tie up that there dog while I get this car started."

The cars sputtered and coughed and shook; the caravan began to move; bright dust filled the air. As soon as he was tied up, the dog began to bark. Jesse's mother came out of the house, carrying a jacket for his father and a sweater for Jesse. She had put a ribbon in her hair and had an old shawl around her shoulders.

"Put these in the car, son," she said, and handed everything to him. She bent down and stroked the dog, looked to see if there was water in his bowl, then went back up the three porch steps and closed the door.

"Come on," said his father, "ain't nothing in there for nobody to steal." He was sitting in the car, which trembled and belched. The last car of the caravan had disappeared but the sound of singing floated behind them.

Jesse got into the car, sitting close to his father, loving the smell of the car, and the trembling, and the bright day, and the sense of going on a great and unexpected journey. His mother got in and closed the door and the car began to move. Not until then did he ask, "Where are we going? Are we going on a picnic?"

He had a feeling that he knew where they were going, but he was not sure.

"That's right," his father said, "we're going on a picnic. You won't ever forget *this* picnic—!"

"Are we," he asked, after a moment, "going to see the bad nigger—the one that knocked down old Miss Standish?"

"Well, I reckon," said his mother, "that we *might* see him."

He started to ask, *Will a lot of niggers be there? Will Otis be there?*—but he did not ask his question, to which, in a strange and uncomfortable way, he already knew the answer. Their friends, in the other cars, stretched up the road as far as he could see; other cars had joined them; there were cars behind them. They were singing. The sun seemed, suddenly very hot, and he was, at once very happy and a little afraid. He did not quite understand what was happening, and he did not know what to ask—he had no one to ask. He had grown accustomed, for the solution of such mysteries, to go to Otis. He felt that Otis knew everything. But he could not ask Otis about this. Anyway, he had not seen Otis for two days; he had not seen a black face anywhere for more than two days; and he now realized, as they began chugging up the long hill which eventually led to Harkness, that there were no black faces on the road this morning, no black people anywhere. From the houses in which they lived, all along the road, no smoke curled, no life stirred—maybe one or two chickens were to be seen, that was all. There was no one at the windows, no one in the yard, no one sitting on the porches, and the doors were closed. He had come this road many a time and seen women washing in the yard (there were no clothes on the clotheslines) men working in the fields, children playing in the dust; black men passed them on the road other mornings, other days, on foot, or in wagons, sometimes in cars, tipping their hats, smiling, joking, their teeth a solid white against their skin, there eyes as warm as the sun, the blackness of their skin like dull fire against the white of the blue or the grey of their torn clothes. They passed the nigger church—dead-white, desolate, locked up; and the graveyard, where no one knelt or walked, and he saw no flowers. He wanted to ask, *Where are they? Where are they all?* But he did not dare. As the hill grew steeper, the sun grew colder. He looked at his mother and his father. They looked straight ahead, seeming to be listening to the singing which echoed and echoed in this graveyard silence. They were strangers to him now. They were looking at something he could not see. His father's lips had a strange, cruel curve, he wet his lips from time to time, and swallowed. He was terribly aware of his father's tongue, it was as though he had never seen it before. And his father's body suddenly seemed immense, bigger than a mountain. His eyes, which were grey-green, looked yellow in the sunlight; or at least there was a light in them which he had never seen before. His mother patted her hair and adjusted the ribbon, leaning forward to look into the car mirror. "You look all right," said his father, and laughed. "When that nigger looks at you, he's going to swear he throwed his life away for nothing. Wouldn't be surprised if he don't come back to haunt you." And he laughed again.

The singing now slowly began to cease; and he realized that they were nearing their destination. They had reached a straight, narrow, pebbly road, with trees on either side. The sunlight filtered down on them from a great height, as though they were under-water; and the branches of the trees scraped against the cars with a tearing sound. To the right of them, and beneath them, invisible now, lay the town; and to the left, miles of trees which led to the high mountain range which his ancestors had crossed in order to settle in this valley. Now, all was silent, except for the bumping of the tires against the rocky road, the sputtering of motors, and the sound of a crying child. And they seemed to move more slowly. They were beginning to climb again. He watched the cars ahead as they toiled patiently upward, disappearing into the sunlight of the clearing. Presently, he felt their vehicle also rise, heard his father's changed breathing, the sunlight hit his face, the trees moved away from them, and they were there. As their car crossed the clearing, he looked around. There seemed to be millions, there were certainly hundreds of people in the clearing, staring toward something he could not see. There was a fire. He could not see the flames, but he smelled the smoke. Then they were on the other side of the clearing, among the trees again. His father drove off the road and parked the car behind a great many other cars. He looked down at Jesse.

"You all right?" he asked.

"Yes sir," he said.

"Well, come on, then," his father said. He reached over and opened the door on his mother's side. His mother stepped out first. They followed her into the clearing. At first he was aware only of confusion, of his mother and father greeting and being greeted, himself being handled, hugged, and patted, and told how much he had grown. The wind blew the smoke from the fire across the clearing into his eyes and nose. He could not see over the backs of the people in front of him. The sounds of laughing and cursing and wrath—and something else—rolled in waves from the front of the mob to the back. Those in front expressed their delight at what they saw, and this delight rolled backward, wave upon wave, across the clearing, more acrid than the smoke. His father reached down suddenly and sat Jesse on his shoulders.

Now he saw the fire—of twigs and boxes, piled high; flames

made pale orange and yellow and thin as a veil under the steadier light of the sun; grey-blue smoke rolled upward and poured over their heads. Beyond the shifting curtain of fire and smoke, he made out first only a length of gleaming chain, attached to a great limb of the tree; then he saw that this chain bound two black hands together at the wrist, dirty yellow palm facing dirty yellow palm. The smoke poured up; the hands dropped out of sight; a cry went up from the crowd. Then the hands slowly came into view again, pulled upward by the chain. This time he saw the kinky, sweating, bloody head—he had never before seen a head with so much hair on it, hair so black and so tangled that it seemed like another jungle. The head was hanging. He saw the forehead, flat and high, with a kind of arrow of hair in the center, like he had, like his father had; they called it a widow's peak; and the mangled eye brows, the wide nose, the closed eyes, and the glinting eye lashes and the hanging lips, all streaming with blood and sweat. His hands were straight above his head. All his weight pulled downward from his hands; and he was a big man, a bigger man than his father, and black as an African jungle Cat, and naked. Jesse pulled upward; his father's hands held him firmly by the ankles. He wanted to say something, he did not know what, but nothing he said could have been heard, for now the crowd roared again as a man stepped forward and put more wood on the fire. The flames leapt up. He thought he heard the hanging man scream, but he was not sure. Sweat was pouring from the hair in his armpits, poured down his sides, over his chest, into his navel and his groin. He was lowered again; he was raised again. Now Jesse knew that he heard him scream. The head went back, the mouth wide open, blood bubbling from the mouth; the veins of the neck jumped out; Jesse clung to his father's neck in terror as the cry rolled over the crowd. The cry of all the people rose to answer the dying man's cry. He wanted death to come quickly. They wanted to

make death wait: and it was they who held death, now, on a
leash which they lengthened little by little. *What did he do?*
Jesse wondered. *What did the man do? What did he do?*—but
he could not ask his father. He was seated on his father's
shoulders, but his father was far away. There were two older
men, friends of his father's, raising and lowering the chain;
everyone, indiscriminately, seemed to be responsible for the
fire. There was no hair left on the nigger's privates, and the
eyes, now, were wide open, as white as the eyes of a clown or
a doll. The smoke now carried a terrible odor across the clearing, the odor of something burning which was both sweet and
rotten.

He turned his head a little and saw the field of faces. He
watched his mother's face. Her eyes were very bright, her
mouth was open: she was more beautiful than he had ever
seen her, and more strange. He began to feel a joy he had
never felt before. He watched the hanging, gleaming body, the
most beautiful and terrible object he had ever seen till then.
One of his father's friends reached up and in his hands he held
a knife: and Jesse wished that he had been that man. It was a
long, bright knife and the sun seemed to catch it, to play with
it, to caress it—it was brighter than the fire. And a wave of
laughter swept the crowd. Jesse felt his father's hands on his
ankles slip and tighten. The man with the knife walked toward
the crowd, smiling slightly; as though this were a signal, silence fell; he heard his mother cough. Then the man with the
knife walked up to the hanging body. He turned and smiled
again. Now there was a silence all over the field. The hanging
head looked up. It seemed fully conscious now, as though the
fire had burned out terror and pain. The man with the knife
took the nigger's privates in his hand, one hand, still smiling, as
though he were weighing them. In the cradle of the one white
hand, the nigger's privates seemed as remote as meat being
weighed in the scales; but seemed heavier, too, much heavier,

and Jesse felt his scrotum tighten; and huge, huge, much bigger than his father's, flaccid, hairless, the largest thing he had ever seen till then, and the blackest. The white hand stretched them, cradled them, caressed them. Then the dying man's eyes looked straight into Jesse's eyes—it could not have been as long as a second, but it seemed longer than a year. Then Jesse screamed, and the crowd screamed as the knife flashed, first up, then down, cutting the dreadful thing away, and the blood came roaring down. Then the crowd rushed forward, tearing at the body with their hands, with knives, with rocks, with stones, howling and cursing. Jesse's head, of its own weight, fell downward toward his father's head. Someone stepped forward and drenched the body with kerosene. Where the man had been, a great sheet of flame appeared. Jesse's father lowered him to the ground.

"Well, I told you," said his father, "you wasn't never going to forget *this* picnic." His father's face was full of sweat, his eyes were very peaceful. At that moment Jesse loved his father more than he had ever loved him. He felt that his father had carried him through a mighty test, had revealed to him a great secret which would be the key to his life forever.

"I reckon," he said. "I reckon."

Jesse's father took him by the hand and, with his mother a little behind them, talking and laughing with the other women, they walked through the crowd, across the clearing. The black body was on the ground, the chain which had held it was being rolled up by one of his father's friends. Whatever the fire had left undone, the hands and the knives and the stones of the people had accomplished. The head was caved in, one eye was torn out, one ear was hanging. But one had to look carefully to realize this, for it was, now, merely, a black charred object on the black, charred ground. He lay spread-eagled with what had been a wound between what had been his legs.

"They going to leave him here, then?" Jesse whispered.

"Yeah," said his father, "they'll come and get him by and by.
I reckon we better get over there and get some of that food
before it's all gone."

"I reckon," he muttered now to himself, "I reckon." Grace
stirred and touched him on the thigh: the moonlight covered
her like glory. Something bubbled up in him, his nature again
returned to him. He thought of the boy in the cell; he thought
of the man in the fire; he thought of the knife and grabbed
himself and stroked himself and a terrible sound, something
between a high laugh and a howl, came out of him and
dragged his sleeping wife up on one elbow. She stared at him
in a moonlight which had now grown cold as ice. He thought
of the morning and grabbed her, laughing and crying, crying
and laughing, and he whispered, as he stroked her, as he took
her, "Come on, sugar, I'm going to do you like a nigger, just
like a nigger, come on, sugar, and love me just like you'd love a
nigger." He thought of the morning as he labored and she
moaned, thought of morning as he labored harder than he ever
had before, and before his labors had ended, he heard the first
cock crow and the dogs begin to bark, and the sound of tires
on the gravel road.

ABOUT THE AUTHOR

JAMES BALDWIN was born in New York City on August 2, 1924. He was the first of nine children and grew up in Harlem where his father was a minister. For six years, after his graduation from high school in 1942, he found work in a variety of minor jobs. When he was twenty-four he left for Europe and lived there almost ten years. During this time, he wrote his first three books: *Go Tell it on the Mountain, Notes of a Native Son,* and *Giovanni's Room.* They firmly established him as one of America's outstanding young writers. In 1957, he returned to New York, where he now lives when he is not on one of his frequent trips abroad.

In 1961, Mr. Baldwin's fourth book, the collection of brilliant essays entitled *Nobody Knows My Name,* brought him broad public recognition as well as distinguished critical attention. Perhaps the most meaningful book ever to discuss being Negro in America, *Nobody Knows My Name* was the recipient of numerous awards and a devoted following. The following year brought similar acclaim for his best-selling novel, *Another Country.* In 1963, the prophetic *The Fire Next Time* jolted both the critical world and the book-buying public. Instantly acclaimed, as Granville Hicks said, as "a great document of our times, in literary power as well as in strength of feeling and clarity of insight," the book rushed to the top of all the best-seller lists.

James Baldwin is also the author of three plays. The first, *The Amen Corner,* was originally produced at Howard University. It had a long and successful run in Los Angeles, later opened on Broadway in 1965, and, as *Going to Meet the Man* is published, another production is touring the world under the auspices of the State Department. A dramatization of *Giovanni's Room* was staged by the Actor's Studio workshop. In 1964, his *Blues for Mr. Charley* opened off Broadway and was published simultaneously in book form. Like *The Amen Corner,* it has been produced throughout this country and Europe.